MONICA LYNNE FOSTER

Bad
CHOICES

A CHANELLE SERIES NOVEL

BAD CHOICES

Cover Design by Jessica Tilles of TWA Solutions.com

ISBN: 978-0-9965825-4-4 (paperback)

ISBN: 978-0-9965825-5-1 (ebook)

For inquiries, contact the publisher. www.monicalynnefoster.com

DEDICATION

This novel is dedicated to my precious grandmother,
Visel S. Nervis
January 5, 1913—April 14, 2013
I still love you with all of my heart...

ALSO BY MONICA LYNNE FOSTER

CHANELLE SERIES NOVELS

Hands Off —Book 2

For Better And For Worse—Book 3

INSPIRATION

Today Is Your Last Day...Say Wha?!: (The first 24 months after you lose your job)

Walk in God's Grace: Faith for Felons

LET'S STAY CONNECTED

Amazon Author Profile and Full Book List:

amazon.com/author/monicalynnefoster

Monica's Official Website and Social Media

www.monicalynnefoster.com

https://twitter.com/authormlfoster

https://bookbub.com/authors/monica-lynne-foster

https://facebook.com/authormonicalynnefoster

https://goodreads.com/authormonicalynnefoster

https://instagram.com/authormonicalynnefoster

THANKS FROM MONICA

I have so many to thank for my labor of love, but, above all else, I thank God. My Heavenly Father has blessed me with a gift for writing and a very active imagination.

I thank my husband and best friend, Keith Foster. You nurture and support me in my dreams, some of which can be a little "out there" and I'm grateful.

Thank you to my mom, Visel Franklin, who is the absolute best. Mom, you have been on my side for my entire life. You've always made me believe that every dream I have is possible.

Thank you to my entire family and extended family. You love me and let me be me.

And thank you to my readers. It is my sincere prayer that this novel is just the beginning of many to come and that you will enjoy reading my work as much as I enjoy writing them.

To anyone I may have missed, please forgive me. I'll catch you in my second book, *Hands Off*, the sequel to *Bad Choices*.

PROLOGUE

FLINGING my suitcase across the room, I lunged for the baseball bat by the side of my bed.

"Chanelle, I can explain," Michael yelled, scrambling to cover himself.

My eyes were red with rage. "You can't possibly explain this." There was no way I'd come home from a business trip to find the love of my life in our bed with his personal trainer. His male. Personal. Trainer.

"I swear to God, this isn't what it looks like." Michael's hands trembled as he held his arms out in front of him. Pfft, as if that would block my major league swing.

I brandished the bat above my boyfriend's head and wondered if I could handle a twenty-year bid. "Don't you *dare* bring God into this. How could I have been *stupid* enough to trust you?"

I slammed the bat on the side of the bed, causing Michael to scrunch his shoulders and squeeze his eyes shut. "Twelve years. I gave your sorry ass twelve years of my life."

I hammered down on the other side of him. He whimpered.

Then I turned my fury on Rocco. "And you. I welcomed you into my home."

Rocco raised his lanky body to his knees, running his finger around his pouty lips. He lifted a perfectly arched eyebrow. "It's not my fault you can't give him what I can."

Michael spoke to his man while keeping his petrified eyes on me."Not now, Rocco."

My chest heaved. My nostrils flared. I adjusted my fingers and tightened my grip around the bat.

With restrained fury, and through gritted teeth, I said, "Get out. Both of you. Get. Out. Now."

They hopped out of the bed and stooped to pick up the clothes that were strewn across my bedroom floor.

"Unh-uh," I shouted, using the bat as a pointer toward the door.

Michael, still bent over, paused, as though contemplating what he valued most. His life or his pants. "Chanelle, it's freezing outside."

His pleas were mute to me. "You say that like it matters. You have exactly one second to be out of my house or I swear to God, I'm gonna catch a case. Now, go!"

I snatched his car keys from the top of my dresser and chased them down the steps and out the front door. Watching them run butt naked and barefoot down the snowy street of my upscale subdivision was suddenly comical. I fell onto the glider on the porch and laughed until I cried as the pain from the betrayal set in. I'd wasted years of my life with a man who never had it in him to commit to me. I was now… alone.

CHAPTER 1

One Month Later

MY EYES GLANCED to the heavens when I opened the front door and saw Michael standing with his lover. "What are you doing here?"

His feminine side was on full display because he matched my eye roll with his own. "Here," he said, his voice higher than it had been when we were together.

I snatched the piece of paper from his hands and frowned. "What's this?"

"You've been served, Honey."

He'd called me 'Honey' throughout our relationship, but this time it wasn't dipped in love. "You're *suing* me?"

Rocco stroked Michael's hand and pursed his lips. "It ain't him."

I looked from one to the other. "Y'all have got to be kidding me."

Rocco whipped his neck as though flicking long hair over his shoulder. "It's no joke, Missy. I'll see you in court."

I waved the paper that cemented Michael's betrayal in his

face. "And you're going to let him do this to me? Like I meant nothing to you?"

"Chanelle, you burned up everything I owned. So, yeah, I'm behind Rocco on this."

I thought about the bonfire I'd had right after he breached my trust. I smiled. He was right. I even received a fine from the city because of the blaze. But it was so worth it when Michael showed up with the moving truck the following day and I handed him a pitcher of ashes. It would've made more sense if *he* was the one suing me. But Rocco? What did I do to him?

I watched Rocco and the man I once loved with everything in me walk down my steps and get into their old Hyundai. Then I groaned and shut the door on a chapter of my life that was closed forever.

"Hurry up. We're going to be late." I called out through the open hall and up the stairs to my best friend, Michele. I loved her like a sister, but she was slow when we were kids, and nothing had changed.

"Where are you going, Auntie Chanelle?" I looked into the bright eyes of my four-year-old godson, Benjamin Jr. and melted as I always did.

"Well, I've been invited to a Christmas party for my job, and your mommy is going with me."

He squinted like he was puzzled. "But Santa already came."

I smiled at his innocence. "Yes, he did. But now, he's coming to my job so he can hang out with us."

He frowned and shook his head. "That doesn't make sense."

He was right, and I wished the party had been canceled. But it was a tradition in our company to celebrate the holidays in January. "Wanna hear a secret?"

BJ's nod was big. "Uh-huh."

I bent down and whispered. "I don't get it either. But sometimes grownups have to do silly things."

"Oh." He paused, as if he didn't understand what I was saying. Then he shrugged. "Is my mommy going to?"

When I nodded, he continued. "Well, who's gonna read me my bedtime story?"

"Now, BJ, who always reads to you when Mommy is gone?" I glanced over at Michele's husband, Ben, who was smiling as he relaxed in his recliner and seemed to be enjoying my conversation with his son.

"Da-ddy."

I playfully tapped his nose. "Right."

"But I want Mommy to do it."

"You want Mommy to do what?" Michele asked, sashaying into the family room and announcing her presence.

"I want *you* to read me my story," BJ whined.

Now, I loved my godson, but I didn't have time for this. We needed to get on the road.

"Sweetie, how about letting Daddy read to you tonight, and I'll do it tomorrow night?" Michele said.

BJ glanced up and tapped his finger against his chin. "Mmm, okay, if you read me two stories."

I couldn't believe they were negotiating, but whatever it took to get us out of this house was fine with me.

"It's a deal. Can Mommy have a kiss?"

BJ ran into Michele's arms and she scooped him up, depositing him into his father's lap. "Honey, we should be back around eleven." She gave Ben a peck on the lips.

He broke their gaze and turned to me. "Don't get my wife into any trouble. I know how you two can be when you're together."

"Whatever, Ben. Michele is the one who's the bad influence."

We laughed as she grabbed her purse, coat, and keys.

Once inside my BMW sedan, Michele turned to the jazz

station. We drove in silence, each of us lost in our separate thoughts.

It was her voice that disturbed the moment. "So, are you okay with this?"

"Okay with what?"

"Don't play with me, Chanelle. This is the first time you have gone out since you and Michael broke up. You've told no one about it, and people are going to be curious when you show up with me as your date."

I shrugged a shoulder, cruising down the on-ramp to the highway. "I'm fine. I mean, I have to be. Right?" I stole a glance at her before returning my eyes to the road. "I thought Michael was my soul mate. That we'd be together forever. But he decided to spend his life with someone who can give him something that I obviously can't."

I pressed my signal light and sailed across the three lanes to the far left. "Oh, and by the way, his new man is suing me."

She leaned away and cocked her head. "You're kidding. For what?"

"Get this. Frostbite and legal fees. When I kicked them out of my house." I stopped and began again. "Correction. Out of my *bed*, without clothes or keys, they were picked up for indecent exposure. But not before his little goodies got too cold and he was hospitalized. He's coming after me for his medical bills."

Astonishment was written in the lines across her forehead. "Unbelievable."

"Tell me about it," I snarled. "I hope his stuff never works right again."

Michele chuckled at that, then twisted in her seat to look at me. "Let me know the court date and I'll go with you. I'm not worried about Rocco. I know you'll handle him. But you still haven't told me if you're really okay."

My pause was long and my sigh heavy. "No." I let the word hang in the air. "I'm not okay. Is that what you want to hear?"

Michele knew me well. She knew that I'd laid in bed for a week straight. Crying until I thought all my tears were spent, then put on a cheerful face and pushed the sting of rejection to the rear of my mind. But still, when I wasn't paying attention, the pain would creep forward and stab my heart.

I blankly stared through the windshield, my car whizzing past the others on the highway. "I thought I'd have a family, a white picket fence, and even a dog at this stage in my life. But I don't." I shook my head. "For the first time ever, I'm by myself. I let my twenties and half of my thirties pass me by. Now, I have to start over."

My bottom lip began to quiver, and now was not the time. "I'm on my way to a holiday party for work and you're my frickin' date."

I paused again, pressing a finger into the corner of my eye, praying tears wouldn't make an unwanted appearance. "I am not okay, and I feel like I have to pretend that I am. On top of everything else, Michele, I got dumped by a guy who was on the down low. Maybe I was delusional. Maybe I should have known after the first year with Michael that I was wasting my time. In hindsight, the signs were there. I just missed them all." I released a long unsteady sigh. "There. Are you satisfied?"

Michele's nods were slow and deliberate. "I am. Because this is the first time you've been open with me. But, more importantly, it sounds like this is the first time you've been honest with yourself."

She reached over and rubbed my arm. "Sweetie, God has someone incredible for you. Be patient. Take this time to get to know you all over again."

"I hear ya. It's just..." I wiped the lone tear that snuck past my finger. "I'm really scared to be by myself. And, I'm terrified to date again."

"It's natural to feel that way. Dating shouldn't even be your focus. The man for you will appear when you're whole."

"Humph. Leave it to a happily married woman to say something lame like that."

Her guffaw at my sarcasm was laced with the sting of her own hurtful memories. "Hey, you know as well as I do, Ben and I weren't always in a good space. We had to work like hell to stay together. And we almost didn't.'"

I thought about what she'd said. They'd been together for over eleven years. But, there was a time, in the honeymoon years of their marriage, when he'd battled a severe gambling problem. Thankfully, the combination of Gambler's Anonymous, counseling, and prayer saved their relationship.

But I didn't see the same fairy tale ending in my future. "Yeah, yeah, whatever. I don't want to talk about this anymore, and besides, we're here." I rolled to a stop in front of the hotel, and waited for the valet to open my door. He handed me a ticket and Michele and I strolled inside.

The grand ballroom was breathtaking. White cathedral ceilings. Four-tiered crystal chandeliers sprinkled throughout. Round tables covered in cream linen with expensive china place settings and tabletop poinsettias. The chairs were wrapped in red cloth with bows tied behind the backs. White and gold floral arrangements adorned the bar and the dessert tables.

The DJ on stage played soft holiday dinner music while a handful of couples enjoyed themselves on the dance floor.

The host tipped his head a bit and greeted us with a warm smile. "Good evening, may I take your coats?"

"Thank you." I slipped my midnight-black full-length mink from my shoulders and into his waiting hands. Michele, an animal activist, did the same with her faux fox. Another host escorted us to our table.

We drew attention from horny husbands and jealous wives as we strutted through the dining area. And why wouldn't they gawk? Michele, in a black glittery wrap dress whose high-low hem flitted as she switched in her Manolo's. Me, in a sparkly off-the-shoulder curve-hugging red dress that put a spotlight on my black girl magic behind and ample cleavage.

As we neared our table, my stomach did two back flips and a somersault. I'd always heard the best way to get over one man was to get under another. If there was any man who could help me forget Michael, it was Sean.

He was a marketing consultant for our company, a technology firm that had survived the tech nosedive several years prior. We were thriving, and several of the accounts we'd acquired were due to the work of Sean's team. He was around so much, we sometimes forgot he wasn't an actual employee.

Though Sean and I worked together, I'd never entertained the thought of him. But since my breakup, I'd been paying closer attention. And I liked everything I saw. Milk chocolate brown. Almost six feet of solid muscle. And he had to wear at least a size thirteen shoe. Hmmm…

I shook my head, hoping to rid my mind of the thoughts that were sure to return frequently before the night ended.

"Good evening." I smiled and introduced Michele to Sean and the other reason why I shouldn't have lustful thoughts. His wife.

Michele extended her hand as we took our seats. "Nice to meet you both."

Cynthia returned the handshake by offering her fingertips. "Likewise."

She then turned her attention to me. "So, Chanelle," her voice affected with the drawl of a woman of wealth. Yet, I knew from conversations with Sean that she was on government assistance and was a hot mess when they'd met. "Where's Michael this evening?"

My back stiffened. This woman made it her business to remind me why I didn't like her. But rather than dance around the issue, I addressed it, so we could move on. I drew in a full breath. "Actually, Cynthia, we're not together anymore." *Because he's banging his trainer,* I thought.

"Aww...that's too bad." She feigned sympathy that I neither needed nor wanted. "He was so sweet. What did you do to run him away?"

The crimson color that settled in Sean's cheeks told me that his wife had embarassed him.

Had we been anywhere else, I would have lit into her. But I knew better than to show out at a work function. Still, my eyes narrowed, and my teeth clenched, her one warning that my measured response wouldn't happen again. "Michael is a very sweet man, which is why we're able to remain friends." That lie was all she was getting out of me.

Benson Jeffries, my firm's CEO, and his wife Phoebe were the final guests at our table.

Mr. Jeffries, forever the charmer, took my hand and brought it to his lips. "Chanelle, it's great to see you."

I grinned at the man who was about forty years my senior and reminded me of my late grandfather.

After the second round of greetings, we engaged in mundane corporate holiday party banter. Cynthia seemed to pick up that I wasn't to be trifled with, and except for eating, she kept her mouth shut.

After dinner, she stepped away when her cellphone vibrated. Michele left to check on BJ. And the Jeffries excused themselves to make their rounds at the other tables.

"Dinner was great," Sean said, sparking up awkward chit chat.

I held a finger in front of my lips before swallowing my carrot cake. "It was delicious."

"So, um, how's the new proposal coming?"

I was pitching a potential client in the coming weeks and Sean had been giving me suggestions. If I landed this multi-million-dollar account, I was sure to make partner. "I'm gathering the final numbers which are a little harder to work through than I'd anticipated."

He drank his wine and leaned back into the chair. "Well, let me know if I can be of any more assistance. From what I've seen, you're on the right track."

"If you mean that, then I'd love for you to review the final draft before I present to Mr. Jeffries."

Sean nodded. "I'll review it for you."

Just then, Cynthia returned to our table. "Honey, I have to leave. An emergency came up at the hospital and I need to be there."

I wondered what kind of emergency came up at a pet hospital that required the technician and not the actual veterinarian.

Sean bunched his brows. "Where's Dave? I thought he was covering tonight."

"Oh… well… he is. But, um, he needs another pair of hands for an emergency surgery."

Was that light mist on her forehead perspiration? I wondered.

"O…K…" He still didn't seem to buy her story, but he raised from the seat, anyway. "I'll get our coats."

"Oh, no," she hurried to say, placing her hand, and a little bit of pressure, on his shoulder and directing him bck into the seat. "Don't bother. I'll take an Uber."

"Why? Don't you want me to take you? Especially, if you're in a hurry." A slight frown settled on his handsome face.

I wondered how she was going to answer. And I wished I'd had some popcorn because this show was getting good.

"I-I-I know this is work for you. I'll be fine," Cynthia said.

"Well, then at least take the car."

After a brief hesitation, she relented. "Fine. I don't have time to argue with you." She brushed her lips against his cheek and scurried out the door.

Wow, was all I could think. And if he believed her story, then I had a bridge I'd build and sell him.

With her gone, the air around us was tense. I diverted my eyes, not wanting to look at him, since his wife had humiliated him for the second time this evening.

Across the room, Michele was in the corner, still on her cell. She was smiling and twirling her hair. Ben must have been reminding her how good it was to be married. I knew she would be ready to get home soon, and though I was happy for her, I had to admit I was a little envious.

"Would you like to dance?" Sean's smooth baritone cut through my thoughts.

His question stunned me, so it took a second to answer. They were playing The Isley Brothers' *"Spend the Night,"* which was one of my favorites.

"Sure." I tried to be nonchalant, hoping he didn't notice the slight tremble in my voice.

My heart went from zero to sixty when his hand touched mine and he led me to the dance floor. I kept telling myself to get it together. This was a dance with a friend. A married friend. Nothing more.

But my common sense fled the building when he pulled me close and pressed my body into his. I inhaled, allowing his cologne, an intoxicating blend of masculinity and power, to seduce my senses. My eyes closed, my lips upturned, my mind a million miles away, I glided across the floor in his arms and pretended this moment was okay.

We didn't talk, we simply danced. Our fingers intertwined as he spun me around to old school Motown, and I listened to the rhythm of his heart as Luther serenaded us. "You're a excellent dancer," he shouted over the bass of the Cha-Cha Slide.

I smiled as I hopped forward. "So are you."

"Don't laugh, but my mother made me take lessons when I was a kid, and I got into it."

"I hear ya. I took lessons from the time I could walk until twelfth grade."

I'd forgotten that Michele was my date until she approached us. "Hey, Twinkle Toes, I hate to bust your groove, but I told my husband I would be home by eleven and it's almost eleven-thirty. I have my own party that I'd like to get started, if you know what I mean."

I knew exactly what she meant, and I hated single life all the more. "Let me finish out this song and then we'll go."

"Cool. I'll grab our coats," Michele said.

After she walked off, I turned to Sean. "I had a great time."

His stare held mine. "Me too."

He looked like he didn't want the night to end, and I had to admit that I didn't either, so I asked, "Do you want a ride home?"

"Thanks, but I don't want to be a bother."

"It's no bother."

"Well, if you're sure, then yeah." We said our goodbyes to those around us. He received his coat from the coat check and the three of us headed to the valet to wait for my car. After giving me his address, which I plugged into the car navigation system, we chatted on our way to his home.

When we stopped in front of his house, he said, "Have a good night, ladies."

"You too," we said in unison.

He exited the car and walked up the steps. I waited until he was in the house before driving off. Then braced myself for Michele's mouth and she didn't disappoint.

"We'll talk about this tomorrow. Right now, I have my husband on the brain."

"What if I don't want to talk?"

"Doesn't matter. We're going to, anyway."

Several moments later, I whipped into her driveway and came to a hard stop.

She opened the door and swung her legs out before looking back at me. "Chanelle, be careful. You're playing a dangerous game."

"I know," was all I could say.

"I'll call you tomorrow. Love you."

"Love you, too."

As I drove off, I prayed that thoughts of Sean wouldn't invade my sleep. But somehow, I knew they would.

CHAPTER 2

THE SHRILL of my ringtone disturbed my deep sleep. "Hello?" I grumbled, not ready to be awakened.

"Good morning, Sunshine!" Michele's perky voice flowed through the speaker of my cell, and called me by my childhood nickname. "Are you still in bed?"

"What do you think? And why are you so dang chipper?" I kept my head under the covers and hoped this would be a brief conversation.

"My, my. Someone woke up on the wrong side of the bed."

I moaned. "I'm not trying to be awake yet. I've got one more hour of sleep before I have to get ready for church. Now, if you don't mind, I'd like to get back to Idris."

"I can't believe you. How can you have these dreams and then go praise the Lord?"

"It gives me something to repent about. See you in a couple of hours. Bye."

I squeezed my eyes tight, wanting sleep to return, but it was useless. I groaned, rolled out of bed, lumbered over to the balcony door, and pulled back the blackout curtains to welcome the daylight. Cracking the door about an inch, the crisp winter air danced into the room.

With a sudden burst of energy, I brushed my teeth, then scooted down the steps to the den where I streamed a yoga class on the theater size television while my coffee brewed. After a zen workout, I sat in the breakfast nook and enjoyed my hot java and a bagel, while scrolling through silly social media posts on my iPad. Then I headed upstairs to get dressed.

I was ready in under forty minutes and called Michele as I raised the door on my attached three-car garage. "Hey girl, you guys doin' the family thing or you want a ride?"

"Yeah, swing by. Ben went to the early service since he has to be at work by noon today. Two employees called in, so he's got to cover their routes."

"No problem. See you in a few." I hopped into the driver's seat of my burnt orange Range Rover and blasted the latest Tasha Cobbs single, starting my church vibe early.

As I pulled into Michele's circular drive and turned the volume down, BJ came running out. "Auntie! Auntie!"

"Hey, Baby. Where's Mommy?" I shifted into park and jumped out, walking around to open the door and helped him inside.

"She forgot her purse." He climbed into the car seat I kept in his spot, and I fastened his seatbelt.

Michele came out as I was getting back into the driver's seat.

"Hey, girl." Out of habit, before buckling her seatbelt, she checked BJ's harness and handed him her phone. "Andrea said she called you, but you didn't answer. Rachel needs a ride to church."

"Why can't she take her?" My sister did this kind of stuff all the time. I checked my phone and there were no missed calls.

"She's not feeling well, so she isn't going."

"Mm-hmm. I wonder if Dante has anything to do with it." Dante was my sister's on-again, off-again, baby's daddy. They'd been together for eighteen years, and the only good thing that had come from their relationship was my niece.

"She didn't say. All she said was come get Rachel."

Michele hated to get involved when it came to Andrea, who was five years older than us, but acted like she was ten years younger. I swear my sister was allergic to responsibility.

"Call her and let her know we're on our way."

"I already told her you'd do it."

I smacked my lips. "What if I'd said no?"

"In the eleven years that Rachel has been on this earth, have you ever uttered that word when it comes to her?"

I sighed in surrender. "That child is my weakness. So anyway, how was your evening?"

Michele's grin broke into a wide smile as memories of her night must have come rushing back. "Girrrl...that brotha is gifted. He was like the energizer bunny. Just kept it going all night. I don't know what got into him."

"I do. It was that dress. You were a hottie!"

"Whatever." She chuckled and pushed me.

"I'm serious. You were working it. He was drooling before you even left the house."

She leaned in a bit, her voice low. "Ben went all out. He turned our bedroom into a romantic retreat." She stopped talking long enough to glance back at her son, who had become one with the kid's video he was watching. "Scented candles were everywhere, and he even filled our Jacuzzi with water and baby oil. And get this, he had dozens of rose petals floating across the top."

My mouth opened as wide as my eyes. "No."

"Yassss," Michele continued. I looked over at her and though her body was in the passenger seat, her mind had clearly drifted to last night. "Guess what was playing to help set the mood?"

"Not The Isley Brothers?"

"You know it. *Spend the Night.* When I walked in, he was lying on the bed with that silk robe I bought him from Japan."

"Keep talking," I prompted her.

Michele recapped the rest of her evening and shared details that only best friends could talk about. "When he slipped off my dress and told me I was the most beautiful woman he'd ever seen, I cried. He kissed away my tears and then made love to me like it was his first time discovering my body." Michele's eyes misted a little.

"Aww... But I ain't gon' lie. I'm stuck on him putting rose petals in the bathtub."

"Channie, it was the most unbelievable experience we've ever had. Although, today he's picking up a bottle of drain cleaner because they clogged the tub. Oops."

We laughed. It was sad that I had to live my love life through Michele, but it was all I had for the moment.

She sighed, as though she were forcing herself to stop reminiscing. "But enough about my evening. What was up with *you* and Sean last night?"

Now, it was my turn to sigh. "I don't know what's going on. But, when Sean and I started working together on this project, we had a few late nights and a Saturday when we worked out of my home office. We started talking about things besides work and connected in a way that we hadn't done before."

"Have either of you said anything about this connection?"

"Nah. I mean, there's this undercurrent that I'm sure he can sense. But it would be a mistake to talk about it."

"Why?" Michele had turned in her seat so she could stare at me.

I kept my eyes on the road because she was making me uncomfortable. Or maybe it was the truth in the conversation. Either way, I didn't want to look at her. "As long as neither of us says anything, we can act like it's not real and nothing has to

18

change. I won't feel like the sinner who's damned to hell and he'll still be a faithful husband."

I pressed the lock button on the door - twice - because we were headed into Andrea's neighborhood. "Once the words are out, one of us may feel obligated to move this to another level. And I'm not even sure what 'this' is. I mean, we work together. I don't want people calling me a home wrecker. Especially when I think about what just happened to me. I can't be known as an adulterer." The thought alone made me cringe.

Michele's brow creased in confusion. "Correct me if I'm wrong, but you seem to be more concerned with what people at work would think than what God would think."

"I wish I *could* correct you, but God is more forgiving than people. He'd be disappointed in me, but at least He knows what I'm going through, and He'd forgive me. The people at work would not. I'm a Senior VP, soon to be a partner. I can't risk that for a fling. When you get right down to it, I'm only feeling all hot and bothered because Michael is gone."

"Is that the only reason?" Michele's words challenged me.

"It's the only one I'm willing to acknowledge. If Michael was still around and remotely interested in what a woman has to offer, Sean wouldn't be a thought."

Michele pursed her lips. "Really?"

"You don't believe me?"

"Nope."

"Why?"

"Because you two have always had chemistry. But after what went down with Michael, I think you opened yourself up to him." My silence prompted her to continue. "There are a lot of qualities in Sean that you find attractive, but Sweetie, he's married. And even if he were available, you still haven't given yourself time to heal. You were in a twelve-year relationship with Michael. Damn near married, but never got a ring. You did everything a wife is expected to do. Took care of him when he lost his job three years ago and never got another one. Let him move in and sponge off you."

Her words made me wince as I turned into Andrea's driveway and blew the horn.

"Chanelle, you saw potential in him that didn't exist. And he repaid you by cheating. With a dude. In your bed. Set me straight if I'm wrong, but that's a pretty clear sign that there wasn't ever a future for the two of you. Matter of fact, I'm glad you didn't marry him and he's out of your life."

Everything she said was true. And I didn't want to talk about it. But she kept on beating that darn dead horse. "I know you. You're still hurting. You're vulnerable. And let's get spiritual. The devil knows it too. Did he tempt Eve with a lemon? No. He got her with an apple. Something sweet."

I was so ready for this conversation to end. "Humph. Technically, the Bible didn't say it was an apple, but I hear ya. And you're right. About everything. Sean is a big red delicious apple, hand-picked for me, and I want to take a bite. A big bite. And even though I know better, just thinking about it makes my mouth water." I wished to God that what I was saying wasn't true. But it was.

Michele's jaw dropped. "Hurry up and let's get your lusty butt to church, 'cause you need Jesus."

"Don't we all?" We laughed as Rachel got in and we headed to church to get the spiritual cleansing I so desperately needed.

CHAPTER 3

"Let the church say 'amen'," Pastor Sharpe commanded from the pulpit.

The congregation responded with a loud, "Amen."

"I said let the church say 'amen'!"

"Amen!"

"Thank you, Lord. You may be seated."

We sat on the cushioned wooden benches, some of us fanning ourselves from the dancing we'd done during praise and worship.

Pastor Sharpe opened her Bible and began reading. "First Corinthians 10:13 says, 'No temptation has overtaken you except such as is common to man; but God is faithful, who will not allow you to be tempted beyond what you are able, but with the temptation will also make the way of escape, that you may be able to bear it.'"

She peered over the rim of her glasses perched on the tip of her nose and scanned the congregation. "Today, I want to talk to you about something we all know about, church. Lust of the flesh."

"Ooh, Pastor, preach it," someone in the back pew piped up.

"The devil is out there, Saints. And he wants to separate you from God." She began wagging her finger at us. "He wants your soul. You have to be strong. Resist the temptation."

"Yes," someone else shouted.

Shifting in my seat, I kept my head glued to my Bible as the message pierced me. If Pastor Sharpe caught my eye, I was certain she'd know the thoughts I'd been having.

"When Satan sets out to destroy you, he's gonna use something he knows you like. He waits with the patience of Job until you are at your weakest point and then he STRIKES! But you have a weapon, Saints. His Name is Jesus!"

More agreement from the congregation. I just wanted this message to be over as soon as she started. But Pastor Sharpe took her time and spent a solid hour, quoting one scripture after another, about the value of resisting temptation and that the payment for sin is death. This was the first Sunday in years that I wished I'd slept in.

After service, I stood in the meet and greet line, expecting her to give me the cursory, "Thank you for coming" handshake. But she didn't. Instead, she covered my hand with both of hers and looked me in my eyes. "Good morning, Sister Chanelle."

"Morning, Reverend."

"How are you doing today?"

Her question felt like a setup. We both knew God had told her I was struggling with my emotions. "I'm fine."

"Are you sure?"

My voice was unsteady. "Um, yes, Ma'am."

"You know God loves you, right?" She didn't blink once. Instead, her stare penetrated me.

"Of course."

"Well, He's telling me to tell you that whatever it is you're contemplating, don't do it. It won't end well."

My eyes darted to my right, to Sister Eunice, who was straining to hear our conversation. That woman would have my business spread before I got to the car. I curled my lip at her, and she snapped her head away from me.

I cleared my throat and looked back at my pastor, whose gaze never left me. "I, I don't know what you're talking about."

"I think you do. I'm not asking you to tell me what's going on. But I'm here for you if you need me. And more importantly, God is here for you."

I slid my now damp hand from between hers. "Uh, thank you, Pastor, but I'm fine."

The creases in her weathered forehead said she didn't believe me. "Be blessed, Sister Chanelle."

"You too." I sped away as she moved on to the person behind me.

"Auntie, what was that all about?" Rachel asked me as we headed back to our vehicle.

"Uh, I'm not sure, Rach."

"She seemed to be warning you about something," Rachel persisted.

"Let it go," I said, still shaken by the uncomfortable conversation. "I don't know what she was talking about. Now, do you want to grab something to eat before I take you home?"

My normally precocious niece would have stayed on me until I gave her a satisfactory answer. But today, she said, "Chipotle?"

"You got it." I unlocked the doors, and we waited for Michele and BJ. The four of us rode to Rachel's favorite restaurant, and I tried to pretend I hadn't just received a warning straight from the Throne.

CHAPTER 4

SITTING AT MY OFFICE DESK, I twirled my pen and rocked in the chair. I couldn't take my mind off Sunday. The conversation with Michele, the sermon, and most disturbingly, my interaction with Reverend Sharpe. She'd been my pastor since I was a little girl. She knew me as well as my family did. I'd expected to receive words of encouragement from her message, but instead, I got a holy beat down.

Last night, as sleep eluded me, I resolved to heed the warning and keep my relationship with Sean professional.

"Good morning." I glanced up to see him standing at my door, scrumptious in a navy-blue Armani suit with a matching winter coat thrown over his arm. Just the sight of him made my breath catch in my throat. I had to remind myself that my goal was to remain all business.

"Good morning." I smiled and gestured for him to come in and have a seat. "What brings you by?"

"I have my weekly one-on-one with Mr. Jeffries and traffic was lighter than usual, so I got here early. As luck would have it, he had an emergency meeting, and pushed our appointment to ten."

"Oh." I wasn't sure what else to say, so I continued to fiddle with my pen.

He asked about the rest of my weekend and we chatted for a few moments before he kicked open the door to temptation. "Since I have some time, I was going to Starbucks. Would you like to join me?"

Say no..., say no..., say no..., I repeated to myself. "Sure." We stood and walked over to the door where my coat hung on the back.

"Let me." He reached for it and helped me slip it on. The velvety blend of his citrus and spice cologne warmed me more than my wool coat.

"Mornin', Boss Lady." My assistant swished into our office suite as Sean and I were about to walk out.

I smiled at the older woman. "Good morning, Patty. How was your weekend?"

"Same as always." She waddled behind her desk, hanging her coat on the hook and unwinding her knit scarf from around her neck. "Grandkids fightin', husband whinin'. And my..."

I cut her off and gestured toward the door. "I hate to be rude, but I'm on my way to Starbucks." I'd grown to love Patty, but she could go on and on about her family issues.

A few years ago, our company took part in a government pilot program where we hired women from abusive situations who were re-entering the workforce. Most of the women didn't work out, but Patty proved to be a superstar. Listening to her problems and fluent Ebonics was a small price to pay for the value she added to my team. And my clients found her refreshing.

"Okay, well, I'll see you when you get back." Winded, she plopped into her chair and turned on her computer.

"Can I bring you anything?"

"Thanks, Boss Lady, but I'm good."

Once outside, Sean asked me if I wanted to drive.

"Nah, it's around the corner. I can use the exercise. Besides, it's a nice day." We each reached into our pockets and pulled out our gloves.

"So, tell me more about the problem you're having," Sean said, as we began our stroll, the snow crunching beneath our feet.

"Well, you've seen most of it, so you know we're bidding to be the technology provider for the new stadium downtown. I've collected the data, but a few of my calculations aren't adding up. That's where I could use your help."

"We'll put our heads together and figure it out." He flashed a perfect smile. "Making you shine is my priority."

"Me?" I pointed to myself, my voice coy.

He stuttered. "I—I mean, Jeffries Technology."

With a bat of my eyes, the warning from yesterday vanished. "What would it take to make me your priority? And I'm not talking about my company."

He gazed into my eyes. "I would love to make that happen. I didn't think you were interested."

"I shouldn't be." I hesitated. "I'm trying not to be." I tilted my head slightly and lowered my voice. "But I am."

By now we were at the Starbucks counter. We paused our conversation, placed our order, then settled at a table for two in the corner.

"So, you were saying that you're interested in me but wish you were not?" He prompted me to continue sharing.

I finished taking a sip of my caramel macchiato and replied. "I'd rather hear how you feel about me."

He let out a slow exhale. "I'm conflicted. I've never looked at another woman since I've been married. But when you and I are together, I feel something I've never felt with Cynthia."

"And what's that?"

"Security. I measure up when I'm with you. When we're working, you don't find reasons to criticize my ideas, even when they're out-of-the-box. If you don't want to go with a concept I've designed, you make it into a joke. You take the sting out of your nos. I don't blame Cynthia for being who she is. I mean, she had it rough growing up." He stopped himself and ran his long fingers around the rim of his cup. "Chanelle, we've had a lot of conversations that had nothing to do with work, right?"

I wasn't sure where he was going, but I nodded. "Yes, we have."

He took a deep breath and continued. "I'm going to tell you some things about Cynthia. Not because I want you to judge my wife, but I want you to understand what's been going on in my marriage. And why I'm feeling more connected to you."

I reached out to touch his hand. "Sean, you're my friend. You can tell me anything."

He glanced down at our hands. "Cynthia used to be an alcoholic. When I met her, she was in recovery and getting her life on track. As long as she attends her weekly AA meetings, she's fine."

I shook my head. "That's good. But I'm still not following why you're sharing this with me."

"I want you to know," he paused before adding, "why I feel obligated to her."

"Sean, she's your wife. No explanation is needed."

"I feel it is. If I thought she'd be okay, I'd leave her."

"Whoa." I pulled back a little. "I'm not asking you to leave your spouse."

"I know. But I'm saying I would leave her for you. That's how much I want to explore a relationship with you."

"Um..."

"I'm not expecting a response. You don't have to figure out what to say." He took another deep breath, then continued. "Cynthia's been offered a job at one of the major animal hospitals in Virginia. She has contacts out there with Handle Marketing and she wants me to set up an interview."

Now, I understood why he was telling me all of this. He was contemplating leaving. "Handle Marketing? Aren't they your largest competitor?"

"Yeah. They're the biggest marketing consultant firm in the industry."

"Cynthia or not, why wouldn't you jump at the chance to meet with them? This is a tremendous opportunity."

"I've been working at Image for six years and I enjoy it. I like Michigan. My family is here. I'm not psyched about the idea of moving to Virginia when Cynthia and I aren't even getting along. Then there's you. I'm not ready to leave you, Chanelle. I want to explore what we could have."

"Sean, you have to take me out of the equation and do what's best for *you*. It sounds like she wants you there with her."

He nodded. "She does. Since this whole thing started, she's been on me to make a decision; and pointing out all the reasons we need to move." He released a weighted sigh before continuing. "She's also been going on these so called work-related jobs at night and staying gone for hours."

"Like at the party on Saturday?" I asked, my voice soft.

"Pfft." He snorted in disgust. "Her excuses are senseless, but I let her think I believe her."

"Do you think she's having an affair?" I kept my voice gentle, so he'd hear my concern.

"My pride would like me to believe she isn't, but I'm not stupid. If she hasn't yet, then it's just a matter of time."

"How would you feel if that were true?" The conversation had evolved into something a lot deeper than I'd expected. We had gone from playful, if not reckless flirting, to a deep discussion about his marriage.

"I've spent many nights thinking about it. Part of me would be relieved."

I knitted my brows. "You'd be relieved that your wife was cheating on you?" I didn't know any man who would be okay with his wife having a side piece. Even if he was doing his own dirt.

He nodded. "Then I wouldn't feel guilty about doing my own thing. But there's another part of me that would feel betrayed."

"Are you still in love with her?"

"I do love her."

"That's not what I asked."

He was silent for a moment that was too long for me. "Yeah. I am."

Ugh! "Well, that makes two things obvious. First, you have to do all you can to make your marriage work."

"That's one. What's the other?"

I hated to even say it. "You need to set up that interview in Virginia. If it doesn't work out, I'm sure Mr. Jeffries and Image would take you back."

"You think so?"

"I do. I'd be sorry to see you leave, but you need to try. Just make sure you help me with my presentation before you go." Although disappointed, I smiled to let him know we were still cool.

He returned the smile. "You got it. Chanelle, I have a lot of respect for you. Not many women would do what you just did."

I shrugged. "Right is right." I knew deep inside that I could never share some other woman's husband any more than I would share mine. Even if he was fine and had big... feet.

CHAPTER 5

I NERVOUSLY CLUTCHED the sides of the defendant's podium. I'd never been a litigant in a court case. And shouldn't have been one now. But, at least, I had Michele in my cheering section, sitting behind the wooden rail. I looked back at her and she gave me a thumbs up and a confident smile. I smiled back before shifting my glance to my traitor of an ex who was on the hard bench on the plaintiff's side of the courtroom. I cut my eyes at him, though he didn't see me. He was too busy watching the back door, probably hoping his boy toy would sashay through the doors with a good reason for being late. Late for a court case that he'd instigated.

"Counselor, where is your client?" Judge Klein tapped a manicured nail against her desk and demanded an answer from Rocco's attorney.

"Your Honor, I don't know," the man stealer's lawyer began. "He was supposed to meet me here this morning. I sent a text and I'm awaiting his response. I'm sure whatever has delayed him was unavoidable. Mr. Colon was eager to have this issue resolved and have Ms. Slate pay the consequence for her reckless actions."

"Counselor, if being on time for court isn't a priority for your client, then hearing his case is not a priority for me. Case dismissed." She banged her gavel.

I whipped my head and beamed at Michele. "That's it?" she mouthed.

I shrugged and mouthed back, "I guess so."

Rocco's lawyer picked up his phone and began texting as he sped out of the courtroom. I was positive he was letting his client know they'd lost.

Michael and the attorney were standing in the hall when Michele and I walked out. The attorney glared at me as we passed him. I didn't care. I was just glad this mess was over. I never should have been sued in the first place, and if Rocco's kahunas never worked right again, it was his own fault.

As Michele and I approached the elevator, Michael called my name. I started not to turn around, but I surrendered to my curiosity and stopped in the middle of the hall to let him catch up.

My hand on my hip, I cocked my head, making it clear he would get no more than sixty seconds of my time. "What do you want?"

"I want to apologize. I've given it some thought, and I understand why you did what you did. I would have thrown me out, too, if I were you."

I squinted at my ex, trying to figure out his angle. "Thank you for the apology." I turned to continue toward the elevator, but he called me again.

"Chanelle, I miss talking to you every day. I was wondering if you would be open to us rekindling our friendship?"

I took a step back and looked at him like he was crazy. "Have you switched to a cheap brand of crack?"

He frowned, puzzled. "Huh?"

"You must be on the pipe to think that we'd ever be friends again. After twelve years of being faithful, you repaid me by cheating. And, you didn't even have the decency to take it away from our home."

I wagged my finger in his face as my anger grew. "Then... you had the audacity to support that homewreckin' son-of-a-biscuit eater when he chose to sue me. *Me!* So, the answer is a resounding hell no. This case is over and I'm moving on with my life. I suggest you do the same."

I spun on my heels, and once again moved toward the elevator. This time, he was wise enough not to stop me. But my luck didn't turn for the better. When the elevator doors opened, Rocco stepped off, almost bumping into me as he furiously texted on his cell phone.

"Excuse you, Rocco," I sniped.

Michele grabbed my arm. "Ignore him, Chanelle. Pretend you don't see him." She escorted me past Rocco and onto the elevator.

But he wouldn't allow me to ignore him. He whirled around, putting his hand on the elevator door jamb, preventing it from closing. "You only won because I got caught in traffic."

My eyes narrowed into slits and I snarled. "No, I won because your case was idiotic, and you should have never come after me in the first place."

"It's your fault I have to have surgery." He stabbed his finger in my direction.

"You have to have surgery because what goes around comes around." I glanced down at what I assumed was his little package and smirked. "And karma bit you in the balls."

Michele gasped.

"Now, move your hand before I force you to move it," I said, ready to make good on my threat.

Rocco backed away, allowing the doors to close, but the last words I heard before we started our descent to the first floor were, "This isn't over, Missy!"

"Yeah, yeah," I muttered. Then looked at Michele. "Can you believe them?"

She shook her head. "I can't."

"And how could Michael think that he and I could ever be friends?" I screwed my face at the sour thought.

"Let's grab a late breakfast so you can decompress," Michelle suggested.

"Nah, I'm going into the office. I still have a lot of work to do on my proposal." We exited the elevator and walked outside.

"Are you talking about the one you've been working on with Sean?"

"Yup."

"Have you seen him since you two went to Starbucks last week?"

"I haven't."

"Do you think he went on the interview?"

I nodded. "I hope so. It's a great opportunity." We reached my car, and I placed my hand on the handle, unlocking the door. "Thanks for being my support system today."

"You'd do the same for me. I'm glad it's over."

"Me too. Although, Rocco sounds like he wants to keep it going." I hugged my best friend and got into my car. "I'll call you later."

"K. Love you."

"Love you, too."

"Boss Lady, Sean is on line one," Patty said through the phone intercom.

"Thanks. Please put him through."

Seconds later, I said, "Hey, stranger. Long time, no hear."

"It's been crazy busy. But, um, do you have time to meet me at Starbucks? I have something I'd like to share with you."

My heart fluttered thinking about what he wanted to say. "Sure. I can be there in about thirty minutes."

"I'll see you then."

After we hung up, I pulled out my cosmetic bag and freshened my makeup. I had no idea what he was going to tell me. Maybe he'd decided he wasn't going to interview, and Cynthia was moving without him.

I sat across from him at "our" table, waiting to hear what was so important.

"Chanelle, Handle hired me on the spot. I called them after you and I talked last Monday and they flew me out the next day. They loved me. I think this will be an excellent move. You were right. I have to do all I can to make it work with Cynthia."

My heart dropped to the bottom of my stilettos. But I didn't want him to know that. I didn't want him to know that I was wishing for something more between us. I took a deep breath and said what I was supposed to say. "I'm happy for you, Sean. You're doing what's best. When do you leave?"

"Things are happening at lightning speed. The position I'm taking has been vacant for almost a year and they're desperate. I start in two weeks."

I nodded and forced down the lump that had lodged in my throat. "Two weeks. Wow. That's fast."

He reached across the table and caressed my hands. "I'll miss you, Chanelle. You're a beautiful woman. You're going to light up some man's world."

I dipped my head, not wanting him to see the tears that were threatening to give away my true feelings. "Humph. That's kind of you to say."

"I say it because I mean it."

I inhaled a long breath, held it for a few seconds, and then exhaled. When I lifted my head, my eyes met his. "Well, you promised to help me with my presentation. And I'm expecting you to keep your word." I gave a weak attempt at a smile.

"I'm not leaving until it's perfect."

We gazed at each other for a few moments, said our goodbyes, and parted ways. I had no idea where he went, but after the roller coaster of emotions I'd experienced in the last several hours, I headed home.

CHAPTER 6

"WHATCHA DOIN'?" I asked Michele when she answered the phone.

"Nothing much. You know BJ is in the Saturday kid's basketball league at the youth center, so he and Ben are gone for most of the day."

"Wanna hit the mall? Nordstrom is having a semi-annual sale."

"Of course, I want to go. You driving or riding?" Michele asked.

"Riding. I drove last time. Besides, you have to pass by my house to get to the mall."

"Okay. I'll see you in a couple of hours. I want to do a little housekeeping before I leave. Once we hit the street, there's no telling what time we'll be back."

"You're right about that. I need to do a little cleaning, too. How about you be here at eleven?"

"Sounds like a plan. Just make sure you're ready."

"I'm not the one who's slow. That would be you."

She chuckled. "Guilty as charged."

As soon as we hung up, my phone rang. I glanced at the

caller ID and sighed. "Hello, Andrea." There was a reason my tone was dry. I knew my sister wanted something.

"Don't sound so excited."

"Sorry. What's up?" Still cautious of her reasons for ringing me this early on a Saturday morning.

"Can't I call to check on my favorite baby sister?" Her voice was dripping with sugar. Whatever she wanted was going to be big.

"I'm your only sister."

"Yeah, yeah, yeah. Look, I'll get right to the point." There. That's the Andrea I was waiting to appear. "I'm 'bout to get evicted. I need you to let me hold a couple G's 'til I get paid."

"Two thousand dollars?" My voice rose a couple of octaves. "Your subsidized rent is five hundred."

"Well, I'm behind on some other bills and I figured since I was askin', I should throw in enough for my weave. It's wrecked and I need it to be tight. Dante is takin' me to Vegas next weekend. You know I gots ta be fly."

I frowned and squinted in disgust. "If Dante can afford to take you to Vegas, then why can't you get the money you need from him?"

"Uh, duh, if he pays for my bills, then how can he afford a Vegas vacation too?"

My sister was simple-minded. That wasn't a surprise. Even so, she lost me every time I tried to follow her logic.

"So, let me get this straight," I said. "You want me to pay for your necessities, including your weave?"

"Yeah."

"And in the meantime, instead of handling responsibilities, your man is paying for your trip?"

"Now, you feel me."

"Andrea, I don't know how to break this to you, but I am not giving it to you."

"Really? Why?" Andrea asked, sounding genuinely surprised.

"Because you're a grown woman. Handle your own business."

"Well. How about five hundred for my rent? Will you let me hold that?"

I sighed. "Will I ever get it back?"

"Truth or lie?"

"Truth."

"No."

I shook my head and chuckled. When my sister and I were kids, we made a pact with each other. Anytime we said, "Truth or lie," we had to be one hundred percent honest. And it worked. It was a strange sister code we shared. "And you're going to bug me until I give in. Aren't you?" I asked.

"You know it."

"Fine. You can have it. When will you be by?"

"Well... how about now? Open ya door."

"Are you kidding me?" I exclaimed, as I stomped through my house and threw open the front door. Sure enough, there was my sister. In a turtleneck, long sleeve minidress, thigh-high boots, and a burgundy weave that went to her butt. I looked past her to the street and saw Dante behind the wheel of his much too big, and I was sure close to being repossessed, Tahoe. I sighed. Maybe one day my sister would wake up and get her sorry act together.

"I knew you would say,' yes'." Andrea grinned, her brilliant smile reminding me that underneath her hoodrat exterior, she was a beautiful woman.

I turned away from the door and headed to my office. Andrea followed. I removed our family portrait from the hook on the wall and took five one-hundred-dollar bills from the wall safe. I handed them to her. "You know this is ridiculous, don't you? You should have money."

"I got jammed up with one of those cash advance places. I'm into them for a lot."

"Well, I'm not bailing you out of that crap like I did last time."

Andrea gave me a devilish smirk as she flashed the money I had given her in my face. "You just did, lil' sis." She began slowly backing out of the room, then hurried to add, "But I promise, this is the last time I get caught up wit' all dat. Love you."

I made a move toward her, but she grabbed my shoulders and kissed me on my cheek. Then she spun on her heels and darted through my house and out the door, leaving me five-hundred dollars poorer and speechless.

I sat on my couch and gazed out the window. My thoughts had shifted from choking Andrea, to how much I was going to miss Sean, who'd given his two weeks' notice to Mr. Jeffries. This coming Friday was going to be his last day. He'd kept his word about my presentation and had taken it home yesterday to review my final draft. I was looking forward to Monday to hear what he had to say about it. I was due to give a dry run to Mr. Jeffries on Tuesday and present it to my client on Thursday.

I glanced at the clock on the living room wall. Nine forty-three. I had already done my yoga, showered, and was lounging in my favorite orange sarong on the couch. Lifetime was having a Golden Girls marathon, and I loved those old ladies. It was a subzero snowy day, and I was no longer in the mood for shopping.

I picked up the phone to call Michele and tell her I'd changed my mind, but before I could dial her number, my doorbell chimed.

"It better not be Andrea coming back for more," I mumbled, marching to the door. I looked through the peephole and butterflies began dancing in my stomach.

My hand flew to my hair and patted my scarf. I snatched it

off and tossed it on the hall table. Then, gave a quick shake to my head to let my curls fall to my shoulders. I smoothed my sarong to make sure it was closed and greeted my guest.

"Good morning!" I gave Sean my brightest smile. "What brings you by?"

"I was in the neighborhood and decided to bring you your proposal. I would have called first, but I left my phone at home. I hope you don't mind that I stopped by unannounced."

"It's fine. Please, come in." I stepped aside and allowed him to enter. Biting my lower lip, I closed the door.

He turned to face me, captivating me with his light brown with flecks of green eyes.

"Chanelle?" He had a puzzled look on his face.

"Huh?"

"So, where do you want to do it?"

"Anywhere you like," I answered. Breathless.

"Since it's your house, I'll let you decide."

"Decide what?"

"Where do you want to go over the proposal? I asked where you wanted to spread out. There were a couple of areas that I thought you could tighten up and I wanted to show you. Overall, it's a winner."

I snapped out of my daze. "Oh. Ah, yeah, right. Ummm, the proposal. Riiigghht. Um, how about here?" I pointed to the living room. "We can spread out on the coffee table and you show me what you're talking about."

I led him into the living room. "Make yourself comfortable. I'm going to change. I'll be right back." I bounded up the stairs to my bedroom. Once inside, I closed the door and then leaned my back against it, scolding myself for acting like a star struck teen. I took several deep breaths in a useless attempt to calm my nerves.

How long had he been talking to me while I gawked at him? Why did this man have such an effect on me? It was ridiculous.

I walked over to my bathroom and turned on the faucet. I hoped that splashing cold water on my face would help. It didn't. I turned off the water and headed to my closet. What could I throw on that said sexy casual? Did I even want to be sexy? Well, I knew I did, but I shouldn't. In the end, I threw on some navy sweats, a fitted yellow T-shirt, and white ankle socks. I said a quick prayer to God and headed back downstairs.

CHAPTER 7

WE REVIEWED every single page of the proposal. His suggestions were on point, and I made notations to make the necessary changes. I was confident that by Thursday I would be more than prepared to land this account.

Michele had called around ten-thirty and said she didn't feel like going out either. She was taking advantage of her afternoon home alone.

"Wow, I can't believe it's noon already." Sean stood, raised his arms, and gave a big stretch.

"I guess time flies when you're having fun." I grinned at him. I put my hands on the back of my neck and gave myself a light massage.

"Here, why don't you let me do that for you?" he offered.

I glanced up at him. "That's okay. I'm a little stiff from bending over those projections for so long." I rotated my neck as I worked out the kinks.

"I insist. I've been told my hands are famous." He wiggled his fingers and gave me a goofy grin.

There was no way that I could not give in so I consented. "Alright."

He sat back down. "Turn your back to me."

I did as instructed and turned to mush the instant he touched me. As his strong hands applied subtle pressure to my shoulders, I let my neck drop, enjoying the tingling sensation on my skin.

I closed my eyes and let my mind wander. It felt so good that I released a slow moan. He must have taken that as an invitation because his soft and warm lips replaced his hands.

Consequences be damned, I thought, smacking away the alarm blaring in my head. I tilted slightly, giving him better access to my sweet spot, then wrapped my hand around the back of his head and played with his hair. He touched my face and eased me around until we were staring into each other's eyes. I glanced down for a moment, thankful that he wasn't wearing his wedding band. Not that it made him any less married; it just made it easier to pretend that what I was about to do was okay.

For two-tenths of a second, the fog cleared and I grabbed his hands before they went any further. But then he leaned forward and whispered, "Please," in my ear and that was it.

We rid ourselves of all clothing as our hands and lips explored each other's bodies. He hovered over me. "Do you want to go to your room?"

"No. I want you right here. Right now." I gazed at him with hunger and waited with anticipation.

We paused while he reached into his pants pockets and pulled out a condom. He must have planned this before he got here. I didn't know if I should be grateful for the protection or pissed that he assumed it would go this far.

But as he entered me seconds later, I decided it didn't matter. I found myself floating to the most magical place I had ever been in my life. And I didn't want to leave.

What in the hell did I do? I held my head in my hands as I stood under the hot shower.

"Do you want some company?" he yelled from the other side of the bathroom door.

"Uh, no thank you," I stuttered. "I'll be out in a minute."

"Okay. Well, let me know if you change your mind."

"Thanks for the offer," I mumbled.

I could not believe that we'd had sex all afternoon and then slept until late evening. Never in all my life had I been intimate with a man who wasn't mine; I was even judgmental of women who did what I'd done.

Life had a cruel way of turning on you. I could hear Michele's mouth when I told her. And I was going to tell her because we talked about everything.

Michael popped into my mind. This was his fault. If he had been who I needed him to be, we would've been married, and this wouldn't have been an issue.

Yeah, right, Chanelle, who are you kidding? I chastised myself. It wasn't Michael's fault. An opportunity had presented itself, and I took it. I probably shouldn't have. I knew I shouldn't have.

But I did. And I loved it. I wished it could happen again. But it couldn't. For one, he was moving at the end of the week. For two, my conscience wouldn't allow a repeat. Now, I had to figure out a way to get him out of my house.

After my shower, I put on my flannel pajamas, the most unflattering thing I owned. The last thing I wanted was to entice him when I emerged from the bathroom.

I touched the door handle and paused. What if he expected us to pick up where we left off? Would I have the strength to say no or would I do it again? I slowly backed away and paced the length of the bathroom, not yet ready to face him. But I couldn't hide all night.

I moved back to the door, took a deep breath, and unlocked

it. Inhaled again, and finally gathered the courage to turn the knob and step through the threshold that separated safety from the unknown.

Sean was sitting on the side of my bed with his head in his hands. He looked up when he heard me. His beautiful eyes that had devoured me with hunger and passion for hours were now rimmed in red.

"Hi."

"Hi."

"I'm so sorry, Chanelle. I don't know what happened. I mean, I know what happened, I'm just sorry that it did. I mean, I'm not sorry, but I am. You know what I'm trying to say?"

He was as tormented by this as I was. He should have been even more so because he was the one who was married. "I feel bad about this, too." I sat next to him and reached for his hand. "Sometimes things have a way of spinning out of control."

"Yeah, they do, but I wanted this to happen. That's why I came over. I could have given you the proposal on Monday. I just wanted to spend some time alone with you."

"I'm not slow, Sean. Don't think that you seduced me, and I didn't know what was up. I wanted to do this as much as you did. You're a good friend and I value our relationship. I'm not going to say anything about this to anyone. Are you?"

"If you mean am I going to tell my wife, the answer is no. She and I have enough issues to work through. But I would be lying to you, Chanelle, if I said I didn't feel something when I'm with you that I don't feel with her."

My heart was so sad. I'd spent a loving and sensual afternoon with a man I cared about, and there was no future for us. "I understand. But you're doing the right thing. You have to give your marriage a chance. Virginia will be a good start for both of you."

He squeezed my hand. "I'm going to miss you."

"I'm going to miss you, too."

He stood and gave me a half smile. "I guess I should head home. I need to figure out how I am going to explain my day."

"Good luck."

I walked him to the front door. I wanted to kiss him before he left, but I was afraid that I wouldn't be able to handle it. Instead, I allowed him to pull me close and hold me like I was his woman. I closed my eyes and inhaled, breathing in the moment, knowing that in seconds all I would have were memories of what once was. But could never be. I held him as long as I could, then peeled myself away from his embrace. With watery eyes, I stayed in the doorway and watched him lumber to his car before driving away. I shut the door and dragged myself back to my bedroom. What a day!

CHAPTER 8

I REACHED my hand from underneath my comforter and grabbed the phone. It took three rings for her to answer. "Hey, Michele. Ride with me to church, okay?"

"Okay. Is everything alright?"

"Yeah," I replied in a low tone. "I just need my best friend."

"I'll be ready when you get here."

We disconnected the call, and I placed my hands over my eyes and groaned. I'd had a tumultuous night, tossing and turning, turning and tossing. Still tired, I forced myself from my bed, skipped my workout, and fixed a jumbo cup of coffee.

"You are such a hypocrite," I said aloud, talking to myself as though I belonged in somebody's institution. "Here you are, getting ready for church. Getting ready to praise the Lord." I raised my hands and twisted them from side to side. "And you screwed another woman's husband. Ugh." I was so disgusted.

Stepping into my bathroom, I cringed. The dated décor of the place that was supposed to bring me serenity was worsening my already sour mood. The former owners had had some love affair with pink and tiny tiled floors with grout that was impossible to clean. I'd dealt with it for much too long, and I was going to have to make a change soon.

It took me longer than usual to dress, and by the time I got to Michele's, we were already late. "What happened to Miss Always On Time?" she joked, getting into the car and closing the door.

"I had a rough morning."

She took a good look at me. "Wow. I can see that. What happened?"

"Let's go to Red Lobster after church and I'll fill you in."

Michele gave me the side-eye as she tried to figure out what was up. "Okay. Sooo... what do you want to talk about now?"

My sigh was heavy. "Nothing. Can we ride in silence?"

"Let me get this straight. You wanted me to ride with you, so we could *not* talk?"

I nodded. "Yes."

Then she nodded. "Okay."

That's the beauty of having a best friend. They understand you in ways that no one else will. We drove in silence and had an uneventful time in church. Although, the message, *Let Your Actions Support Your Words*, made me feel awful. Humph, my actions these days were a long way from what I professed. But I made it through the morning, dodged Pastor Sharpe after service, and now Michele and I were seated at Red Lobster, nibbling on our cheddar bay biscuits, artichoke dip, and drinking strawberry daiquiris.

She chomped on the buttery bread. "What's going on?"

"Sean and I had sex all day yesterday," I blurted.

She stopped chewing. "Come again?"

"I did. Many times."

"Whoa. How did *that* happen?"

I filled her in on the details of the day before, starting with him knocking on my door and ending with him leaving hours later.

"Wow... How do you feel about all of this?"

I shrugged. "Guilty. Sad. Like I lost a good friend. Like the worst Christian ever."

Michele was quiet and I kept talking. "It never should have happened, Chele. I knew better."

"Yeah, you did," she said, and I rolled my eyes. "Am I lying?"

I shook my head. "No."

"Hey, what's done is done. Lamenting about it doesn't change it."

"But you remember what Pastor Sharpe said to me a few weeks ago, right?"

"You mean, the warning about whatever you were planning to do, don't do it? Because it won't end well?"

"This has to be what she was talking about."

Michele seemed to ponder what I'd said. "The question is, what are you gonna do, now?"

I took a slow sip of my daiquiri. "Keep it moving. I asked God to forgive me, and I believe He did. One day I'll forgive myself. Sean will be gone at the end of the week, and I'll get my focus back."

Michele nodded. She scooped some lobster artichoke dip onto a chip and shoveled the entire thing into her mouth. She held up her finger while she finished chewing. "You'll be fine, girl. You just have to take some time for yourself. Get your head right."

"Yeah, and pray that karma doesn't get me too bad. God says we reap what we sow. This is a messed-up crop I planted."

"It is. But it's not the end of the world. You'll bounce back from this."

I fell into the plush leather seat of the booth and blew the air out of my cheeks. "Lord knows I hope so."

CHAPTER 9

"HEY, CHANELLE," Sean said when he phoned me in my office the Wednesday following our tryst.

"Hey."

"Would you mind meeting me at Starbucks in about an hour?"

Good Lord! I was starting to hate Starbucks. "Is it something we can talk about here? Maybe before your going away party?" Mr. Jeffries had arranged a final farewell for Sean around three.

"Um, I was hoping to see you alone."

"Why?"

"What I need to say can't be said in the office."

I wondered what God-awful news he was going to drop on me now. "Sure. I can be there in an hour."

"See you then."

I hung up and tilted forward, placing my elbows on my desk and my head in my palms.

"Thank you for meeting me." He stood as I approached the table.

"You're welcome." I allowed him to kiss my cheek, before scooting into the booth.

"I ordered your favorite, a caramel macchiato." He pointed to the steaming hot cup in front of me.

"I didn't realize you noticed what I drink."

"I notice a lot of things about you."

Why was he doing this to me? "So, what did you want to talk about?" I asked, wanting to get to why I was here and trying to pretend that my heart wasn't being shredded.

He reached for my hands. "I wanted to make sure you were okay. After what happened on Saturday."

"Why wouldn't I be? We both knew what was up." I slid my hands back and placed them in my lap, underneath the table.

"Chanelle, I want to apologize again. I never should have let it happen."

"Look, Sean. We've already had this conversation. I said we're good. If this is all you wanted to say, then you could have saved your breath." I made a move to stand, but he leaned forward and touched my arm.

"Please, don't leave. Not yet. Please." His eyes pleaded with me to stay put, and against my better judgment, I sat back down. He exhaled. "Thank you. The reason I asked you to meet me was because I wanted to give you this." Reaching into his pocket, he pulled out a small jewelry box, then slid it across the table next to my cup.

I stared at it like I'd be electrocuted if I touched it. "What is it?"

"Open it and see," he prompted.

Did I want a gift from him? Yes. No. Yes. Shoot, I didn't know. I moaned inwardly, then opened the box. Inside was a two-carat diamond and platinum tennis bracelet. I held it in my hands, fingering the jewels. "Sean, this is beautiful," I whispered.

"I'm glad you like it."

"I love it," I said. "But I can't keep it." I handed it to him, but he wouldn't take it.

"Why?"

"It wouldn't be right. You're married."

"I told you, I care about you. My situation is my situation. But I want you to know you'll always be in my heart. Please. Keep it." He slipped it from my hand and fastened it around my wrist.

I was admiring it and wondering if I should remove it when a woman walked up to our booth.

"Hi, Sean," she cooed.

Tiny beads of sweat appeared on his upper lip. "Oh, uh, hi, Bianca."

"So, who's your little friend?" She crossed her arms in front of her flat chest and cut her eyes at me.

"Um, this is—" he began, but I interrupted him.

I unclasped the bracelet, letting it drop onto the table. "No need for names. I was just leaving." I slid out of the booth and exited the restaurant. This was without a doubt the last time I would ever step foot inside of a Starbucks!

"You're kidding me," Michele said, when I'd called her as soon as I returned to my office.

"I wish. She walked right up to us and stared me down like I was trying to take her man or something."

The call waiting tone chimed for the fifth time since I'd left Sean. I didn't need to look at the number to know who it was.

"I didn't expect that from him." She commiserated with me.

I shook my head, ignoring the beep. "I didn't either. And here's the worst part. He's not mine. So, I can't even be upset. I thought I was special. The exception. But nope, I was a side chick, probably in a long line of side chicks."

"Well, at least now you know."

"Yeah, but his going away party starts in less than twenty-five minutes. How am I supposed to act normal when I'm so angry? And hurt."

"You fake it. You can't be the jilted woman at work."

My sigh was loud. "You're right. This is my bread and butter. Look, I'll call you later. I need a few minutes to get my head right before I go into this party."

Seconds after we hung up, Mr. Jeffries knocked on my door. "Chanelle, did I catch you at a bad time?"

"Of course not." I welcomed him in with a smile.

He sat in the cushy seat in front of my mahogany desk. "I wanted to compliment you again for the work you did on your presentation. I believe we'll secure this account tomorrow."

"Thank you. I'm confident things will go well."

"Sean helped you, right?"

I twisted in my seat. "Yes. Yes, he did."

"I'm going to miss him. He was an enormous asset around here."

I swallowed hard. "Yes. Yes, he was."

Mr. Jeffries, oblivious to my discomfort, kept talking. "I was thinking it might be a good idea for you to say a few words. You worked with him more than anyone else around here."

"Uh," I began, my eyes larger than the coaster on the corner of my desk, "uh, I, I think that's a great idea." I cleared my throat and continued. "I—I'd be happy to say a few words."

"Good." He stood. "I need to make a quick call, but I'll see you in a few."

I nodded. "Yes, Mr. Jeffries."

As he was walking out, Sean was approaching my open door. "Well, if it isn't the man of the hour," the older gentleman said.

He slapped Sean on the arm, like a father proud of his son, and then kept going.

"Hello, Sir," Sean said to his retreating back, before entering my office. He was lucky. If Mr. Jeffries had been a few steps further away, I would have slammed the door in his face.

"Hey." He closed my door and began walking toward me but froze in mid-step when he saw the daggers coming from my eyes.

"What do you want, Sean?"

"I want to explain what that was back there."

"No need for explanations. I'm not your wife."

"Chanelle, please listen. Bianca means nothing to me. I'd forgotten all about her. She's a woman I met a couple months ago when I was having a lonely moment, and she was company for the evening."

"You paid for sex?" My lip curled in disgust.

"No, I didn't. I met her in a bar. It was a one-night thing. That's it."

I stood. "That's nasty."

He blew off my comment and continued. "Like I said, it was one-night that she wanted to be more. And she pops up from time to time. Like she has my schedule or something. But what am I gonna do? Report her?"

"So, you're saying she's following you? This must be the day I wore my dumb clothes." I moved toward the door, brushing past him, but he caught my arm.

"It's the truth. My feelings for you are too deep for me to lie to you."

I looked down to where his hand was holding me and then looked into his eyes. Our faces were so close, I could feel his breath. "Sean."

"Chanelle," he whispered my name, and every ounce of resistance I'd had was washed away in a flood of lust. Then with his other hand, he cupped my chin and dipped his head to slip his tongue into my mouth.

His kisses grew forceful as he backed me against the wall. I was glad my office was on the fourteenth floor and there were no interior windows. When his lips moved down to my neck, he unzipped his pants, then hiked up my skirt and pushed aside the only barrier between us. The next twenty minutes were explosive, both of us surrendering to the passion that gripped us and refused to let go.

Somehow, we pulled it together in time to walk into his party as it was beginning. I made it through my impromptu speech, though I was clueless about what I'd said, since my mind kept replaying what had just happened. And I was still a little tingly. The one time I looked at him, he licked his lips and my body shuddered. But whatever I said must have been okay, because I got a few laughs and applause.

I mingled for a moment, then slipped out when no one was paying attention and dashed back to my office to grab my belongings. I was ready to go home and sort out this wild day.

When I entered my office, a sparkle on my desk peeked out from underneath a piece of paper. I walked over and realized Sean had left the diamond tennis bracelet and a note. *"Chanelle, thank you for being a wonderful woman. I would never hurt you. I love you."*

The note wasn't signed, but it didn't need to be. I fastened the gems around my wrist and sighed. The sooner this man moved, the simpler my life was going to be.

CHAPTER 10

"Since you ignored my advice about taking time for yourself, you need to start dating," Michele said, over a cup of coffee and a chicken caprese sandwich at the now infamous Starbucks, that I'd sworn to myself was off limits. "Sean has been gone for what, three weeks?"

I absently stirred my coffee, glad to be out of my office for a quick lunch. "Yeah, yeah, yeah. I'll get out in my own time."

"If I set you up on a blind date, would you go?"

A blind date? Me? I turned up my nose. "I don't know about that."

"It would be with one of Ben's friends. And you know he's got good friends. I wouldn't set you up with a loser."

"Hmm... Let me think about it."

"Well, well, well. Look who we have here," a vaguely familiar voice taunted me.

Michele and I turned toward the sound, and I groaned inwardly. Sean's one-night stand.

"What do you want with me?" I asked as she stepped to our table.

"Sean. I'm letting you know right now. Stay away from him."

Her slow neck roll, combined with her full puckered lips, and raised brow, let me know this heifer thought I would be easily intimidated.

The frown across my forehead deepened. She was about to learn that I was not the one. "One, I don't know you, so you need to back up. Two, he's a colleague. A colleague who doesn't even live here anymore."

"Humph. Like I said. Stay away from him."

I wiped the corners of my mouth with my napkin and threw it down. Then placed my palms on the table, pushing myself away and ready to pop up. "You have one more time to talk sideways to me and it's gonna be on and crackin'." I summoned my inner Andrea and forgot I was a professional woman.

"Chick, I'm like the Incredible Hulk. Don't make me angry. You wouldn't like me when I'm angry."

My scowl intensified. "Who says stuff like that?" I jumped up and opened my arms wide, inviting her to come at me. "But if you're feeling froggy, then jump."

But Michele also rose and placed her hands in front of me to block me from swinging. "Chanelle, no. This is not who you are." She faced the woman who was about to receive a beating. "For your safety, you need to leave."

The woman paused, and I could see the hamster wheel turning in her brain. "This ain't over. Believe that."

I patted my chest like I was ready for a schoolyard battle. "Pick the place and time. I'll be there," I yelled as she backed away.

Returning to our seats and pretending that patrons weren't gawking at us in horror, Michele said, "You've never had a fight in your life. What in the heck was *that* all about?"

For the first time in a couple minutes, I breathed easily. Lord knows, all of that was nothing but bluster. Michele was right. I hadn't ever been in a fight. "Girl, I have no idea, but that's who I was telling you about. She's the one who walked up on Sean and me the last time we were here. Seeing her again set me off."

"You are not a housewife on one of those reality shows. Pull it together." Michele wagged her finger, chastising me.

I held up my hands in surrender. "You're right. I lost my cool. But I'm back to normal now."

"Good." Her posture relaxed, obviously relieved. "So why is she acting like Sean is your man?"

I shook my head and raised my shoulders. "How am I supposed to know? This is the second time I've ever seen her in my life."

Through a snicker that grew into a full belly laugh, she managed to squeak out, "And did you say, 'if you're feeling froggy, then jump'?"

I howled with her. "Girl, you know I think I'm gangsta." We laughed until tears streamed down our faces. "Anyway," I said, my chuckles subsiding. "I have a meeting in twenty minutes, I need to get back. I'll call you later."

"K. I'm going to finish my coffee, run some errands, and pretend I didn't see what I know I saw."

"Right. And I'll pretend I didn't do what I know I did." I stood and bent down, kissing her on the cheek. Then went back to work.

Mr. Jeffries was going on and on about who knows what. But sitting in this meeting was torture. I was kinda rattled by my interaction with that woman at Starbucks and my insane response. Why did she think Sean and I were a couple? And why did she even remember me? And why was I so ready to knock her out? I doodled in my notebook, as though I were taking notes from the meeting, and prayed like a kid in class who didn't do her homework, that Mr. Jeffries wouldn't ask me any questions.

Finally, the meeting concluded, I said my goodbyes, packed up my laptop and went home.

Pulling into my driveway and waiting for the garage door to lift, gave me a sense of comfort, and I exhaled the tension of the day. I entered the kitchen through the side door of the garage, tossed my keys on the counter and kicked off my shoes. I grabbed an ice-cold beer from the fridge, selected a bland pre-packaged dinner from the freezer and popped it into the microwave. Then I headed upstairs to my bedroom to change into my favorite beat up sweats.

Coming back down the steps, I made a pit stop at the front door to grab the mail that had been slipped through the slot. I threw it on top of the pile that had been accumulating for the past three weeks and went back into the kitchen. Four minutes later, my meal, if I could even call it that, was cooked. I took it and my beer into the den, where I fully intended to be parked for the rest of the evening.

I washed down what was supposed to be a piece of chicken with a swig of the frothy beverage and flipped through the cable channels, looking for mindless entertainment. When my phone chimed, I almost ignored it, but then thought it might be important.

I answered without bothering to check the caller ID.

"Hey, Chanelle, how's it going?" Sean asked.

My heart froze as I popped up on the couch. "Hey. Things are going well."

"I hope you don't mind me calling. I tried calling you before I left, but you wouldn't answer."

Of course I didn't answer, I thought. "I didn't see the point."

He cleared his throat. "Um, did you win the account?"

"Yes. Thank you for your help."

"Congratulations and you're welcome."

We listened to the sound of each other breathing as we struggled to hold a conversation. "How's the new home?" I asked.

"Virginia is beautiful... I love the weather... My new job is good... Challenging, but good."

"Oh," I said. More silence as both of us danced around what I wanted to know but was afraid to ask.

"Cynthia and I aren't doing so well," he volunteered.

"Oh. Um, sorry to hear that," I lied.

"Yeah, I thought the change of scenery would be good for us, but things seem to be getting worse." He paused. "I miss you, Chanelle. I miss working with you and seeing you almost every day."

I didn't know how to respond. I missed him too, but I wasn't going to say it. It wasn't like we dated. "Well, things will get better. Look, I'd love to talk more, but I have to go. I wish you all the best."

"Oh, okay." The slight elevation in his voice said he was surprised I was rushing him off the phone. "Well, I guess I'll talk to you later."

I inhaled a deep breath and released it. "Sean, I don't think that's such a good idea. We should have a clean break. You're building your life there and I'm living my life here."

"I'm not ready to let you go." His voice, full of his yearning for me tugged on my emotions. But I had to be strong.

"You have no choice. I was never built to be a side piece. I made a mistake. A couple of mistakes. And now I'm moving on. I suggest you do the same."

"Wow, I didn't expect this."

"I'm sure you didn't. As much as I care about you, Sean, and I do, I really care about you. But I care about myself more. You have a wife and a life that's separate from me. I'm not going to sit around and be the cleanup woman, taking whatever I can get. I'm worth more than that. Don't you agree?" I put him on the spot, but I needed him to acknowledge that playing with my feelings wasn't cool.

"Yes, Chanelle, you are worth so much more."

"Thank you for that. Please, don't call me again. Goodbye Sean." I clicked the "off" button. Then immediately turned the phone back on and dialed a familiar number.

"Hey, Chele, I'm ready for that date."

CHAPTER 11

"MICHELE, I hope you did right by me," I said aloud, walking into J. Alexander's for my first-ever blind date.

She was excited that I was willing to give it a try and set me up with Lawrence, the brother of one of Ben's closest friends. She said I'd met him before, though I couldn't remember. Ben had given him my number and when he called, I thought he was silly. But I chalked it up to nerves and decided to give him a chance, anyway.

He was already there when I arrived. The hostess escorted me to the table and Lawrence stood when he saw me approach. One thing I could say about him was that he was handsome. He had smooth caramel skin and a body that would make a body builder jealous. Though, it was a little hard to get past the short s-curl he was sporting and the electric blue and cream pinstripe suit. I glanced at his feet and noticed he had on matching blue and cream gators. The smile he saw on my face as I greeted him was masking laughter. This was going to be an interesting night, I thought.

"Hey, Chanelle." He leaned forward to kiss my cheek, and I

didn't want his lips on me. So I extended my hand. I was grateful that he got the message and didn't press the issue.

"Hi, Lawrence, how are you?" I continued to stand as he pulled out my chair and allowed me to sit down before pushing it back toward the table.

"I'm fine, Baby. You look incredible. It's like you knew what I was going to wear," he slurred as he sat across from me.

It was true; I was looking good in my cream knit dress and matching boots, but I was not his baby. And I was not trying to be color coordinated with him. The last thing I wanted was for someone to think we knew each other that well.

"What do you recommend?" he inquired, taking his time to scan my body.

Feeling uncomfortable, I shifted in my seat and did my best to remain cordial. "Well, I love the grilled salmon, mashed potatoes, and their house salad. I order it every time I come."

He gave me a lazy grin. "I like the way you say that. 'Every time I come.' Yeah, I like that."

My eyes narrowed at his inappropriate comment. Why in the heck had Michele hooked me up with Supa Fly? And why was I only now noticing that gold front tooth?

"So, have you been here before?" I asked, pointedly changing the subject.

"Nah, this is my first time. But it won't be my last."

"I was hooked after my first time."

"I hope you get hooked after yo' first time wit' me." There he goes again with that idiotic grin.

My limit with him was fast approaching. I inhaled, telling myself to keep it together. I was not going to create a scene in another restaurant. Even Andrea wouldn't do that. "Don't you think it's a little soon to talk about a 'first time'?"

"It ain't never too soon. It's like this, Chanelle." He leaned back, rested his arm on the back of his chair, and sucked his teeth. "This is a nice restaurant and I expect to be repaid."

This fool was out of his mind. I squinted. "And how do you expect me to repay you?"

He let his eyes drop to my generous cleavage and then back up to my face. "You know the answer to that question."

That's it. I was now prepared to make a scene. But I never had a chance. Out of nowhere a shrieking female voice said, "Ah ha. I knew I'd find you here with some skank."

We both turned to see an enraged and very pregnant woman barreling down on our table.

"Heyyy, Baby." He threw up his hands to fend off her swinging fists.

"Don't you 'baby' me," she screamed, drawing attention from nearby tables. "Here I am, 'bout ready to have yo' baby and you sittin' here with some chick. Buyin' her a dinner you won't even buy me."

I looked from Lawrence to his wife or girlfriend or at the very least his baby mama, while he said, "Baby, it ain't like that. She my cousin."

My eyes widened, offended and amused at the same time.

"Unh-uh. You done this for the last time." Then she turned her rage on me. "Look. I been with this man for seven years. You hear me? Seven! And I ain't 'bout to give him up. If I ever catch you with him again, you ain't gon' like what I do to you."

Had I stepped into the ghetto edition of the Twilight Zone? "Um, you don't have to worry about me and your man. I promise you, I don't want him." I stood and smoothed the front of my dress.

"If you ain't want him, then why you havin' dinner with him, huh?"

Instead of going into details and delaying my exit from this bad dream, I said, "You have a good evening."

"Look here, you man stealing hussy. If I catch you with my dude again, I'll cut yo skinny little—"

I had a pretty good idea how she ended her sentence, but I

missed it. I was already on the other side of the restaurant doors and sprinting to my car.

Once inside, I instructed my Bluetooth system to dial Michele's number. "Hello?"

"You are soooooooo on my list," I said. "You are going to have to kiss up to me for a long time before I forgive you for this one."

She feigned offense. "My, my, that's a lot of hostility. And from such a sweet, demure young lady. I take it your date didn't go well?"

"Considering it started five minutes ago and I'm back in my car, you take it right. Why didn't you screen him?"

"I did." She defended herself. "Leonard is a sweet guy. What happened?"

"Who in the world is Leonard? I had a date with Lawrence." Now, I was confused.

"Lawrence?" She repeated his name a couple of times and then suddenly, uncontrollable laughter filled the interior of my car.

"What's so funny?" I was steaming at the fact that she found anything humorous about my train wreck of a date.

"Ben must have given your number to the wrong brother. I am so sorry. Lawrence is a jerk."

"Tell me something I don't know. And this is not funny." I was yelling in my car.

She snickered, unable to stop. "Yeah, right. You know this is hilarious and if it had happened to anyone else you would be laughing, too."

As she continued gasping for air through her giggles, my frustration subsided, and I saw the humor that had tickled her. We laughed while I described the events of the evening, including his outfit, gold tooth, S-curl, and girlfriend who looked like she should've given birth five months ago. I had to pull over. I was chuckling so hard, I couldn't see the road. To appease me, she told me to come over and she would buy me a pizza. I told her to have it delivered to my home. If I saw Ben tonight, I was liable to choke him.

She understood, and I arrived at home moments before my pizza was delivered. I stopped by the kitchen and grabbed a beer, then took my drink and the entire box to my bedroom. I changed into my 'I'm home alone so it's okay to have this on' pajamas and got in the bed with my food and my drink, turned on the TV, and had a great Friday night.

And this was my first date post, Sean? Ugh…Ay yi yi.

CHAPTER 12

Seven Months Later

"Good morning, Patty," I said to my assistant as I entered our office suite.

"Morning, Boss Lady. How was ya night?"

"Same as usual, but it was alright. How was yours?"

"Fine. But are you sure about that? You been lookin' a little tired these days. You sure everything is cool?"

Leave it to Patty to call me out. "I'm fine. Please hold my calls this morning. I have a couple things I need to get out by noon."

"You got it, Boss Lady."

I entered my office, set my briefcase on the floor, then powered up my computer, following my usual routine.

My mouth dropped when I opened my email, and the first message that popped up was from Michael. *"Hi, Chanelle. It's been awhile since we last spoke. I've been thinking about you a lot over the past several months. I'm emailing you because I figured you wouldn't accept my call. I'm genuinely sorry about what happened with Rocco. I was confused at the time, and things with him aren't what I expected. I think maybe I made a mistake. You said you weren't interested in remaining friends when we were at the courthouse, but months have passed and I'm hoping you'll reconsider. I'd love it if we could have drinks one day after you get off work. I'd like to talk about us."*

Wow. I rested in my executive chair and scrutinized his email, re-reading the words over and over. I hadn't expected to hear from him again. Ever. I wondered how I should respond. Or *if* I should respond.

I swiveled in the chair, rested my elbow on the arms and laced my fingers. Whenever I had an issue, I'd take in the beautiful skyline and I'd always feel better. But today, as I gazed through the floor-to-ceiling windows, I felt... nothing. The last seven months had been so lonely. Many nights of frozen dinners and mindless TV. A couple of pitiful dates as bad as the one with Lawrence, who by the way I'd run into at the gas station and we'd talked at the pump. Until his off-her-meds baby mama came charging out of the store connected to the station and started screaming at me to stay away from her man.

I sighed heavily, looking back at the computer monitor. It was in my best interest to ignore Michael's email. I pressed the delete key and watched the message vanish from my screen, then sighed again and went back to work.

CHAPTER 13

"HOW'S MY FAVORITE AUNTIE?" Rachel's voice was sweet enough to give me cavities.

I rubbed the sleep from my eyes and yawned. Still tired and not ready to get out of bed. "Seeing as how I'm your only auntie, you must mean me, and I'm fine. How's my favorite niece?"

"Well..." she hedged. "I would be doing a whole lot better if I could spend the weekend with you."

I sat up and fluffed the pillows behind me. "You know you're always welcome to stay with me. But what's going on at home?"

"You know it's the first of the month and Mom is gonna get her check, which means Dante is gonna be up in the crib all weekend and I don't feel like dealing with him anymore."

I understood her frustration. I hated visiting my sister when Dante was there. He was a loser, and so was my sister, for allowing him to make her child feel out of place in her own home. Rachel didn't even refer to him as her dad. "Did you check with your mom to see if it's okay?"

"She said she'd be glad to have the peace and quiet, so she's cool with it."

"Okay. You want me to pick you up after work?"

"Yes, thanks, Auntie. I'll be ready." I could hear the big smile on my niece's face as she hung up. I decided to make it a girl's weekend and we would have a blast.

Before I could set it down, the phone rang again.

"Hey, girl. Whatcha got up for tonight?" Michele asked.

"Rachel called and wants to spend the weekend, so I was thinking about taking her to a movie and going to the spa tomorrow. Why? Did you have something in mind?"

"Nah. I was being nosey. Ben wants to take BJ to the movies too, but I'm sure our movie will be different from yours." Michele chuckled.

I giggled with her. "Rachel would have a fit."

"It definitely wouldn't be the weekend she wanted. Anyway, since you have plans, I won't try to rope you into coming with us."

"Even if I didn't, I would've passed. I haven't felt like doing much of anything these days."

"I've noticed and I'm worried about you. Why—"

I cut her off. "Hey, Chele, I still have to finish getting ready for work. I'll call you later."

"Don't rush me off the phone. I want to know—"

I interrupted her again. "I'm not rushing you, but I have to go. My first meeting is at nine-thirty and I'm almost running late. Call you later. Love ya. Bye." I clicked the "off" button and tossed my phone on the bed. Michele was worried about me, and while that wasn't my intention, I didn't feel like being social. I was much happier at home. Alone.

I glanced over at the clock on my nightstand. I had less than thirty minutes before I needed to leave for work. I didn't have a meeting. Actually, my schedule was clear, so I decided to play hooky and do something just for me.

After calling in to the office and letting Patty know I wouldn't be in until Monday, I walked into the bathroom, placed my hands on my hips and let my eyes journey around the sea of pink. It was time to tackle my last home improvement project and create a personal oasis. The more I thought about it, the more amped I became. I went back into my bedroom and turned on the jazz station, then moved over to the closet to find something to wear. I settled on a pair of capris and a tight-fitting burgundy tank top, with a scoop neckline. After my shower, I slathered on my favorite body oil, did my makeup, styled my hair and dressed. I grabbed the keys to the Rover and headed for the garage.

For the first time in a long time, I was feeling pretty good, so I turned on the local R&B station and rolled down all of my windows on the short drive to Lowe's Home Improvement store. Once inside, I made a beeline for the bathroom displays in the center of the store. There were so many styles and themes that I was lost on where to start. As I stared at a two-person Jacuzzi jet tub, I heard a voice behind me. "You should buy it."

I spun around and blinked a few times. Rick. We'd met the summer after my first year of college and dated until my senior year. Every part of me was in love with him. And not because he was gorgeous, but because he had a thuggish lifestyle; and in my younger years, I found that attractive. I think back now on how foolish I was to love someone like him, but at the time it felt right.

"Hi, Rick." This man still had the power to take my breath hostage. Six foot five. Golden brown. Almond-shaped hazel eyes framed by the longest lashes I'd ever seen on a man. He hadn't aged one day in the thirteen years since I'd last seen him.

"It's so good to see you, Chanelle." He pulled me into a spontaneous hug and I 'bout lost it. It had been months since a man touched me. When he released me, I wobbled a bit. "The years sure have been good to you." He eyed me and smiled.

I blushed. "Thank you. And they've been just as good to you." I checked out his muscular frame underneath his black collared polo shirt. "So, what brings you here this morning?"

"Supplies. I own a home remodeling business."

"You gave up the street life, huh?" I'd never pictured Rick doing something worthwhile with his life. I had always assumed he would either be in prison or become a victim of the streets.

"I had to. All my boys were gettin' locked up or dyin'. You remember, Tommy?"

I nodded. "Wasn't he your roommate?"

"Yeah. He got pinched on a murder charge and they gave him all day." When I frowned, he clarified. "Life. That was it for me. I had to make some major adjustments, or I was going to be right behind him. I took my money and got out the game. I started my own company."

"Very impressive." I nodded my approval. "I'm glad to know you made a career change."

"Thanks." He beamed at my compliment, which surprised me.

"Do you have a specialty, or do you remodel everything?"

"I do it all, but bathrooms are what I enjoy most. More specifically, master baths. I don't know why, but people love their bathrooms. It's like their private sanctuary or something. I get a high off creating designs that fit their lifestyles and personalities."

"It's funny, you should say that. I decided this morning that it was time to remodel mine. It's so hard, though. How do you narrow the choices? I mean, I thought I knew what I wanted, but now I'm not sure."

He chuckled. "That's natural. Most people stand in the middle of their space, whether it's the bathroom, bedroom, kitchen, whatever, and they dream up what they want. Then they get to the store, see all their options, and panic. A lot of times they scrap their entire project." He waited a beat before adding, "I could give you some tips if you like."

"I would love that." I jumped at his offer. He didn't know it, but I was seconds away from doing what he'd said. Looking up at him through my lashes, I asked, "When can you come by?"

He hesitated before saying, "I was talking about giving you some pointers here, but I could stop by and take a look."

My cheeks stained with embarrassment. How had I jumped to the wrong conclusion? "Oh, I'm sorry. I didn't mean to be presumptuous. I guess I'm in desperate need of help."

"It's no problem. It's what I do for a living, remember?"

He squeezed my shoulder and an electrical current flowed from his hand, sending shock waves through my entire body. I couldn't believe the effect he was having on me after all these years. "Thank you. When is a good time?"

"How about this evening? I should be done with my job around six. I could swing by around six-thirty, if that works for you."

I thought quickly. Rachel would be there, but since it wasn't a date, that wouldn't be a problem. "Six-thirty is fine." I gave him my address and home and cell phone numbers. He teased me about still having a landline but understood when I told him that was the only number my grandparents would dial when they were alive and couldn't bring myself to disconnect it.

"It was good to see you again, Chanelle." He stared into my eyes and the moment was a little too intense for me, so I blinked and glanced away.

I cleared my throat before turning back to him. "Um, it was good to see you too, Rick."

"Well, I guess I'll see you tonight."

"I look forward to it."

After we said our final goodbyes, he strolled away, and I went back to looking at the Jacuzzi tubs. But I couldn't focus. This was the first time I'd felt a connection with anyone since Sean.

Since I was no longer in the mood to look at bathroom fixtures, I left Lowe's and headed to Michele's. It had been a while since we hung out and I missed her. I knew she would want to talk about my life and when I was going to snap out of my funk, and even though I didn't want to have that conversation, I wanted to spend time with her.

On my way to her house, I stopped by the supermarket and picked up a few steaks, a couple of chicken breasts, and pasta salad.

Michele opened her front door and stepped aside, giving me room to enter. "Hey, Channie, what brings you by? And why aren't you at work?"

"I called in today. The place won't fall apart without me. And I missed you guys. I haven't had a hug from my godson in ages." I moved toward her kitchen with the groceries, setting the bag on the counter.

"If you want to see him, you'll have to go by my parents."

"What's he doing there?"

"My mom was missing him too, so she came by earlier this morning and picked him up." Michele began removing items from the bag. "What's with the raw steak?"

"I had a taste for some barbecue and good conversation. And you grill up a steak like nobody else."

"Flattery will get you everywhere. Hook up a couple daiquiris while I get the fire started." She opened her junk drawer and pulled out an aim-n-flame before walking to the deck in her backyard.

"You got it, girlfriend." I made the daiquiris and met her outside.

"So, what's been going on with you? I can't believe we haven't seen each other in a few weeks." She spread charcoal briquettes around the bottom of the grill.

I plopped into the wicker chair and took a drink of my daiquiri. "I know, right? Emotionally, it's been a little rough."

Michele's voice was soft. "You haven't been your usual

upbeat self in quite some time, but what tipped you over the edge?"

"This whack dating life!" I chuckled even though I saw nothing funny. "I spent too much time thinking about it, and it messed with my head. So, I kinda retreated into myself."

"But how could you shut me out? We've never done that to each other before." I heard the hurt in her voice and felt guilty.

We had been best friends for over three decades, and she was right. "I apologize. I needed to be alone. But days turned into weeks. And before I knew it, so much time had passed..."

Michele shook her head. She squinted like she was trying to see what wasn't clear. "I don't understand. You're a beautiful woman. You have family and friends who love you, a gorgeous home, a wonderful personality, a body that twenty-year-old women envy. And you made partner."

I gave her a half smile. "But none of that matters when you're lonely and want to be with someone special. Maybe you can't relate. You have Ben and BJ. *You're* the one who has it all. Don't get me wrong, I enjoy my life and I'm grateful for it, but I'm not getting any younger. I want the next phase to start."

"What does God say in His Word about waiting? Doesn't He say something like we are to be content no matter what our circumstances? The next phase of your life will come, but you shouldn't spend this phase waiting for it and letting life sail by without you."

"Yeah, yeah." Her psychobabble wasn't helpful.

Michele smiled. "You know I'm right."

I rolled my eyes at my bestie and her Mary Poppins attitude. "Whatever. Guess who I saw today?"

"Who?" she asked, allowing me to switch topics.

"Rick."

"From college?"

"The one and only. He owns a remodeling company. He's

coming by tonight to check out my master bathroom and give me some tips on what I could do to change it up."

"Is he as fine as he was in college?"

"He looked better, if that's even possible."

My iPhone vibrated, and I pulled it from my purse and checked the screen. "Hey, Pumpkin," I said to Rachel. "Is everything alright?" I looked at my watch and became alarmed. It was eleven twenty-seven. She must have been calling from school.

"Hi, Auntie Chanelle. Oh, yes, everything is fine. I wanted to tell you that my friend, Maria, invited me to spend the weekend with her. I called my mom and she said it was okay. Maria's family is really cool, and she has lots of movies and games. Are you disappointed?"

"Of course, I'm disappointed that I won't get to spend time with my favorite niece. But I want you to have a good time with your friend this weekend."

"Thanks, Auntie Chanelle. You're the best." Her jubilant attitude was infectious.

I smiled. "Mm hmm. Love you."

"Love you, too. Bye."

"Bye, Sweetie." I set my phone down on the glass patio table. "Well, guess my plans have changed."

"Rachel's standing you up?" Michele added some lighter fluid, trying to get the fire to catch.

My laugh was lighthearted. "Yup. She has a friend who has, in her words, 'lots of movies and games'. How can I compete with all of that?"

"It's a losing battle." Michele joined my laughter before a hush fell over us. She was the first to speak. "Since your chaperone bailed on you, can you be trusted alone with Rick?"

My eyes widened in disbelief at the question. "Of course. Why would you even ask me that? Besides, it's not me he wants; it's my business."

Michele ignored my offended tone. "You don't believe that any more than I do."

I'd taken note of the way he'd looked at me. "Alright, maybe it's a combination. But for me, it's business. And Rick is someone I know and trust."

"No. Rick is someone you *used* to know and trust. You haven't seen him in over a decade. You have no idea what he's like. For all you know, he could be crazy."

"You're right," I conceded. "I'll tell you what; I'll text you as soon as he gets there and call you after he leaves."

"Sounds like a plan. Hey, where are you going?" Michele asked as I raised from the chair. "You haven't even eaten yet."

"I don't have much of an appetite anymore. I'm going to head up to the mall. I need a couple of suits for work, and since I don't have to pick up Rachel from school, now is a good time to hit the shopping center. Wanna ride?"

"I wish, but since BJ is with my mom, I'm going to tell Ben to come home. We have to take advantage of these moments when we get them." She pursed her lips. "Besides, someone is leaving me with a crap load of meat that I have to finish barbecuing. I can't believe you bought all of this food and aren't going to eat any of it."

I gave her a sheepish grin. "Sorr-eee." I reached down to pick up my purse and phone.

"This is a total flake move and you know it."

I shrugged. "It is. But you love me anyway. Talk to you later." I blew my bestie a kiss and left.

CHAPTER 14

"HELLO, CHANELLE?" a male voice asked as I grabbed my shopping bags from the back seat of my truck and walked toward the door.

I kept the phone pressed to my ear and jiggled the key in the lock of the door leading to my kitchen."Yes. Who's asking?"

"This is Rick." His tone relaxed. "I wanted to let you know I'm on my way."

Stepping inside, my stomach fluttered at the richness of his tone. Even through the phone, I could hear his swag. "I'll see you when you get here. Do you need directions?" I asked.

"I'm good. I've done a couple of jobs in your subdivision so I should be there in about thirty minutes."

We hung up, and I dashed up the steps with my bags, hung my purchases, and walked into the bathroom. My plan had been to take a relaxing bath, so I'd be chilled before he arrived. But the clock said I only had time for a shower. I undressed and tossed my clothes in the hamper, then stood under the spray of hot water, unwinding my mind and my body.

This wasn't a date, but I was still anxious. I wanted him to be interested in me, even if I didn't want him back. With Michael using me for my money, Sean accepting me only as a mistress, and Lawrence seeing me as a potential booty-call, my self-esteem had plummeted over the last several months. I needed the attention of an attractive man to boost my ego.

After my shower, I layered on jasmine scented cream with a body mist, then sauntered into my closet sifting through options. I wanted to give the impression of being put together without looking like I spent a lot of time—especially since I only had ten minutes.

I needed an outfit that said, "Thanks for coming over to give me some tips and, by the way, if you wanted to go out for a bite to eat, I'm ready." I settled on a pair of curve-hugging dark blue denim jeans and a printed halter top. If he invited me to dinner, I could throw on the matching denim jacket and my heels.

My doorbell chimed the second my foot touched the bottom stair. The last time I let a man in my home, I slept with him. I hoped this time I'd behave myself.

I took a full breath, then plastered a smile on my face before swinging the door open. "Hi, Rick."

"Hey, Chanelle. You look fantastic." He stepped inside and for the second time that day, he drank me in with his eyes.

"Oh, stop…" I waved away his compliment. "I can't even believe I'm letting you see me like this. I wish I'd had time to change." Why did I lie? Did I need a compliment that badly?

"Well, you look great. Like you just stepped out of the shower."

"Ha. Right…" I gave a nervous laugh. "Um, let me take your jacket."

"Thanks." He handed me his black jean jacket, and I hung it on the banister. He had on the same outfit he wore in Lowe's and smelled a little tart. My expression must have been a traitor to my thoughts because he said, "I apologize for not changing, but my job ran a little longer than expected and I didn't want to be late."

"Mm hmm. Not a problem. As long as I remember not to inhale too deeply." I winked to let him know it was okay that he was funky. This was definitely not turning into a date. I didn't even want him sitting on my couch.

He chuckled. "It's nice to know you haven't changed."

"I have where it counts." My smile was demure. "Can I get you something to drink?"

"Pepsi would be great."

"One Pepsi coming up. Follow me."

I led him to the kitchen and gestured to the dinette set in the breakfast nook. "Have a seat, and I'll get it for you."

He sat on one of the oak chairs. "So, how have things been? What have you been up to?"

"Life's been good. No complaints." I removed a couple of cans of Pepsi from the refrigerator, filled two glasses from the cabinet with ice, and sat across from him. I took a small drink of my Pepsi, then told him about my job and how I was steadily moving up the food chain. "How about you? Tell me about your business."

"Business is great. I run it with my brother, Max. Do you remember him?"

"Oh my gosh, of course I remember Max." I smiled, remembering the fun times we'd had with his younger brother and whatever girl was his flavor of the week. "Is he still a playboy?"

He rolled his eyes and guffawed. "Would you expect him to be any different?"

I snickered with him. "I guess not. How's the rest of the family?"

"Everyone is good. Believe it or not, my mom still asks about you."

"Get out. Seriously?" I'd loved his mom and the way she'd welcomed me to their Sunday family dinners.

He nodded. "To this day, she still says you're the one who got away."

"Oh, stop." I felt my cheeks turning as red as ripe cherries. "I'm sure there's a Mrs. in the picture."

"There was. But I'm divorced." He raised his hand to show me his bare ring finger.

"I'm sorry to hear that." Somehow, I managed to twist my face into an empathetic frown. Because that was the lie of all lies. I was ecstatic that he was available.

"Thanks. We got married not long after I graduated from college. When our marriage hit a rough patch, we tried working it out before calling it quits a few years ago. Best decision I could have made."

I tilted my head, wanting to know more. "What makes you say that?"

"I do what I want, when I want. But more than that. I have peace in my life." His eyes clouded over. "When I was with my ex, we didn't click on the major issues. And we didn't communicate well. We argued about money. I liked to make it,"—he rubbed his thumbs across his fingers—"and she liked to spend it."

I thought about how my sister was always in my wallet. "I can see how that would be frustrating."

"It was. When I turned my life around, she wasn't supportive. She wanted the money and didn't care what I had to do to make it happen." He paused while he gulped his drink. "You know what was ironic?"

"What?"

"Do you remember why you dumped me?"

How could I forget? We'd been wildly in love. If I wasn't hanging out with Michele, I was with Rick. But I hated that instead of focusing on pursuing his degree in architectural engineering, he was selling dime bags of weed and other pharmaceuticals. Breaking up with him was one of the hardest decisions I'd ever made. "Of course, I remember. I came to my senses and realized the way you were living wasn't acceptable. But you wouldn't give up your street life for me."

His nod was small. "And when I was finally ready to make that change, my wife didn't want me to."

I gave a light chuckle. "Irony at its finest."

He sighed. "I was so in love with her, Chanelle. I did whatever I could to keep her happy. And then one day, I couldn't do it anymore. The stress of dodging the cops, watching my boys get picked off, it got to be too much." Though his body was sitting across from me, I could see in his eyes that he had gone back in time, to days of unpleasant memories.

"I remember the day I told her I was shifting careers and putting my degree to use," he continued. "I'd laid out my entire business plan. She looked at it and laughed in my face. She wasn't down for me and gave me an ultimatum. I wanted to choose her, but I knew if we stayed together, she'd keep juicing me for my money and I'd never get out of the game."

"Is that why you divorced?"

He moved his head slowly from side to side. "Believe it or not, it wasn't. With all we were going through, I *still* wanted to be married to her; believed that we could work it out." His hands tightened around his glass. "And then she cheated on me."

I shifted a teeny bit and reminded myself that I was not the one who had cheated on him and he wasn't talking about me. "Your marriage ended because of an affair?"

His eyes grew stormy dark. "If you don't have trust and a solid commitment, then why be with someone? My parents have been married forever and they've always stressed fidelity. It was drilled into me since I was a kid. Although, their message seemed to be lost on Max, it wasn't lost on me. But you know that from when you met them when we were in college."

I nodded, unable to speak. What would he think of me if he

knew about what I'd done with Cynthia's husband? I may not have liked the woman, but she didn't deserve what I'd done.

He must have sensed my discomfort, though I'm sure he didn't know it was because of my life and not his. He let out a nervous laugh. "I apologize for telling you all that. I'm sure I said way more than you wanted to hear."

"That's okay. Sometimes it's good to get it out." I mentally shook my head, returning my focus to him.

"Maybe, but I'm still embarrassed."

"Don't be." I reached across the table and covered his hand with mine. First, he glanced down, and I wondered if I was being too forward, but then he looked into my eyes.

"Thank you, Chanelle."

Quietly, I said, "Rick, no matter how much time passes we will always have a friendship. Besides, back in the day, we used to talk about everything."

"We did, didn't we?"

"Yeah." I nodded. "The only problem we had in our relationship was the way you made money. If you'd have given up the drug dealing, we probably would've stayed together." *And I'd have my white picket fence, my kids, and my dog,* I thought to myself, but wouldn't dare say out loud.

He continued to use my eyes as the window to my heart. "I appreciate your listening. Like I said, my mother always knew you were a very special woman. I agreed with her back in college and I agree with her now." His words made me blush, and I pulled my hand away and turned from him. I was trying to understand this crazy chemistry we still seemed to have.

"Thanks." I didn't know what else to say. "Are you ready to see my bathroom?"

He seemed to read my cue because he said in a business tone, "Sure. Lead the way."

We stood from the table, and he followed me up the stairs.

Once inside my bathroom, he began his inspection. "Do you have any ideas on what you want?"

I shook my head, my gaze traveling around the spacious room. "All I know for sure is that I want a two-person Jacuzzi tub."

"Two-person, huh? Is that because you're planning for your future or because there's someone in your life?"

I tilted my head and raised a brow. "That's a presumptuous question."

"Hey, I spilled my guts in five minutes flat. I'm hoping you'll share something too, so I don't feel like such a fool."

"As your friend, Rick, you don't need to feel like a fool around me." Then I added, "But as your potential client, my reason for wanting a two-person tub is my business. Okay?"

The way Rick's body tensed, my response seemed to stun him. "Message received."

He cleared his throat, and in what was probably his most professional voice, shared some options.

I tried to listen, since it seemed that he had some solid suggestions. But I couldn't concentrate on what he was saying, because I was too busy replaying our conversation. He'd shared so much about his relationship and I'd shut him down.

And I didn't know why. All I knew was that I was officially confused. I'd been anxious, excited even, about him coming over and now I needed him to leave. I wondered if I could even hire him because things were weird with us. Or maybe it was only me.

"Chanelle? Chanelle?"

"Huh?"

"Are you okay? I've been talking to you, but I'm not sure you were listening. I was asking what you thought about shades of green."

"Green? Hmmm. Can I think about it? Actually, can I say something?" I faced him and, although he seemed puzzled, he

84

bobbed his head. "I feel a little awkward. First, you tell me about your broken marriage, and I felt you needed to let it out, so that was okay. Then, you ask me a playful question and I have a reaction I can't explain. Rick, you've been in my house less than thirty minutes and my head is spinning." I laughed slightly.

Rick paused a moment. "I agree that our conversation was different. How about we start over? No more personal questions or discussions. I'm good at what I do, and I want your business. I believe I still know what you like." When I lifted my eyebrow, he added, "You know what I mean. You had excellent taste in college and judging by your home decor, you still do."

"Thank you. This bathroom is the only part of my house that I haven't redone. How about you draw a sketch of your plans and bring them by next Saturday? If I like it, and your quote is reasonable, then the job is yours. Deal?" I extended my hand.

"Deal." Instead of shaking my hand, he grabbed it, pulled me toward him, and gave me a hug that short-circuited my senses.

I didn't know what to do, so I squeezed him back and felt the same electrical current that I'd felt earlier. We stood for a moment locked in a warm embrace until I reluctantly pulled away and held him with my eyes. "I think you'd better go."

His voice was deep and raspy as he forced himself to release me. "I understand." He cleared his throat again. "I'll call you once the drawings are complete. Do you mind if I take a few pictures of your bathroom?"

"Sure. Take all the time you need. I'll be downstairs." As he slipped a small camera from his pocket, I darted down the steps to safety. Rick came down about ten minutes later, picked up his jacket, and headed straight for the front door.

I followed him, and he faced me before opening the door. "It was great to see you again, Chanelle. I hope you know that I'm not the same man you dated years ago. I've grown and matured and I'd love to take you to dinner. But I'll understand if you have a man or you're not interested."

His eyes pierced straight through me. I knew he wanted some kind of reassurance from me, but I couldn't give it to him.

"Let's stay focused on the job. Okay?" My eyes pleaded with him to drop the subject of us and stick to business.

"Okay. I'll call you sometime this week." And with that, he let himself out.

CHAPTER 15

I GAZED out of my office window, working through a problem. Only this time, my issue had nothing to do with work.

It was all about Rick. It had been three days since his visit and I was as confused now as I was the day he was there. He'd been on my mind a lot. I realized I'd turned the entire night into a huge deal. I'd decided that when he called, I would act like all was normal and move forward, and if he asked me out again, I would say yes. Michele told me I'd made an issue out of nothing. And she was right. Rick had always treated me well.

Patty lightly tapped on my door. "Boss Lady? You have a delivery." She wore a smile that almost touched her ears, and I wondered what it could be.

I rose and trailed her out of my office. The bright floral arrangement that sat atop her desk left me without words.

I searched the two dozen yellow and white roses for the card, curious to find out who I needed to thank. Patty stared at me, waiting for me to read the card aloud, but I chose to read it by myself, so I said, "These are gorgeous. I'm taking them into my office."

"Gorgeous is an understatement, Boss Lady! Some dude

must really be feelin' you." Patty winked at me. "You betta give him an extra special 'thank ya'."

I smiled, then hurried inside my office, and kicked the door closed with my foot. Briskly stepping to my desk and placing the bouquet on the corner, I pulled the card and plopped on my couch.

The card simply read, "What if..."

That was it.

I flipped it over. Nothing. Puzzled, I got up and searched the bouquet for some sign of who could have sent it. Still nothing. I sighed deeply and returned to the couch. There was no one in my life who would send me flowers. I leaned over and picked up the phone on the table next to the couch and called Michele.

"Hey, girl. What you got up for today?" I asked.

"Nothing much. Working on the books for work while BJ is at preschool."

"Wanna meet for lunch?"

"How about Champs since it's halfway between me and you?"

"Cool." We agreed to meet at the bar and grill at noon, giving me almost no time to do any work. Which was good. I couldn't concentrate, anyway. I kept staring at my flowers and the cryptic card.

"What if? What if?" I whispered to myself, tapping the card against my hand. What if what? What if we were together? What if I love you? What if I'm crazy? What on earth did "What if?" mean?

Patty buzzed me on my office line. "Uh, Boss Lady... you have a call on line one."

"Who is it?"

"He won't leave a name. But he says you'll know what it's about and you'll want to take his call."

"Okay, put him through."

"Yes, Ma'am."

"Hello?"

"Is this Chanelle Slate?" a gruff voice asked.

"You placed the call. Shouldn't you know?"

The caller's laugh was chilling. "You want to play it like that? Okay. My client hired me because they want revenge against you."

"Yeah, right. Is this a joke?"

"I'm far from a joke."

I ignored his serious tone and rolled my eyes. "Sure you are. Did Michael set this up? If so, you tell him it's not funny."

"Look, I don't know who Michael is. My client prefers to remain anonymous. But understand this, Ms. Slate, at the right time, you'll know exactly who sent me."

"Mm hmm." I smacked my lips. "Well, Mr. Scary man, I'm very busy. So either you tell me who's behind this unfunny joke or I'm hanging up."

"I don't think you understand, this is not a—"

I clicked the on-hook button, ending the call. I didn't know who thought it would be amusing to prank me at work, but it was highly unprofessional, and it agitated me.

I buzzed Patty and told her to hold all my calls, then I snapped a picture of my flowers, put the card in my purse, and headed out to meet Michele.

"You will not believe my morning." I slipped into the booth across from Michele and reached for the drink menu.

She elevated an eyebrow. "Um, aren't you still on the clock?"

"What? You mean this?" I pointed to the menu in my hand. "When I tell you about my day, you'll understand why I need this." We chuckled and placed our orders with the server who'd arrived with our silverware and water.

She sipped her water. "So what's going on?"

"Look at this." I pulled out my cell phone and showed her the picture of my flowers.

"Those are gorgeous! Who sent them?"

"Beats me. This is all that came with them." I handed her the card.

"What if?" She flipped it over.

"I did the same thing. That's all there is. Two words."

"Do you think they're from Rick?"

I shook my head and frowned. "Why would Rick send me flowers? Especially after our evening ended so weird."

"What about Sean?"

I raised and lowered my shoulders. "I thought about it and if it was right after he moved, then maybe. But too much time has passed for it to be him. And besides, when we last spoke, I told him not to call me anymore. And he didn't. Which honestly, I thought he'd try at least one more time."

She nodded. "You have a point. What about Michael?"

"Humph." My hand swatted the air. "Maybe *black* roses, but not yellow and white."

Michele snickered. "Rocco would have a fit if he found out Michael sent you flowers of any color."

I hooted with her. "Exactly. Especially if he knew that Michael was thinking he may not be gay after all." My laughter subsided. "So, I have no idea where they came from. And if some guy doesn't have enough swag to step to me, then you know I'm not interested." I changed the subject, finished with trying to solve the mystery. "Oh, guess what? Somebody prank called me today."

"Who's playing games on the phone at our age?"

"No clue. They said some craziness about being hired to get revenge on me."

"That's nonsense." She bit into her jalapeno popper appetizer that had been placed on our table.

"I know, right? I tried to find out who was behind it and then got so irritated I hung up."

"Do you think the call is related to the flowers?"

"Hmm, not really. I mean, the flowers were beautiful. The call was strange. Maybe the flowers were delivered to me by accident."

"I'm sure they were for you. You just haven't figured out who sent them yet."

An unfortunately recognizable male voice interrupted our conversation. "Hey, Chanelle, it's great to see you, Baby!"

I felt like a rock had settled in my stomach as I dragged my eyes upward. "Hi, Lawrence."

"You ready to go out on another date with Big Daddy?" He sucked his teeth, the disgusting gold tooth on full display.

I had to choke back the vomit that was suddenly in my mouth. "Lawrence, you have a woman. And besides that, we have nothing in common." I held up my thumb and forefinger in the shape of a circle to emphasize my point.

"Oh, so it's like that?"

I frowned. "If you see me again, pretend you didn't."

"Okay, okay," He held up his hands, backing away from the table. "Hey, Michele, how you doin'?" He jerked his head up. "You alright?"

"Yes, I'm fine." She gave him the same smile I'd seen her give the homeless people who begged for dollars at stoplights.

"Alright. Cool, cool. I'll holla." He turned and pimp walked back to his bar stool.

Michele and I looked at each other, shaking our heads. "That was bizarre," she said.

"Bizarre has been my life lately."

We giggled as the waitress brought our meals and my drink.

I raised my glass, the liquid sloshing around the rim. "Now, do you see why I need this?"

"Girl, with your life, you should have made it a double."

CHAPTER 16

I TAPPED my pen on the office desk, my mind back in my thoughts. Since that first call on Monday, I'd received multiple calls every day after. I was thankful that it was Thursday and the weekend would soon be here, because I was beginning to stress.

Initially, I thought it was a joke, but the tone and frequency of the calls had escalated, and I worried this was becoming serious.

"Boss Lady, you have a call on line one," Patty announced through our intercom.

The hold light flashed and with each blink, my stomach muscles clenched. "Is it the same guy?" I whispered.

"Sounds like it. Do you want me to take a message?"

"Yes. And bring me the Simmons file, please."

"You got it, Boss Lady."

I watched the light until it went out, then, breathing a sigh of relief, I went back to the document I was reading. A moment later, my cell vibrated across my desk. I glanced at the number and it said, "Unknown".

I answered, cautiously. "Hell-o."

"So you're avoiding my calls now?" that nasty voice said.

I kept my voice strong and solid, even though I was petrified. "What do you want with me?"

"I told you before. My client has paid me to get revenge on you."

I started shaking internally. "And I've asked you before, who is your 'client' and what do they think I did?"

"You should already know." His cackle made the tiny hair bumps on my arms pop.

I knew I should hang up. Common sense told me so. But there was something in me that thought maybe, just maybe, I could appeal to his humanity. "Well, is there anything I can do to make it right?"

"It's too late for that. For now, my warning to you is to watch your back. I know where you live. Where you work. What you drive. And who's important to you. And if you think about calling the cops, you and your precious little Rachel will pay the price. I'll be in touch. Make sure you take my call." He hung up.

I still held the phone, my mind racing through the list of people I knew. Who would want to hurt me? I was a good person with a ton of friends and no known enemies—till now. Tears pooled in the corners of my eyes while I gulped air, trying not to hyperventilate at work.

Looking down at the papers in her hand, Patty entered my office. "Boss Lady, here's the file you requested. Do you need anything else?"

I mumbled, "That'll be all. Thank you."

She finally brought her attention to my face and gasped. "Boss Lady, you white as a ghost. Are you okay?"

I blinked several times, trying to focus on Patty. "Uh… yeah… yeah… I'm fine."

"Do this got anything to do with the man who keep callin' you?"

I whimpered and nodded. "I think he wants to kill me."

"Why would someone want to kill you?" Patty wailed.

I leapt from my chair and crossed the floor in three steps. Pushing the door shut, I said, "Shh… keep your voice down. I don't want the whole office to know."

"I'm so sorry. I hate that someone wants to hurt you. You're one of the sweetest people I know. Do you think it's real or is somebody pullin' your leg?"

I collapsed against my office door and shrugged. "I have no idea what's going on, Patty. I thought it was a horrible joke. Even up until today, I didn't want to believe the threats were real. But now I—I just don't know." I felt my legs betray me as I slid down the door.

Patty ran to my side, put her arm around my waist and led me to my couch. After she helped me sit, she said, "Stay right here. I'm gonna get you some water." She left my office and was back in what felt like seconds.

"Here, drink this." She handed me the cup, but my hands were trembling so badly that I spilled half of the liquid in my lap. Patty took the cup from me and held it to my lips so I could take a few sips of what remained.

"Thank you."

"You don't need to thank me. I'd do anything for you, Boss Lady," Patty said, as she sat next to me and opened her arms. I tipped into them, put my head on her shoulder, and cried.

"Chanelle. Are you okay? What happened?" I must've been delirious because I could swear I heard Michele's voice. But when I looked up, she was standing in front of me. How long had I cried on Patty's shoulder?

"How—how did you know something was up?"

"Patty called me. She said you got a threatening phone call."

I pushed away from Patty, narrowing my eyes into thin slits. "Why did you call Michele?"

"I'm so sorry, but I know Michele is your best friend and she would know what to do. I called her when I went to get your water."

Michele interjected and chastised me. "Don't you get mad at Patty. She called me because she cares about you. And you would have called yourself if you weren't crying. Now, what's going on?"

Michele attempted to sit next to me, but I was suddenly antsy and popped up, pacing the floor. "No clue. Every day this week, I've been called by this, this *man* who keeps threatening me." I wrapped my arms around myself and tried to stop the cold that was overwhelming me.

"Are you talking about the prank phone call you got on Monday?"

I nodded.

"Why didn't you tell me he called again?"

"I don't know." I snapped. "I—I thought if I ignored him, he'd go away. But today, when Patty asked if I wanted to take his call, I said no. And then, he called me on my cellphone. He has my personal phone number. This isn't a sick joke. It's a sick reality."

Michele let out an audible breath. "Oh, Lord."

My tears resumed their paths down my cheeks. "I know," I said, my voice an octave above a whisper. "He said he knows where I live, what I drive, who my family is." I stopped pacing and faced my best friend. "Michele, he called Rachel by her name…"

"I'm calling the police," Michele said as she rose from the couch and moved toward my desk phone.

"No." I screamed and raced in front of her, snatching the phone out of her hand as she picked it up.

"Are you crazy?" Michele looked at me as though I'd lost it.

"No, I'm not crazy. But he knows my family. And they're in danger if I say anything. Let me handle this on my own. Please." I pleaded with her.

"Well, you can't be a sitting duck, waiting for him to hurt you. That's nonsense. And you're too smart for that."

I folded my arms tightly across my suit jacket. "I'd rather he hurt me than do something to my family. No police. Period. I'll handle this on my own."

Michele was silent for what felt like hours. "Not on your own." When I opened my mouth to object, she raised her hand. "Let me finish. Not on your own. But no police. For now. I will not promise you that I won't call them at some point." She mirrored my posture. "And I am telling Ben."

"Just make sure he doesn't call the cops. I'm serious, Michele. This is my life." I moved over to my desk chair, plopped down, and fell back. My sigh was big.

"What I'll promise is this: if Ben and I decide to call the authorities, we will tell you first. What you have to promise is to tell me everything."

I nodded to indicate that I agreed with her terms.

"Do you have any idea what this could be about?"

I shrugged and shook my head. "I honestly don't. I'm lost on this one. I mean, maybe Rocco,"—I opened my hands—"but I can't imagine he'd go this far."

"Do you think it's business related?" Patty interjected, reminding me that she was still in the room. "Ever since you won that huge account earlier this year, you've had a lot of your competition mad as heck."

I paused and puckered my lips. "I hadn't thought about that."

"Even the Simmons' account was a major score and upset a lot of people when they switched firms and signed under you," she continued.

I glanced at the file she'd placed on my desk. Patty was right about my growing portfolio. The account that I closed earlier in the year with Sean's help had opened a lot of doors for me and aggravated many of my rivals in the industry.

I ran my hand through my curls. "I don't know, Patty. Yes,

people were angry, but we're all professionals and everything was just business."

"Boss Lady, people lost millions of dollars because of you." She hesitated. "I didn't say anything before because I know you don't get into office gossip, but I was talkin' to Sandra in the break room the other day. She was tellin' me, that Heather told her, that Marisa was madder than a wet hen when Mr. Jeffries promoted you to partner and started giving you the larger accounts."

"Are you kidding me?" A look of surprise swept across my face. "I did nothing dirty or underhanded to win these clients." I jabbed my finger at the file. "Nor did I do anything shady to make partner. And besides, Marisa's in line to be promoted, but she has to pay her dues like everybody else."

"Calm down, Boss Lady. You probably right. Maybe that was a stretch. Or maybe someone don't know that you've been winning your accounts fair and square." She stood. "Anyway, I'll give you two some privacy. But please let me know if there's anything I can do."

I was touched by Patty's genuine care for me and found a smile to give her. "Thank you. But this is my battle to fight."

"Well, let me know. Me and my ol' man got yo back fo sho."

I giggled a little. "I know you do. And I appreciate you both."

It was times like this when I was glad I'd decided, against conventional wisdom, to keep Patty onboard.

She returned my smile and left my office, closing the door behind her. But as Michele and I settled onto the couch, Patty burst in, wild-eyed, and in a panic. "Boss Lady, Michele, you gotta see this."

Michele and I jumped up together and rushed out of the office and into the open area. At the entrance to my office suite was a dead rat with a note pinned to its lifeless chest and held in place by a sharp pocketknife. Just the sight before my eyes tied my gut into several small knots.

"I'm going to be sick." I clutched my stomach, the cold sweat of nausea filling my body.

"Boss Lady, if anybody sees this, it's gon' kill your career." She snatched a sheet of copy paper and her trash can. Holding her breath, she used the paper to pick up the rodent and threw it in the garbage, but not before unpinning the letter. "Do you want me to read it?"

I was in a trance. "This is a nightmare."

"Yes, and it's ridiculous that you won't let us call the police," Michele said, snapping me out of my comatose state. "Chanelle, this is serious. Someone is sending you a very strong message. Are you sure you don't know who's behind this?"

"I don't lie to you. I may not tell you everything, but I don't lie. As God is my witness, I know as much as you do. But Patty is right. I can't let anyone see this."

"At least your office is at the end of the hall," Michele said.

I nodded. "There's no big risk of anyone passing by." But I was still worried the delivery hadn't gone unnoticed. How would I explain what was going on if someone asked?

I turned and went back into my office, with Patty and Michele right behind me.

Michele held out her hand to Patty. "Let me see the note, please." Patty handed it to her, and she read it silently.

I tapped my foot. "What does it say?"

"Well...." she hedged. She looked back down at the note and took a deep breath. "I despise you, Chanelle. You will pay. And you'll pay with your life."

I gulped and sank into my chair, while fresh tears slid back down my cheeks.

CHAPTER 17

AFTER MICHELE READ THE NOTE, I realized I physically couldn't take anymore. What the heck? I wanted to be alone, but I was sure they wouldn't leave my side, so I said, "Patty, you should go back to your desk so we can look as normal and possible. And Michele, would you mind getting me a bottle of water?"

"No problem," they said in unison.

"Michele, the vending machine is at the end of the hall," Patty said, giving her directions.

I waited for them to leave, pulled my purse from the desk drawer, and hightailed it to the bank of elevators. I heard Patty call my name but turning around wasn't an option.

When I reached the elevators, I pushed the "down" button multiple times, even though it had already been pushed by the person who was standing there looking at me like he was watching a lunatic. As soon as the doors opened, I stepped in and pressed the button for the parking garage. When I reached my BMW, my cellphone buzzed, and I knew it was Michele.

I pushed her to voicemail and sent her a quick text, letting her know I was going home and that I needed time to myself. I'd call her later. We texted back and forth a few times until I was comfortable she wouldn't follow me.

It was no surprise that I arrived home faster than a NASCAR driver. I parked in my garage and scurried inside my house, setting the alarm and darting up the stairs. I needed the sanctuary of my bedroom. I left a trail of clothes from the bottom of the stairs to my bed. I put on my most comfortable flannel pajamas, even though it was eighty degrees outside. As I was contemplating never leaving my house again, I drifted off to sleep and was awakened by the shrill of my home phone ringing.

Dazed, I said, "Michele, I don't feel like talking."

"Excuse me? Chanelle?" a melodic, deep voice responded.

"Oh, I'm sorry. I thought you were... never mind. Who's calling?" My head felt like it had traded places with a bag of bricks, and I didn't have the time—or patience—for whoever was on the line.

"This is Rick. Chanelle?" He sounded puzzled.

I tried to think of something clever to say, but my mind was fried. The most I could come up with was a halfhearted apology. "I'm sorry. I thought you were someone else, and I didn't check the caller ID before I answered."

"Oh, no problem. Is everything okay?"

"Uh, yeah." I toyed with the idea of telling him what had happened today but decided against it. "I—I just had a very long day, that's all. So, what's up?"

"I have the designs for your bathroom. I've created three different options and I wanted to set up a time to show you."

"That's great, Rick. Um, I thought we were set for Saturday?"

"We are, but I was kind of hoping to show you sooner. I think you'll be very pleased with the designs. I thought maybe I could come by tonight unless you have plans."

I was in no mood to entertain. But now that the adrenaline of the day had worn off, I was afraid to be alone. Maybe having

Rick come by would be a good thing. "I guess tonight is okay." I sighed. "What time?"

"I'm around the corner. Have you eaten? I could grab some Thai food and be there in twenty."

Despite my awful day, I had to admit to myself that I was excited to see him. And maybe focusing on my bathroom redesign was what I needed. I felt my mood lifting. "I haven't eaten, and I love Thai food. There's a good restaurant down the street from me. It's called Thai Chi. Have you heard of it?"

"Have I heard of it? It's my favorite. I'll see you soon."

"Sounds good."

I desperately wanted to keep on my flannel pajamas, but I knew better. I dragged myself from my bed and went to my chest of drawers. I threw on some old workout clothes and mismatched footies and laid back across my bed. I dozed off again and was startled by the ding of my doorbell. Before I headed downstairs, I searched for my cellphone and remembered that I had left it on the kitchen counter. I made a mental note to grab it.

I licked the last of the sweet and sour sauce off my fingers. "That was delicious."

Rick smiled. "I'm glad you enjoyed it."

"It was exactly what I needed." As we sat on the sofa in front of my glass cocktail table in the den, I glanced over at Rick and noticed he was studying me. "What? Why are you staring at me?" I used my fingernail as a toothpick, thinking maybe I had a piece of chicken satay stuck between my teeth.

"Nothing."

"Don't say 'nothing'. You were staring at me for a reason." It was at that moment that I glanced at my reflection in the table and noticed my hair was matted and my eyes were red and puffy. "Never mind. Why didn't you tell me I was hit?"

"Because I don't see a 'hit' woman, as you describe yourself. I see a beautiful woman who had a rough day."

His compliment warmed my heart. "Thank you. It was pretty bad."

"Do you want to talk about it?" Rick's voice was gentle. Soothing. He must have sensed my hesitation because he added, "You're obviously in distress."

I took a deep breath and contemplated for the second time that day about what to tell him. "Maybe some other time we'll discuss it. Right now, you being here and keeping me company is helping me more than you realize." I lowered my chin because I didn't want him to see my eyes well up.

But he leaned toward me, cupped my face, and searched my eyes. "I'm here for you."

"I know you are, Rick. And I thank you." I squeezed his hand and composed myself. "Now, let's look at those drawings."

Rick stood. "I left them in the truck. I'll be right back." As he walked to the front door, I gathered our empty plates and dropped them off in the kitchen. When I saw my phone on the counter, I noticed I'd missed seven calls.

That was a bit much, even for Michele, and I wondered why she didn't call me at home, but I dialed my voicemail ready to hear her fuss at me for taking off and not calling the police.

The first five messages from Michele, Ben, and Patty, were no surprise. It was the sixth message that sent chills from my head to my mismatched socks. "I saw you pull into your driveway. How'd you like your special delivery?"

Oh, my God. This nut was telling the truth when he said he knew where I lived. And he was outside my house. I pressed nine to save the message, and then I listened to message number seven. "So, is that your new boyfriend? He can't save you from your fate."

Rick strolled into the kitchen and stopped short when he saw me. He sprinted to my side and asked, "What happened? You look like something spooked you."

My lip trembled. "Someone is stalking me. I don't know who it is or why he's doing it. But he knows where I live and he's watching me. For all I know, he could be outside now because he left me a message and said he saw you."

Rick raced back to the front door with me right behind him. Standing on my porch, we glimpsed a dark-colored four-door sedan speeding off.

"That must have been him," I said, as we came back into the house and I led him to the den.

"Why would someone be following you?"

"I already told you I don't know," I snapped.

"When did it start?"

"Monday." I held back my tears and recapped the events of the last four days.

Without words, Rick wrapped his arms around me. I was consoled by his strength and the dam inside me broke. I cried harder than I had ever cried in my life and, when I finished, he wiped away my tears.

I looked at his tear-soaked chest, and felt like a little girl when I sniffed, and said, "I'm sorry I got your shirt wet."

He smiled at me with tenderness in his eyes. "It's just a shirt." Then his countenance changed. "I know you said you weren't calling the police, but I think you need to reconsider. This man is dangerous. You can't handle this by yourself."

I pushed away from him and shook my head. "I can't call them! He said he'll hurt Rachel. Whatever I did, or someone thinks I did, or I'm doing, I can't let my family pay for it. No, I have to figure this out on my own."

He pulled me back to him. "I'm spending the night. And before you bother arguing with me, it's not up for discussion. I'll sleep on the couch in the den. Where do you keep the sheets?"

I remembered how protective he was when we were in college and there was no way I'd win if I protested. It was reassuring to know that at least some things about him had remained the same. So I said, "I'll get them."

I picked up the trail of clothes I'd left when I got home, and went upstairs to grab linen for the sofa bed. Rick went out to his truck and came back in as I was making up his home for the night. When I finished, I thanked him for staying and kissed him on the cheek. As I headed up the stairs, I heard a thud on the table. I turned around to see a nine-millimeter handgun. Yup, some things remained the same.

CHAPTER 18

"WAKE UP, Sunshine. It's time for you to get up and face the day."

"Go away," I mumbled, even though I was flattered Rick remembered my nickname. I was face down under layers of blankets and I wasn't ready to re-enter the world.

"Come on. It's two-thirty."

"Why are you waking me up at two-thirty in the morning?"

"It's not a.m. It's p.m."

My eyes opened as wide as I could get them since I was still tired. "You're kidding."

Rick sat on the side of my bed and placed his hand on top of my back. "I'm not kidding. I've been checking on you every hour on the hour. Did you know you snore like a sailor? And you drool a little, too." He laughed.

I peeked my head out from under my blankets and gave him a playful push. "I do not snore... and I definitely do not drool."

"That's what you think. But your wet pillow says otherwise."

I cut my eyes at him and smirked. "Whatever."

He tapped my leg and stood. "Come on. You have to get up and eat something."

I sat up and relaxed against the cushioned headboard, pulling the comforter up my lap. "I'm not hungry. Did you see the car again last night?" I asked, afraid to hear the answer.

The smile left Rick's face. "This morning. He was here around five-thirty. I was able to get a better look at the car. It's a late model Buick. Either navy blue or black. With a big dent by the left fender."

"Did you see the license plate?"

He shook his head. "I don't think he was expecting to see my truck in your driveway because he sped past."

Tears dropped from my eyes every time I blinked. "I'm glad you were here, Rick. I don't know what would have happened if I was alone."

Rick knelt in front of my bed, and with his thumbs wiped away my wet fear. "I won't let anything happen to you. Until we get to the bottom of this, you've got a live-in houseguest. And before you object, it's not up for discussion."

I vehemently shook my head. "I can't ask you to do that."

"You didn't ask. I'm going to be honest with you." He stalled, like he was debating whether he should say more. "When I saw you in the store, I found myself attracted to you all over again. And I do want to get to know this Chanelle. But that's not what this is about. I don't want to see anything bad happen to you."

I waited a beat before releasing a long, grateful sigh. "Okay," I said, simply.

"What? That's it? No more fight?"

I gave him the brightest smile I could muster. "That's it. I don't have any fight left in me. I'm scared. So, if you're offering to protect me, then I'm going to accept."

He kissed my forehead and tremors pulsated all the way to my toes. "Thank you for trusting me. Now, I have something planned for us today. So, get up and get dressed." He rose to his feet and strolled toward my bedroom door.

I thought about work. "Oh, no. I didn't call my job."

He stopped moving and patted his hands against the air. "Relax. Patty called to check on you. I answered your phone because I didn't want to wake you and figured your friends were worried. Anyway, she told your boss you had an emergency and wouldn't be in today and next week. She also got rid of the rat but took a picture of it and kept the note in case you needed it. Michele called you, too. I told her you were sleeping, and you'd call her when you woke up. I'll see you downstairs." He winked at me and left my room.

I called Patty to thank her and let her know I was okay, and then I placed a quick call to Mr. Jeffries. It was my responsibility to make sure my job was protected.

"Hi, Alana," I said to his executive assistant. "This is Chanelle. Is Mr. Jeffries around?"

"Hi, Chanelle. Yes, hold on a moment." I waited while she transferred my call.

"Chanelle, how are you? Patty said you had a family emergency. I hope everyone is okay."

"We're fine. I, um, have a couple things I need to handle. I'll be back as soon as I can."

"No worries. If something is keeping you away from the office, it must be serious. I'm here for you if you need me."

"Thank you, Sir."

After a couple minutes of small talk, I hung up and called Michele.

"Hey, how are you doing today?" she asked, her voice brimming with worry.

"Eh, I've had better days." I crossed my ankles, getting comfortable. "Last night that guy was outside my house."

"Oh, no. Did you see him?"

"I didn't. Rick is here."

"I figured that out when he answered your phone."

I grinned. "He came by last night and I told him what's been going on. He offered to stay with me for a few days."

I could hear her raising her eyebrows. "Oh, really?"

"Yes, really. There's nothing going on. And this is a blessing, so don't worry. I'm a lot safer with Rick here than being by myself."

"You know I've got your back and I support you. But I still disagree with you about the police."

I sighed, exasperated. "Now, you sound like Rick. And it's not that I won't ever do it. I just have to think this through. I can't put any of my family in danger. I'd never forgive myself."

"What about Steve?"

"Your brother?"

"Yeah. What if we call him? He's a cop. He might have suggestions on what to do."

That could be a good idea. Steve was like my big brother. "Let me think about it."

"That's fair. I won't push it right now. Especially, since you have a houseguest."

"Thanks. Rick says he has something planned for us today."

"Oooh, a date."

"I doubt that. Knowing Rick, it could be anything." We chuckled and lightened the mood.

After agreeing to check in with her throughout the day, I hung up and hauled myself out of bed.

I desperately wanted to stay in my room, but I was curious to know what Rick had planned. I showered, dressed, and made my way downstairs. As I sat at the kitchen table, Rick brought me a grilled ham and cheese sandwich, a cup of tomato soup, and a glass of apple juice. "Aren't you going to eat?" I asked when he sat across from me with a cup of coffee.

He crossed his legs, resting his calf on his thigh, and took a sip. "I ate a little something earlier."

"Oh. Well, thank you." I blessed my food and took a big bite of my sandwich. "Mmm... This takes me back to my days as a child. I ate it almost every Saturday at my grandparent's home."

"I remember. You used to eat it when we were in college."

I paused with my sandwich in midair. "I had forgotten about that. I can't believe you remembered."

"I remember a lot of things about you, Chanelle. You've been in and out of my thoughts since college. I'm glad we have a chance to reconnect."

I was too, but I wasn't sure what to say, so I said, "What do you have planned for us today?"

He grinned. "It's a surprise."

"Oooh... I like surprises."

"I remembered that, too. While you finish eating, I'm going to make a couple calls for work and then do a quick walk around the house."

I was grateful to Rick for everything he was doing for me and I was eager to get to my surprise, so I wolfed down my meal. After reassuring me that no one was around my house, I grabbed my purse, and keys, then dashed to his truck.

I was happy that for at least a little while, I could concentrate on something other than the madness that was happening to me.

"Are you serious? This is my surprise?" I asked, staring straight ahead.

"Yes. This is something you need to learn how to do."

I could feel Rick's eyes on me, but I refused to face him. "There's no way I'm going inside." I folded my arms.

"There's no way you're *not* going inside." He unfolded my arms. "Now, come on." He unlocked the doors and got out.

I stayed seated. I was not going inside that building. Rick

walked around to my side of the truck and opened the door. "Come on. This is going to be good for you," he said.

"I'm scared. I've never done this before."

"There's a first time for everything. And I'm going to help you. But this is something you need to do."

I released a long, slow breath.

While I considered my next move, Rick extended his hand. "Do you want my arm to fall off?"

I tried my best not to crack a smile. "Do not quote Billie D. Williams in *Lady Sings the Blues* to me. This is no time for jokes." I refolded my arms.

Rick reached inside, unfolded my arms again, and tried to coax me out of the truck. After about five minutes of bantering back and forth, I had no choice but to give in. I was stubborn, but this man had me beat. "I'll go in on one condition," I said.

"What's that?"

My eyes pleaded with him. "We go at my pace. No matter how slow that may be."

"Deal."

I finally got out and together we walked inside the "Firing Line," a top-notch gun range. I'd secretly always wanted to learn how to shoot, but guns terrified me. And I was even more afraid of the implication. Rick must have believed that I was in danger. Otherwise, why else would he force me to learn how to shoot?

As soon as we walked through the door, I saw cases upon cases of guns. Different styles and calibers. The sight unnerved me, and without thinking, I reached for Rick's hand. He glanced down at our entwined fingers and smiled. In the background, we could hear shots in the practice area and every time I heard a gun fire, I flinched. This was not the kind of surprise I had in mind.

Rick told one of the associates this was my first time and we needed to rent a practice gun. Rick suggested I start with a twenty-two caliber, so I could get used to the feel and power. I followed his lead, since I had no idea what he was talking about. He also rented ear and eye protectors for us and then took me to the range. Metal partitions separated each practice space. After Rick gave me a lesson on the proper way to load, reload, and hold the firearm, it was time to shoot.

"Okay, Chanelle. Pay attention. Do you see how I'm standing?" I nodded, and he continued. "You stand with your legs a little apart so you can keep your balance. Now, notice how I hold my hands." I watched him intently and wondered how in the world did he expect me to imitate what he was doing. The sound of him firing that first round startled me. But with each shot, I relaxed a little. That is, until he turned and asked, "Are you ready?"

"No, but I'll try," I said, with great reservation. He handed me the gun, and my entire body tensed.

"You'll do fine." He hovered behind me and put his arms around me. He placed his hands on top of mine, as he positioned me to fire my first round.

I was trying to concentrate on what he was saying, but I was jittery; partly because I was about to shoot my first gun, but mostly because we were so close. His body heat. His cologne. His breath tingling my neck. I shivered. Focus Chanelle. Focus.

"Go ahead. Pull the trigger."

I forced air through my parted lips. "Alright." I closed my eyes and squeezed. The kickback from the gun made me jump.

"Not bad. How did it feel?"

"Different from what I expected."

"Now, do it again," he commanded.

"Okay." I closed my eyes and squeezed again. With each shot, I became more comfortable.

After a few rounds, he came from behind me. "This time, you do it on your own and I'll watch."

I took a deep breath and nodded, then repeated my same process.

"Good job, but were your eyes closed?"

"Yes."

"Why?"

I shrugged. "I dunno."

He lifted a brow and cocked his head. "Don't you think your eyes should be open so you can see your target?"

"But I don't want to see who I'm shooting." I bit my lip. That sounded a lot smarter when it was in my head.

His lips puckered, and he squinted. "Chanelle," he began, as if talking to a five-year-old. "You have to keep your eyes open when you are shooting a lethal weapon. Can you do that?"

I hated his patronizing tone, so I glared at him. "Yes."

"Good girl. Now, do it again. And this time I want you to look."

"Whatever." I turned to face my target and fired an almost perfect shot.

His mouth opened wide. "Wow. I didn't expect that."

I gave him a sassy smirk. "I guess I'm a natural."

"I guess you are."

"Can we leave now?"

"Empty the clip and we can go."

"Bet." I assumed the position and shot four more perfect shots. At least perfect for an amateur. I set the gun down. "I'll meet you outside."

I knew Rick was watching me walk out, so I added a little extra sway in my hips. I was happy my first lesson was successful, but the prospect of needing to shoot someone made me shudder.

I stood outside of the front door while I waited for Rick and watched the traffic. Was it my imagination, or was the guy in that navy-blue Buick across the street watching me? Then I felt my phone vibrating in my pocket. I pulled it out and glanced down at the number. I didn't recognize it, so I looked back at the man in the car. He waved his cell in the air and put it to his ear. I clicked the answer button. "Yes?"

"You think owning a gun will prepare you for me? My client wants you handled. And I always finish my job."

I didn't answer. Everything around me faded into the background as I sprinted across the street toward the car. I didn't hear horns honking as tires screeched so I wouldn't be splattered across a windshield. My sole focus was the man who wanted to destroy my life. Destroy me. "Who are you? What do you want with me?" I screamed.

Just as I barreled down on the car, he hit the gas and sped off. All I had time to do was bang his trunk. "What did I do?" I shouted. "Please, please tell me what I did."

"Chanelle," Rick yelled my name, dodging moving cars as he raced toward me.

I was shaking like a leaf on a windy day. I thrusted my finger the direction of the now vanished car. "That was him. That was the man. He was right here. Watching me." I placed my hands on my temples and forehead. "Oh, my God. Rick, what kind of psycho follows a person to a gun range," I wailed.

"Why would you chase after him? Have you lost your mind?" His voice elevated to a decibel I hadn't heard since college. He pulled me out of the street and led me to the safety of the sidewalk.

"It was a knee-jerk reaction. I wasn't thinking."

"He could have killed you."

I continued to wail. "Don't yell at me. Don't you think I know that?"

Rick took a couple deep breaths in quick succession, bringing his temper in check. "I'm sorry. I shouldn't have yelled, but he could have hurt you, Chanelle." He enveloped me in his arms and stroked my hair, trying to get me to stop trembling.

"He was here, Rick." I sobbed into his shirt. "He doesn't care that you're with me. He's waiting for an opportunity to get me. And I have no idea why." I sobbed harder.

"Shhh," he whispered into my hair and continued to hold me. "Let me get you out of here."

I sniffed several times and nodded as he led me to his truck and took me home.

CHAPTER 19

"CHANELLE, HONEY?" I heard a soft voice. But I didn't answer.

I was lying in my bed, staring straight up at the ceiling. I had no idea how long I had been like that. All I knew was that I was never leaving my bedroom again. And no one was going to force me. If I had stayed in my bed earlier, then The Stalker wouldn't have followed me. Although, for all I knew, he was outside my window right now.

"Chanelle?" the voice repeated my name. I turned my eyes in the direction of the voice.

"Hi," I muttered.

Michele took that as an invitation to sit on the edge of my bed. "I called your cell and Rick answered. He filled me in on what happened this afternoon."

"Is he downstairs?"

She shook her head. "He had to make a couple runs, so I offered to come by and stay with you for a bit. He also said when he brought you home, you barricaded yourself in here and told him you were never coming out."

I moaned. "I'm not. What's the point? To make myself an easier target?"

"We need to call the police."

I shot straight up in my bed. "We can't. Think about Rachel and my sister. My parents. What about you and Ben and BJ? How do I know he doesn't know stuff about you? No. No police. Period."

She ignored me. "I have someone here I want you to talk to." She stood and opened my bedroom door, and positioned outside the doorframe was her brother.

"Hey, Chanelle, what's going on?" Steve asked, stepping inside before I'd extended an invitation.

I glared at Michele as she sat back on my bed. "I don't care if you're angry with me. This is serious. And someone who can help needs to know," she said.

I thought for a moment, then peered at him. "Steve, are you obligated to report anything I say to you?"

He waited a beat before he spoke. "Let's just say, I'm here as a family member who happens to have knowledge of the law. And I'm not here as a cop taking your statement."

"So… does that mean that what we talk about stays between us?"

"It means that if I have to escalate it, I'll tell you first."

"Now, you sound like your sister," I said, still smarting from the ambush.

He overlooked my salty attitude with Michele. "Can you think of anyone who might want to harm you? Have you met anyone new lately?"

I let out a deep breath and wilted against my headboard. "Just, Rick. And I know it's not him."

Steve perched on the edge of the wing-backed chair across from my bed. "Michele said you received some flowers. Do you know who sent them?"

I shrugged my slumped shoulders. "Like I told her, I don't."

"Steve," Michele said to her brother, "I was thinking the stalking and the flowers are related."

He nodded. "There's a good chance they are. It could be someone who's jealous about the flowers and wants to send you a message. Chanelle, are you involved in any kind of love triangles?"

I screwed up my face. "Absolutely not," I said, more offended than I should have been when I thought about my not too distant past. "I, uh, accidentally ended up in a couple messy situations, though. My ex's current lover was angry and sued me."

"Are you talking about Michael?"

"Yes. But that was so long ago it wouldn't make sense for him to be doing something against me now." I paused as another thought came to me. "Although, Michael did email me the other day."

Steve tipped forward. "What did he say?"

"That maybe he'd made a mistake, and asked if we could talk. I deleted his message and never responded."

"Did he contact you again?"

"Nope, not to my knowledge."

"Is there anyone else?"

"Well, Chele set me up on a blind date with a friend of Ben's." I frowned at Michele as unpleasant memories of my date with Lawrence flooded my mind. I shifted back to Steve. "But it lasted less than five minutes. Although his girlfriend thought there was more to it and threatened me."

"Have you heard from him recently?"

"Kinda. Chele and I saw him earlier this week. But I tell you, all of my interactions with him totaled less than ten minutes, and he knows I'm not interested at all. It would be ludicrous to think he's the reason I'm experiencing this."

"Anyone else?"

I delayed my answer. What did I want to say about Sean? "Umm... I had a brief sexual relationship with a guy who was involved with someone else. But that's been over for months and he doesn't even live in the state anymore." It was embarrassing enough to tell him all I had with Sean was sex, I wasn't about to tell him that he had a wife. I peeked at Michele whose forehead had creased but she kept quiet.

"Do you think any of these situations could be the cause of what's going on right now?" he asked.

I sighed and shook my head again. "I don't. Not one of these situations would warrant *this*. That's why I'm at a loss."

He stood. "Well, give it some more thought and let me know if anything comes to mind."

I nodded. "I will. And you aren't making this an official discussion, right?"

His eyes darted from me to Michele and back to me. "Not at this time. But you need to be very careful, Chanelle. This person, whoever it is, is serious. And if they contact you again, then I will take official action. One, it's my duty. And two, you're as much my sister as Michele is. I wouldn't forgive myself if something happened to you. I'll stay here until Rick gets back." He bent down and kissed me on top of my head."

I felt a sense of relief, knowing that I had so much support. "Thank you."

He tousled his sister's hair and then went downstairs.

Michele re-fluffed her Afro puff before sheepishly asking, "Are you mad at me?"

I shrugged and pulled my blanket up my legs. "Nah. I was expecting it after what happened today. Thanks for not saying anything about Sean's wife."

"Do you think it could be her?"

My sigh was heavy. "I doubt it. Sean said he wouldn't say anything to her, so how would she know? And you know it didn't come from me. And, besides that, what happened between us was almost a year ago, so why would she wait until now?" I shook my head, the familiar lump in my throat signaling the tears that were coming. "But I guess at this point, anything's possible."

The melody of the water flowing down the side of my slate fountain in the corner of my bedroom soothed my frayed and frazzled nerves. After several minutes I said, "Michele, I love you. You are my best friend in the entire world. And I know you want what's best for me. But I need to be alone. I don't feel like talking. I'm a mess on the inside and out and I just want to go to sleep. Tomorrow is a new day, and maybe I'll be able to think better. Or maybe I won't leave my room. Either way, it's my choice and right now I choose to be by myself."

Michele rose from her spot on my bed and touched my shoulder, then kissed the top of my head, just as Steve had done. "You are *my* best friend. And I'm not leaving you alone." She went inside my closet and emerged seconds later with an oversized down blanket and pillow. She walked over to the couch on the far side of the room and made a pallet. "We're in this together. Sleep tight," she said as she laid down for the night.

I reached over and turned off my lamp. In the shadows, she never saw my appreciative smile as I nodded off to sleep.

CHAPTER 20

"Knock, knock," Ben said, holding a pizza box in one hand and a two-liter of Pepsi in the other; Michele, right behind him with plates and cups.

My face lit up as I waved them in. "Oooh, pizza. Yummy. What brings you by?"

"Michele said you refused to leave your room." He set the box down on the dresser. "So we thought we'd come to you and hang out for a while."

"You guys are the best. But it's only been a couple of days since Michele spent the night. It's not like I've been hiding out forever." I sat in my lounging pajamas on my bed and held out my hands to accept the ooey-gooey goodness from Michele.

"Yeah, but what are you going to do? Wait here until the boogeyman comes and gets you?" Michele said, sitting on my bed and taking a drink of her soda.

I narrowed my eyes at her. "Of course not."

"You sure about that? Because hiding in your room is not going to work forever."

"I don't expect it to."

She pursed her lips. "Mm hmm. When was the last time you heard from him?"

I glanced away from her, knowing that she'd be able to see through me. "Not since the incident at the gun range."

"Truth or lie?"

"That's something I do with Andrea."

"Well, you're doing it with me today. Truth or lie?"

"Okay, fine. I may have received a call or two." There was no way I was telling her that he'd called me at least six times, with each call sounding the same. Threats on my life and my family, but never giving me a clue to the reason for the threats or who was paying him.

"Chanelle! Why didn't you say something?"

"So you and your brother could call in the cavalry? Nope. I already told you. I'm handling this myself."

"Did you tell Rick?" Ben interjected.

"Um…"

"That would be a 'no'," Michele said, speaking for me.

"I didn't want to stress Rick."

"Stress me about what?" he said from the doorway.

"Hey, I didn't hear you come in," I said, the shine on my face announcing to everyone how I was feeling about my houseguest.

"Stress me about what?" he repeated.

"Chanelle received calls from her friend that she didn't tell anyone about," Michele said.

"You know, Michele, you can quit speaking for me."

Rick's stare bored through me. "When did he call?"

"Yesterday, and he didn't say anything he hadn't said before. So what was the point in mentioning it?"

"How did he call, and I knew nothing about it?"

I hung my head and mumbled, "I put my phone on vibrate and kept it under my bedspread."

Everyone looked at me with irritation and I felt like I was

being scolded by my parents, which put me on the defensive. "Look, this is my life. My drama."

"Snippy, snippy," Michele said.

"I'm serious. Everyone needs to stop treating me like I don't know how to handle my business. In case you've forgotten, I am a partner at a Fortune 100 corporation," I said with attitude designed to get them in check.

Michele gave me a sistah-girl neck roll and challenged me. "And you call locking yourself in your room, handling your business?"

If this had happened when we were teenagers, I'd kick her off my bed. Literally. "At this moment, yes I do. Now, can we please enjoy a nice meal of junk food and talk about something else?"

Ben turned to Rick. "I got to give it up to you, man. You have your hands full with this one." His finger stabbed the air in my direction.

"It's all good. I'm not letting anything happen to her," Rick said, taking a seat next to me on the bed and snagging a pepperoni off my slice of pizza.

"You're a good dude," Ben said.

I beamed at Rick and felt my heart melt like ice cream in a desert. We'd been back in each other's lives for about a couple of weeks, but with what we were going through together, I felt connected to him. Knowing that Ben approved of him helped me settle into our growing friendship.

The trio of wardens allowed me to change the conversation, and we talked about lighter topics for the rest of the evening. I was thankful to have all of their support, but they were right. I couldn't hide forever. Eventually, I was going to have to figure out my next move. And at the present time, I had no clue what that was going to be.

CHAPTER 21

A FEW MORE DAYS HAD PASSED, AND I was pretty sure Rick wasn't letting me spend one more day in my room, so I mentally started preparing myself to re-enter the world and face this issue.

"Chanelle?" He called my name from the other side of my closed door.

"Yes?"

"Are you leaving your room today?"

"I was thinking about it," I sat up on an elbow and flipped through TV channels.

"I'd love to see you today in something other than mismatched flannel pajamas." He chuckled.

I rolled my eyes, even though he couldn't see me. "Whatever."

Rick cracked the door and peeked in. "And maybe, just maybe, you might wanna take a shower."

With that, I let out a loud, offended laugh. "I can't stand you." I exclaimed, hurling a pillow at him.

Laughing with me, he closed the door. "I'm glad you have

your spirit back." I listened as his footsteps moved farther away from my door, as he retreated down the stairs.

Heading toward my master bath, I was grinning like I'd won the lottery. I hated what was going on, but I loved having Rick in my house. In my life. I was still smiling after my shower. It had been days since Rick saw me in something presentable and, for my own confidence, I needed to look and feel attractive.

In my closet, I chose a denim wrap dress with the tags still hanging on it and a new pair of platform sandals. I completed the outfit with a colorful chunky necklace. I applied my makeup and styled my hair in a casual ponytail. I took one final glance in my full-length mirror. Perfect.

"Well, well, well. You look fantastic, Chanelle." Rick sat in the recliner in front of the television and eyed me when I sauntered into the family room.

I lowered myself onto the end of the couch, suddenly shy. "Thank you. And thank you for coaxing me out of my room."

"Any time." He continued staring.

The heat between us filled the space of the room and threw my nerves off balance. "Um, you've been my babysitter for a while now. Are you ever planning to go back to work?

Sensing my discomfort, he looked away and at the television. "Max has everything under control so I can keep my schedule clear for you. And I was thinking that maybe we could go out for breakfast and..."

My brow edged upwards. "And what?"

He slowly rotated his head to me. "And go back to the gun range." He raised his hand to stop my protest. "I know what happened last time. But this is something you need to be able to do. And you learn with practice. Plus, I'll be there with you. So, I signed you up for a CPL class. They will perform your background check while we're there and when you leave, you'll be licensed to carry a gun."

I closed my eyes, massaging my temples. I knew he was

right, but what if we were tailed again? For that matter, what if he was outside now? What if he'd been outside my house for days? What if? What if? What if? It was the "what ifs" that were driving me cuckoo. And the reason I said, "Okay. Let's do it."

"That's it? No more push back?"

I shook my head. "Nope. You're right. You have your own life to live. I can't expect you to continue protecting me."

"I enjoy being your protector, Chanelle."

It was the way he said "protector" that caused me to blush. He made me feel like such a girl. In a good way. "I know you do. And I appreciate you, Rick. But I need to become independent again. Hiding like a wuss isn't who I am. So if it means I have to learn how to shoot a gun, then that's what I'm gonna do." I paused, gazing at him through my lashes, before adding, "Besides, I like it when we shoot together."

The way his eyes widened told me he was thrown by my flirtatious comment. And the way he jumped up said he quickly recovered. "Come on, woman! Let's go."

Laughing, I let him lead me out to the garage and tossed him the keys to my Range Rover. "I feel like taking Gigi today. Do you mind driving?"

"Of course not. Why do you call her Gigi?" he asked, opening my door for me before going around to the driver's side and starting the motor.

"It stands for 'God's Gift'. It was something I always wanted and in an impulsive moment, I bought her."

"That's pretty cool. Where do you feel like eating?"

"I'm flexible. And it's my treat."

"Leo's Coney Island?"

"Works for me." I tuned my audio system to my Kurt Carr playlist. "I hope you're okay with gospel music."

"I love gospel music. Marvin Sapp. Kirk Franklin. Old school Winans."

Hmmm... I thought. The Rick from college days would have

never listened to gospel music. But back then, I didn't either.

We drove, neither of us talking, enjoying the scenery around us and the inspiration piping from my Meridian sound system. When we arrived at Leo's, we seated ourselves and waited for our waitress to arrive.

"When did you start listening to gospel music," I asked, browsing the menu that had been behind the sugar shaker on the table.

"It's been quite a few years. Max was in a nasty car accident and the doctors said there was nothing they could do for him. I used my street money to buy him the best medical treatment I could afford, and it still wasn't good enough. As a last resort, I went to church, and something happened. I can't explain it, but I gave my life to God and started praying for my brother. And God healed him."

"Wow." His words gave me goosebumps. I'd only heard of those kinds of stories before, but I didn't know anyone who'd actually experienced a miracle.

"Sorry to keep you waiting," the waitress interrupted us as she placed water and straws on the table. "Can I get you started with something else to drink?"

"Yes, please. I'll have a cup of coffee," I said.

"I'll have the same."

"Two coffees coming up," she said. But not before giving Rick the once over.

I couldn't blame her. There was no denying that he was hot. Even in a simple collared shirt and jeans, he was sexy. But she was rude for checking him out in front me since she didn't know if I was his wife or girlfriend. However, since I was neither, I didn't comment.

"What about you? When did you start listening to gospel music?" he asked, returning to our conversation.

"Not long after I left college. My parents have always been big into church. I strayed while I was away at school. Then after I graduated, I guess you could say I returned to my roots."

He grinned. "Nice. So you've been living a Godly life for a long time then."

"I try. But nobody's perfect," I thought about how I lived with Michael for years and had an affair with Sean. An affair that would have continued if he hadn't moved out of town.

"Maybe this Sunday, you and I could go to church together," he suggested.

I studied him, struck by how much he'd changed. "I'd love that."

He leaned back into the pleather seat. "Then it's a date."

Our waitress returned with our beverages. "Here you go. Two cups of coffee. Are you ready to order?" she asked, her eyes fixated on Rick.

"Chanelle, you go first," he volunteered.

"I'll have a veggie omelet with hash browns and turkey bacon."

"Mm hmm," she said, all but dismissing me. Then eyed Rick again. "And what can I get you, Sweetheart? The Hungry Man special?"

I didn't want Rick to see me show my butt, but my eyes narrowed. I was close to sticking out my foot, so she tripped.

He ignored her flirtatious tone. "I'll have the short stack of blueberry pancakes and sausage."

"Got it." She flashed more teeth than any one person should have.

When she sashayed away—my foot safely under the table—I said, "You know she was flirting with you, right?"

"I don't pay any attention to women like her. "His hand cut through the air as he dismissed her. "I'm here with you. You're who I want to get to know better. Not some trifling woman

127

who's disrespectful to my date. But I don't want her playing hockey with our food, so I let it go." He chuckled.

I was glad to know he'd observed what she was doing, and he'd blown her off because of me. And I was glad I hadn't acted a fool. "Thank you. I appreciate that."

"One thing you'll learn about me is that I'm a one-woman guy. I was that way when we were together in college. I was that way when I was married. And I'm that way now. Cheating and straying are words that aren't in my vocabulary. And I hope they aren't in yours."

Not anymore. "No, those words aren't in my vocabulary either."

"I'd be surprised if they were." He smiled at me, having no idea I was becoming increasingly uncomfortable with our conversation.

"Uh, tell me about today. How long do you think we'll be at the gun range?" I asked.

He proceeded to tell me how the rest of the day would unfold and after a few moments, I was able to set aside thoughts of our discussion about fidelity. We enjoyed breakfast, and our waitress got the hint that he wasn't interested. Thankfully, our food had already arrived before she figured it out.

At the gun range, I gave them the information needed to start my background check, and Rick rented a nine-millimeter, like the one he owned.

"Why didn't you get a twenty-two caliber again?" I questioned as we made our way back to the practice area.

"Those are starter guns. I want you to be able to shoot a gun that can do some damage. With a twenty-two, if a guy has on a heavy coat, he might not even feel it."

"Oh, I didn't know that."

He winked at me with a sexy grin. "That's why you have me to teach you. We have about an hour before your class starts, and I want you to get comfortable with it." He repeated the lesson he'd given me days earlier, and I quivered when he stood behind me. It was kind of nice to be so attracted to someone who was equally attracted to me. And I was gaining confidence in my ability as a shooter.

Toward the end of our lesson, Rick said, "Okay, now I'm not going to talk you through it but, I want you to show me what you've learned."

"Yes, Coach." I mimicked the stance I'd been taught and cocked the gun. I closed one eye and when my target came into focus. I pulled the trigger.

Rick pushed the button that brought the target paper to us. I had landed a bull's eye. He stared at the paper in amazement and then looked at me.

I was just as shocked as he was, but I shrugged and played it cool. "I guess I'm a natural shot."

"You have no idea how sexy you are to me right now."

"Mmm, I think I have an idea." I scanned his body, noticing his rise of excitement.

He chuckled and shook his head. "I can't even hide it. You're definitely ready for class."

"You're right. You can't hide it." I joined him in laughter. "And yes, I'm ready."

The four-hour lesson was a breeze. When we returned our equipment, the clerk said my background check came back clear, handed me a temporary certificate, and informed me that my permanent card would come in the mail.

I was feeling pretty good, but when Rick went to talk to the instructor, I waited inside the building. No way was I standing outside by myself again. He came back and told me the instructor said I was one of the best female students he'd ever seen.

I was on a high as we stepped out into the bright daylight. I got into the Rover as Rick received a phone call and excused himself. When he returned, his brows were furrowed.

"What's wrong?" I asked, with concern in my voice, as Rick got into the driver's seat.

He shut the door and pressed the ignition button. "It's nothing major. I have a guy working for me and he ran into a problem on a job that Max can't handle." He swiveled in his seat. "I hate to do this to you, Chanelle, but I need to check it out. Do you wanna ride or do you want me to drop you off at home?"

Fear swept over me. I hadn't been home alone since Rick had basically moved in, but I didn't want to be a tag-along. Besides, I didn't think it would be professional for me to go with him. "I'll be fine at home," I lied.

"Are you sure? Do you want me to call Michele?"

I shook my head. "I have to be comfortable taking care of myself." I placed my hand on top of his and gazed directly in his eyes, hoping he would see that I was confident. Even though I wasn't. "Go. Handle your business."

Rick hesitated before speaking. "I'll work as fast as I can."

"I know you will. Now, let's go. Okay?"

"Okay." He put the SUV in reverse and backed out of our parking space.

The ride to my house was quiet. I didn't want Rick to know how worried I was, so I gave myself a mental pep talk, which was not working. As we pulled in my driveway, my head was going around like a corkscrew. Even though there was no sign of the dark sedan, Rick went inside and checked every room on every floor. Once satisfied that I was home alone, he marched toward the front door. "Make sure you set the alarm."

"Please, stop worrying, Rick. You're making me nervous. And besides, the sooner you leave, the sooner you'll be back."

"You're right. I'm sorry. Okay, I'm leaving. My job is about twenty minutes away, but if you need me, call me."

"You are so sweet." I kissed him and pushed him out the door. "I'll be here when you get back."

"Promise?"

"I promise."

Closing the door behind him, I prayed that was a promise I would be able to keep.

CHAPTER 22

THE DISTANT RINGTONE of my cell in the kitchen pulled my eyes away from the movie I was watching. I glanced at the time on the cable box. Rick had been gone about three hours. Thinking it might be him, I sprang from the couch in the den and sprinted through the house to catch it before the ringing stopped. Looking at the caller ID, I tensed. I didn't recognize the number. It chimed a few more times while I debated swiping right. Thinking that maybe Rick was calling me from another phone, I tentatively answered. "Hello?"

"Chanelle?" a male voice asked.

The poor connection caused static on the line, making it difficult to hear. "Who's calling?"

His answer was inaudible.

"I'm sorry, but I can't hear you. Who's this?"

Through the choppy reception, I heard a male voice ask, "Is this better?"

My stomach touched my feet. With the line clear as crystals, I knew who was calling. And I wished he wasn't. "Sean?"

"Yeah. Um, is now a good time to talk?"

My eyes traveled around the room and I slowly lowered

myself onto the wooden chair at the table in the breakfast nook, keeping the kitchen door in full view. Not that I was doing anything wrong, but I didn't want Rick popping up on me. "Um. I guess so."

"How are you?"

"Fine. You?"

He didn't answer right away, and that surprised me. "I've been alright. I'm planning a trip to Michigan and I was wondering if, maybe, we could get together for dinner."

"Sean, the last time we spoke I thought I was clear. We made a clean break. Dinner wouldn't be a good idea."

"I understand. But I want to see you. I have something I need to tell you." I heard his nerves and didn't understand it.

"Can you tell me now?"

"I'd prefer to tell you in person."

I sighed my frustration with this conversation. "Sean, I have a lot going on these days."

"I understand," he repeated himself. "But I've missed you and we need to talk."

With my elbow on the table, I held my head in my hand. "I don't want to hurt your feelings and I'm sure you're still a great guy, but I'm not interested in having dinner with you. That time in my life has passed. I hope you will respect my decision."

"Cynthia and I aren't together anymore," he blurted.

I popped up straight in the chair. If this had been eight months ago, I'd have jumped up and danced around the room. But now, his declaration did nothing for me. "Okay... If you're happy, then I'm happy for you."

"I don't think you get it. We're not together. That means you and I have a chance to explore a real relationship."

"Like I said, I'm happy for you, but I have no desire to be with you, Sean. I'm embarrassed by what happened between us and, quite honestly, I want to forget it."

"Did you like the flowers?"

My blood turned to ice. "What did you ask me?"

"Uh... uh...," he stuttered. "The flowers. I know how much you like yellow roses. And I added some white ones. I wanted you to know that my love for you is pure."

Oxygen stopped flowing to my brain and had I not been sitting, my legs would have failed me. "Are you telling me you sent me flowers with a card that read 'What if'?"

"Yes. Did you like them?" This was the first time since we began talking that he sounded like the Sean I remembered.

"Sean, did you tell Cynthia about us?" I spoke slowly because I didn't want the answer.

He stalled. "Why do you ask?"

"Just answer me," I snapped. "Did. You. Tell. Her?"

"I may have said something about it." Then he added, "But it was after I told her that I wanted a divorce."

I collapsed against the back of the chair and took several cleansing breaths.

"I wanted to send you something to show you that I still think about you," he continued.

I closed my eyes and pinched the bridge of my nose. "Sean. Cynthia knows you sent me flowers."

"Why do you think she knows?"

I wanted to scream. "I *know* she knows because she sent me a dead rat."

"What are you talking about?" I heard his confusion.

"I got the flowers. And that same day, I received a threatening phone call from some man who said he was paid to seek revenge on me for what I did. Only, I had no idea what he was talking about." I took a deep breath and continued. "And then a few days later, I received a dead rat... *at work*. Sean. All this is happening to me because you decided to tell Cynthia something. And I may not know exactly what you told her, but whatever it was, it was enough for her to think I'm the reason her marriage is falling apart!"

"I am so very sorry. I didn't know she would do something like that."

By now I was in full-blown anger mode. "My life has been flipped upside down and turned inside out, and all you can say is you're *sorry* and you didn't know? Are you nuts? You told me you weren't going to tell her!"

"I wanted to do something nice for you. Telling her just kinda happened."

"How are you going to fix this?" I had several emotions running laps inside me. I was relieved to know what started all of this. But I was also petrified. Cynthia was a woman scorned. And scorned women knew no boundaries. I placed my hand on my belly. Nauseous. For the first time since this drama began, I considered calling the cops.

And my career. What would happen if I went to the cops and somehow Mr. Jeffries found out? How would he respond if he knew a partner in his firm had an affair with a consultant? Even though it had happened before my promotion, would he fire me for violating the ethics clause in my employment agreement? I looked at my Viking stove and other high-end appliances. All the things my career afforded me. I didn't want to lose that.

And Rick? How could I tell him all this was happening because of an affair I'd had? What would he think of me? Would he be able to see beyond it? Or would he judge me based on one indiscretion? Well, two indiscretions.

The sound of Sean's voice snapped me out of the rabbit hole of despair. "Chanelle, I'll talk to Cynthia and find out what she did."

"I appreciate that. But more importantly, I need you to call her off me."

"How do you expect me to do that?"

I hopped up and paced the length of the kitchen. "How am I supposed to know? But you better do something. Tell her that you changed your mind about the divorce."

"But I haven't. Cynthia changed when we moved to Virginia. She never connected with an AA group. She's been behaving erratically. She quit her job. She's spiraled out of control and she doesn't talk to me."

I disregarded him. "I need you to at least try. Do you realize that I have been living in fear for my life since you sent me those damn flowers? I haven't been able to work. I barely eat, sleep, or leave my house. Heck, it's hard for me to leave my bedroom. And this is your mess. Now clean it up!" I bellowed.

"I'll see what I can do." He stammered before saying, "Does this mean that I won't be able to see you when I get to Michigan?"

I rubbed my forehead. Was this fool for real? I swear his IQ dipped when he moved out of state. "The next time I hear from you, you better be tellin' me you have your wife under control."

"I understand, Chanelle." Sean sounded dejected. "I also need to tell you the reason I'm coming to Michigan. I'm interviewing to get my job back at Image."

My migraine was instant. "You're what?"

"I'm moving back to Michigan if Image has a spot for me."

"Oh." This was getting worse by the moment.

"Anyway, I'll be in touch."

"Unbelievable," I muttered and disconnected the call.

CHAPTER 23

IT HAD BEEN close to an hour since I hung up with Sean, but it felt like five minutes. As I slumped against the kitchen counter, plotting my next move, the phone in my hand chirped.

"Boy, am I glad you called," I exclaimed to Andrea. "I have so much to tell you."

"And hello to you, too. But I called because I need a favor."

"It'll have to wait because right now I need my sister. Can you come over?"

Andrea's flippant tone became serious. "What's goin' on, lil sis?"

"I'll tell you when you get here."

"I'm on my way."

I was happy to spend some time with my sister. We didn't talk often because about the only thing we had in common was blood. But that blood was thick. Andrea was the perfect person to talk to about what was going on. She might not have a solution, but she'd be a good sounding board.

I set the phone on the counter and went into my main floor bathroom to splash cold water on my face, and then back to the kitchen to prepare a snack. I didn't have an appetite, but I knew

I needed to put something in my stomach. I settled on a platter of cheeses, crackers, grapes, strawberries, and a bottle of Riesling. I was carrying the goodies into the den when I heard my front door open. My heart skipped a few beats until I remembered Andrea had the alarm code and a key to my house.

"It's just me," she called out.

"I'm in here. How'd you get here so fast?"

"I was around the corner. What's up?" She strolled into the den and flopped on the couch. "What's with the bougie food? You ain't got no wings?"

"Andrea, I'm going to need you to focus on me for a change. Now, have a drink. You'll need it because you won't believe me when I tell you what's been going on." I proceeded to fill my sister in on the last several months of my life, starting with Sean.

"You gotta be kiddin' me." She swigged her wine.

"I wish."

"You was kickin' it with some married dude? That don't even sound like you."

"Pfft." I rested on the couch and ran my hand over the top of my hair. "What can I say? I got caught up. And now I'm paying for it."

"So what you gon' do?"

"I don't know." I snagged a handful of grapes and popped one into my mouth, then tucked my feet beneath me on the couch.

"You tellin' Rick?"

"Which part? The affair? I know who's stalking me? Sean may be moving back?"

"All of it."

I chewed on my fingernail. I had been asking myself that same question for the last hour. "I don't know yet. What do you think I should do? Everyone is telling me to call the cops."

She pursed her lips. "Girl, you don't need no cops."

"You don't think so?"

"Nah. We got the same blood. If I wouldn't need no cops, then you don't need no cops," she said, then continued. "But you can't keep hidin' in your room like some little bi—"

"Don't say it." I cut her off. "But I hear you. I'll handle it."

Andrea rolled her neck. "You sure?"

I glared at my sister. "I said I'll handle it."

"Let me know if you need help. And if he comes near my daughter, I'll take him out myself."

That's why I loved my sister. I could always count on her to be hood. "Thanks, Sis."

"So, you and Rick are kickin' it again, huh?"

I blushed and grinned. "I don't know what we're doing. But he's been amazing to me since this whole ordeal began. We've gotten very close in a short amount of time."

"That's cool." She turned her wrist toward her and looked at the time on an Apple watch I knew she couldn't afford. "But if we done talkin' about you, I need to get to that favor."

I shook my head. "You listened to me longer than I thought you would. What do you want?"

"I need you to let me hold a few hundred. And before you say no, it's for Rachel."

There she goes. Attacking my weakness. "What's going on with Rachel?"

"She wanna take swimming lessons and I ain't got no money for 'em."

"Wait here." I dashed upstairs to my bedroom and searched inside the jewelry box on my dresser. I returned with the bracelet from Sean. "Here. Pawn this and keep the money." I handed her the unpleasant reminder of the mistakes of my past.

She lit up like a gold digger who'd found her mark. "Straight up? You givin' me this?"

I stood with my back to the arched doorway between the den and the hall. "Yeah. Take it before I change my mind. And I can't think about this anymore today. I'm sure Rick will be here soon, and I don't want to have this on my mind when he arrives."

"Don't want to have what on your mind?"

I jumped and turned, startled to see Rick. "Oh. You have to stop appearing out of nowhere. You almost gave me a heart attack." I clutched my chest, feeling my heart pulse against my dress. How long had he been standing there?

"I'm sorry, Chanelle. I thought you heard me. I announced myself when I came in. So, what don't you want to have on your mind?" he questioned me again.

"This whole insane situation." My response was the truth. It had consumed my life and I had to find a way to let it go.

But now I felt guilty when I looked at him. He was so concerned about me. I saw it in his downturned mouth and the wrinkle in his forehead. "Rick, I have something I need to tell you."

But Andrea interrupted. "Hey, Rick, it's good to see you again."

"You too, Andrea. You're still lookin' good. Beauty must run in your family." He stepped past me to hug her, then turned back to me. "What is it that you need to say?"

Andrea coughed. "It'll have to wait. I'm gettin' ready to go. Sis, walk me to my car?"

I frowned, unsure of what she was up to. I patted Rick on his chest. "I'll be back in a minute."

I trailed my sister through the house and out the front door to her car with red tape over the tail lights. "Why did you stop me?"

"Because you was 'bout to screw up a good thing. It took me two seconds to see he is checkin' hard for you. You tell him what you did with ol' boy, and poof," she snapped her fingers, "Rick'll get ghost."

I folded my arms, leaning against her trunk. "You think so?"

"Sis, I know so." She poked me in the chest. "Keep yo mouth shut and handle yo business."

I smacked her hand away and rubbed the tender spot she'd jabbed. Was she right? I thought talking to her would help me sort things out, but instead I was more confused than before she arrived.

"What am I supposed to say when I go back inside?" I asked.

She shrugged. "I dunno. You'll come up with somethin' good." She kissed my cheek. "I gotta go. Call me if you need me."

I smiled with wry amusement. "Thanks."

I watched my sister drive off, wishing I was in the passenger seat, then realized I was standing outside alone and sprinted back into the house. Andrea was right. I had it in me to take care of this myself. I couldn't risk losing Rick. We were building a solid foundation for a lasting relationship. And it was within reach. There was no way I was going to jeopardize it.

"Is Andrea alright?" Rick asked when I'd returned to the den and scooted close to him on the couch.

"Yeah. She's the same as she was when you knew her before. She was keeping me company while you were gone."

He leaned away from me so he could see me better. "What was it you wanted to tell me?"

"Um… it was nothing serious. Just that I missed you and couldn't wait for you to get home." I looked up at him and twirled my hair around my finger. "I'm scared when you're not here."

His voice was soft. "It'll be over soon. I promise you; I'll find out who's doing this to you."

"That's why you're my protector. Would you like a glass of wine?" I asked, while pouring myself my first glass of the evening. And knocked it back in three gulps.

His eyes popped open. "Nah, I'm good. But you need to slow down. It's wine, not water."

"I need something to take the edge off." I poured and downed my second glass.

"That's it. You're cut off." Rick snatched the bottle and my empty wineglass, while I wiped my mouth on the back of my sleeve. "Would you like me to fix dinner for you?" he asked.

"Oh, no." A belch crept past my lips. "Excuse me." I giggled. More from embarrassment than because it was funny. "I couldn't ask you to do that. You had a long day. I'm sure you must be tired."

"You didn't ask. I volunteered. And I don't mind. I'll do a quick check around the house and we can fire up the grill."

"But the grill is outside," I whispered.

With a humored smile, he whispered back, "That's usually where people keep them. No one is going to hurt you while I'm around."

I beamed at my guardian angel. "Then barbecue would be great. I have a pack of Amish chicken wings in the refrigerator. I'll whip up a quick marinade, while you start the grill. There's a big bag of lump charcoal in the garage."

"Perfect." Rick marched to the kitchen to drop off the glasses and the remaining wine before opening the door that led to the garage. I wobbled to my feet, caught my balance and followed him into the kitchen. Once he was out of sight, I hurried and swigged my third glass of wine, then created a teriyaki marinade for the chicken.

Dinner was delicious. The chicken fell off the bone and the lemon pepper grilled asparagus melted in my mouth. For dessert, we enjoyed juicy slices of grilled pineapple. I was extra chatty, thanks to the wine. He was a gentleman and pretended not to notice.

After dinner, Rick gathered the dirty dishes. "You rest while I clean up."

I gazed at him, grateful and thankful to God that he had re-entered my life.

I relaxed on my lounger and shut my eyes. My thoughts were so jumbled, and I longed to be me again. For a fleeting moment, I thought about leaving the country. Maybe The Stalker didn't have a passport. I chuckled to myself.

"It's nice to see you smile."

I gradually opened my eyes to see Rick grinning down at me. "It feels good, too."

Rick had turned on my stereo system and the sounds of smooth jazz filled the room.

He extended his hand to me. "Let's dance."

I welcomed the chance to be close. He helped me to my feet and tenderly took me in his arms. We swayed to the sensual rhythm. I rested my head on his chest and again closed my eyes. The cascade of the water flowing from my fountain in the den, combined with the seductive tunes, and the security of his embrace lulled me. For the first time that day, all traces of tension floated out of my body. I knew I had decisions to make, but for now, I was going to enjoy the peace in my soul and pretend my world was perfect.

I gazed up at him. "Thank you."

"For what?"

"For being such a friend to me. I don't know how I would have made it without you."

He tightened his embrace. "Thank you for trusting me enough to keep you safe." He positioned his finger under my chin and tilted my head up as he bent down to give me the sweetest kiss I'd ever experienced in my thirty-plus years of living. His lips were so soft that I felt my body melt into his.

I stroked his head as he pulled me even closer, and our kiss deepened.

"Chanelle?" Rick called my name, his voice thick with desire.

"Yes?"

"I want to make love to you."

My heart fluttered. "I—I would like that. But it's too soon."

"I knew I still loved you when I saw you in Lowe's. I'm in this with you for the long haul. I'll wait as long as it takes for you to trust that I'm not going to hurt you and that I'm not going anywhere."

I prayed he was being honest with me because I knew I could love him, too. "Rick, I just need more time. I'm emotional right now and a little tipsy," I added with a light laugh. "When we make love, I want my head to be clear."

"Like I said, I can wait as long as it takes."

"Thank you." I whispered as a lone tear meandered down my cheek.

He gently kissed it away. Then he kissed my closed eyelids, my cheeks, my nose, and finally my mouth. Our kiss intensified, and I was about five seconds from changing my mind.

"We need to stop before we go farther than we should," I said, my voice ragged as I pushed away from him.

"You're right," he said with his mouth, but his eyes were pleading with me to keep it going.

I listened to his mouth. "I'm going to bed and I'm sleeping alone." I paused before adding, "Tonight."

"Does that mean you won't be sleeping alone tomorrow?"

I smiled and shrugged a shoulder. "I dunno about tomorrow. I guess you'll have to wait and see." I leaned in and kissed him on his cheek. "Good night, Rick," I said and sauntered out of the room.

I felt him staring at my backside. "Good night, Chanelle. I love you."

I stopped walking and turned to face him.

"Too much?" he asked.

I nodded. "Yes, too much."

"Okay. Then just good night."

I smiled with my eyes and left the room.

CHAPTER 24

"HEY, Boss Lady, how are things going?" Patty asked when she called my house.

I set the novel I was reading in my lap and crossed my legs. "Patty! It's good to hear your voice. Things are fine. How's work?"

"It ain't been the same without you. People askin' if somethin' is wrong."

I glanced out the living room bay window, watching the wind tickle the tree leaves. "What are you telling them?"

"That it ain't none of their business." Patty snickered. "I'm just teasin'. I say you're on an extended vacation. You have any idea when you'll be back?"

"I don't." It had been a couple days since my call with Sean. I hadn't heard anything from The Stalker since we spoke, so maybe Sean had gotten through to his wife.

"Well, I got good news for ya."

"Please share. I could use some good news right about now."

"Sean may be coming back."

That wasn't good news. "Oh."

"Yeah, Mr. Jeffries told me yesterday," she continued,

oblivious to my lack of enthusiasm. "He's pumped about it. I guess Sean called and told him he was coming back to Michigan and asked if he could get his spot back. Mr. Jeffries said he would hire him in a New York minute."

My head began to pound. "And Mr. Jeffries just volunteered that information?"

"Yeah. That's how excited he was. He came by to tell you and then remembered you were out. So, he told me."

Breathe, Chanelle, breathe. "Well, I hope things work out."

"Ain't you happy about this, Boss Lady? You and Sean were like the dynamic duo."

"I'm happy. Look, I have to go. But thanks for telling me," I said, rushing her off the phone.

"Oh, okay. Well, I guess I'll talk to ya later."

I sighed and threw my head against the back of the chair as I continued gazing out the window. This unfolding travesty was becoming exponentially worse.

It was the snail's crawl of a white Impala as it rolled past my window that grabbed my attention. The driver paced the street twice before coming to a stop in front of my house. I tipped forward in my chair to get a closer look inside the car. I squinted. Then blinked. Cynthia?

She wore shades and a wide-brimmed hat, but when she lowered her head and pulled her glasses down on her nose, our eyes locked. She tossed her head back and swigged from a bottle that looked like it contained whiskey or some other brown liquid and sped off. My eyes followed the car until it was out of the sight of my window and I could no longer see it. I snatched my phone from the side table and launched myself from the chair, my book falling to the floor. Then, scurried out of the room and up the stairs, tapping on numbers on my cell.

"Hey, Steve, it's your other sister," I said, slamming and locking my bedroom door.

"What's going on, Chanelle?" I heard his smile. "Are you alright?"

It must have been because I didn't give a quick response that his tone switched to worry. "Spit it out."

I sat in the center of my bed and whispered. "I saw a woman in front of my house, and I think she may be connected to what's going on."

"What makes you think that? Can you describe her?"

"Um..." What was I going to say? Of course I could describe her, but I hadn't told him about Cynthia. Now, I could hear Andrea's voice in my head telling me to man up and leave Steve out of it.

"Chanelle? Are you still there?"

"Yeah, I'm here. Uh, it was a false alarm. I—I missed the pizza sign on top of the car. Probably a lost delivery driver."

"Mm hmm. You sure?"

"I'm positive. I was just being jumpy. Sorry to have bothered you. I'll call you if I need you."

I hung up before he could ask me any more questions.

"Okay, Sherlock," I said to myself. "Now, what are you gonna do?"

"Chanelle, dinner was scrumptious. You keep cooking like this and I'm never leaving." Rick licked his lips, savoring the last bites of his smothered pork chops, collard greens, and rice.

"Is that a promise?" I smiled at him from across the table.

"It could be."

I sipped my wine, hoping the liquid would calm the ripples that overtook me when Rick's eyes beheld me. "You ready for dessert? I fixed an apple pie."

"What I'm ready for is a conversation about us." 2He reached across the mahogany wood and caressed my fingers, sending yet another tremor to my center. "I'm ready to talk about us, Chanelle. I want there to be an 'us', don't you?"

I looked at his hands, then allowed my eyes to travel up his arms, stopping momentarily at his ripped chest and finally to his gorgeous face. "Yes, I want there to be an 'us'."

"Just you and me. I don't have a desire to date anyone but you."

I wanted to move forward and tell him I wanted the exact same thing, because honest to God, I did. I wanted to be with Rick and only Rick. But I couldn't do it until I'd resolved my Sean and Cynthia issues. "I... I can't focus on a relationship right now. Not until I get my life straightened out. Can you understand where I'm coming from?"

He slid his hands back to his side of the table and his lips turned down, but he nodded. "Yeah. Yeah, I can understand."

"Um, I'll get dessert. Why don't you unwind, and I'll bring it to you?" Slowly, we stood. He went into the den without speaking another word, and I picked up our plates, went into the kitchen, sliced the pie, and scooped vanilla ice cream.

"Here you go," I said, meeting him in the den and handing him his bowl while sitting next to him on the love seat.

The mood was noticeably awkward, but I didn't know what to say. So, I said nothing and hoped he'd get over it and go back to being the Rick I enjoyed, instead of the one I'd just hurt. We were about halfway through a boring program on the Military Channel—which was his favorite—when the cordless phone rang. I tensed when I picked it up and saw "unknown" on the caller ID.

I peeked at Rick before I put the phone to the side of my face that was farthest from him. "Hello?"

"Hi, Chanelle. It's me. Sean." The only heat I felt when I heard his voice now was my anger. But I had to play it cool, because Rick was laser focused on me.

I pressed the phone closer to my ear and subtly turned down

the volume on the side of the receiver. "Oh, hey," I glanced again at Rick, who was watching me intently.

"Is now a good time to talk?"

I crossed my legs, tilting my body away from Rick. "Uh, not really."

Rick mouthed, "Is that him?"

I shook my head and looked away. Rick was going to have questions the second I hung up. And I had no answers that I could share.

"Okay, well, I was calling to let you know I haven't been able to talk to Cynthia about you. She moved out and changed her phone number when I told her I got the job at Image."

He dealt me a double whammy. My dreams of having him call her off plummeted and my anxiety about him returning shot through the proverbial roof.

"Did you hear me?" he asked.

"Yes. I appreciate the heads up."

"I'll see you soon, Chanelle. And I'm not giving up on us. We could have something very special if you'd give us a chance."

"Thanks again for calling. I'll be sure to keep that in mind."

"Huh?"

"Gotta go now. Bye."

My finger had barely touched the "on hook" button before Rick asked, "Who was that?"

I chewed on my bottom lip. Thinking. I answered with a shrug before I gathered the courage to say, "The office. Patty was giving me a quick update. No big deal."

Rick peered at me out of the corner of his eye. I knew what was happening. He was wondering if he should believe me. "You know, when we were in college, I could always tell when you weren't being straight with me," he said.

"What are you talking about?" The furrow in my brow deepened as I chewed my lip like it was a continuation of dessert.

He massaged his chin with slow, methodical, deliberate strokes. "Whenever, you told a half truth or you out and out lied, you would bite your lip... sorta like what you're doing now."

I promptly stopped. Then swallowed. Hard. "I'm being straight with you. It was work."

"Mm hmm." He turned his attention back to the television, but I knew he wasn't watching. He was trying to guess what I was up to. And I was trying to figure out how to fix my disastrous life.

CHAPTER 25

"Hey, wanna come over?" I said to my best friend, the afternoon after finding out Sean was definitely returning.

"Sure. What time?"

"Whenever's good for you. Rick's not here and I don't want to be home alone. I was thinking we could have a little girl time."

"Well, aren't you the little housewife? Seems like you're never going back to work."

I giggled. "I have to admit, I could get used to this kind of life. You know, minus the stalker part."

"I'm glad to know you can joke about it. I'll swing by after I pick up BJ from preschool and drop him at my parents."

"Cool."

We hung up, and I called my sister. "I want you to come over."

"Why?" Andrea didn't know how to answer the phone without an attitude.

I glanced up and shook my head. "Why can't you just say, 'yes, my favorite baby sister, I'm on my way'?"

"'Cause I don't roll like that. But since you did me a solid when you gave me that tennis bracelet, gimme an hour."

"Thank you. Love you."

"Yeah, yeah, yeah," she said, then hung up.

Even though morning had long passed, I'd taken my time in starting my day, so I said my daily prayer to God, took a shower, dressed, and walked downstairs. I was enjoying a cup of tea and a bowl of oatmeal when my cellphone buzzed. I hated that I felt compelled to answer when I was sure I didn't want to talk to whoever was on the other end of the line. But without fail, I said, "Hello."

"Humph. So, you think you can ruin my marriage and den go on like nothin' happened, huh?"

I sat up straight in a chair in my great room. "Cynthia?"

"Who else would it be? Who else marriage you jack up?" she snarled.

I ignored her biting words. "Cynthia, I'm sorry your marriage is ruined, as you say. But I didn't do that."

"Ha! Yeah, you did." The slurring of her words made it clear she was having her own happy hour.

I inhaled a deep breath. Maybe if I could just reason with her, she'd leave me alone and go on about her life. "Cynthia, I *truly* apologize to you if I hurt you in any way. What happened between Sean and me was a mistake. And will never happen again."

"You damn right it was a mistake. It's your fault he's leaving me."

"I don't know why you say that. Sean and I haven't spoken since you moved." My comment wasn't completely true, but it wasn't like I wanted to talk to him when he called.

"He moved all right, but he wasn't the same. He kept talkin' 'bout how he wanted to get back to Michigan and I couldn't understand why. And den one day, he comes home from church and he's feelin' all guilty and he start tellin' me 'bout you. And how he miss you. And how he don't wanna be married to me no more because he wanna try and make it work wit' you." Every time she emphasized "you," her voice escalated. And so did my fear.

I was floored, but apparently there was no need for me to speak because she kept talking. "So den I said to myself, 'self, if we got rid of her, den Sean will stay wit' us'. And me and myself liked dat idea. So guess what?" She paused and let a moment pass before she added, "I'm 'bout to get rid of you."

My voice was strong when I said her name. Much stronger than I felt as I tore through the house to the living room. "Cynthia."

I crouched down on the floor and parted the curtains at the base of the window. I inhaled a couple of quick breaths. Cynthia was parked in a silver Impala in front of my house, but this time she didn't see me. Fortunately, her car was pulled up far enough for me to get a view of the license plate.

Staying low to the ground, I opened the desk drawer next to the recliner and grabbed a pen and piece of paper. "I told you I was sorry for what I did." I said, cradling the phone in the crook of my neck and jotting down her license plate number. "And I feel bad for you because your marriage is on the rocks. But that's between you and Sean. And if you come at me, I will defend myself." I hesitated before saying. "I'm not afraid of you." I knew that part was a complete and total lie, but she didn't.

"You shouldn't be afraid. You should be terrified."

My home screen reappeared as our call disconnected. I returned the pen and paper to the drawer and resolved right then and there that this nonsense had to end. Now.

CHAPTER 26

I FLUFFED the pillows on the sofa in the den and took a final inventory of the snacks I'd prepared. I'd laid out wine, cheese, and crackers for Michele. Beer, pizza rolls, and ranch dip for Andrea.

Michele arrived first and followed me back to the den. "What's going on?"

"Girrrl, a lot. I'll wait for Andrea, so I only have to say it once."

Michele plopped onto the sofa and kicked off her shoes. She poured a glass of white wine, popped a cheese chunk in her mouth and tucked her feet beneath her. "It must be serious."

"More than you know."

The doorbell chimed, signaling Andrea's arrival. Using her key, she breezed in seconds later. "What you got to eat?"

I pointed to the table.

"That's what's up." She flopped down next to Michele.

"Now, talk," Michele said, snagging one of Andrea's pizza rolls and drawing daggers from my sister.

I sat on the floor, relaxing back on my hands behind me and

crossing my legs at the ankle. I filled them in on Cynthia's crazy call.

"She was actually outside your house?" Michele asked.

I nodded. "Yup. That's the second time that I know for sure she's been here."

"Why didn't you tell me sooner?"

"So you could call Steve?" I shook my head. "No, thank you."

Andrea spoke up. "Why would you bring Steve into this?"

"Why wouldn't she?" Michele asked.

"She wouldn't because she can handle some drunk veterinarian with a grudge," she said to Michele, then turned to point her beer at me. "You're a punk if you bring in the cops."

"Look, I didn't call you two over here for that. I called you to tell you that Sean is definitely returning."

"What?" they said in unison.

"You heard me. He's moving back to Michigan. And he got his job back as our consultant. *And...* he wants us to pick up where we left off."

"You might as well quit now," Andrea said. "Because this 'ish is messy."

"Who you tellin'?" I raised to my knees and poured my own glass of wine, then sat back. I downed an unladylike gulp. "But there's no way I'm giving up my job. I've worked too hard to build my career to watch it vanish." I snapped my fingers.

Michele said, "Your career is worthless if you're dead."

I glared at her. I was beginning to wish I hadn't called either one of them. "You're not being helpful, Michele."

She raised her brow and puckered her lips. "Calling it the way I see it. But anyway, what about Rick? Does he know about Sean?"

I shook my head. "Last night, he told me he wants to be exclusive. And then later in the evening, Sean called. While I was sitting next to him."

"Oooh, what you do?" Andrea asked.

"I pretended like I was on the phone with work."

"Did he buy it?"

I shook my head again. "I don't think so. But he let it go."

"Chanelle, you can't build a relationship on lies. It'll kill it before it starts," Michele said.

"Don't you think I know that? But what was I going to say?"

"Here's a novel idea. How about you tell him the truth?"

"Yeah, right." My laugh was cynical. "How's it supposed to go? 'Hey, Rick. I know you think I'm a sweet girl and all, but I slept with a married man and by the way, we'll be working together again soon. You still wanna be my boyfriend?' Is that what I'm supposed to say?"

"See, Sis, that's why I told you to handle yo business by yourself. 'Cause ain't no man stickin' with you if you tell him that."

"Chanelle," Michele began, calling my name and forcing me to look at her instead of Andrea. "If you keep being secretive, then it's going to blow up in your face. You have to tell Rick. You can handle everything else that's happening if you start with talking to him. He'll understand. It's not like you two were together when you slept with Sean. But what he won't understand, is you intentionally deceiving him. Don't make a bad situation worse. I'm just sayin'...."

The three of us continued to talk about my problems and eventually gravitated to other topics. But in the back of my mind, I kept replaying Michele's warning. "Don't make a bad situation worse." And that was exactly what I was already doing.

"Hey, Sweetie, come on downstairs. I have something for you," Rick yelled up.

It had been a couple hours since the ladies had left. After a long conversation with myself, I'd decided to tell Rick everything, and deal with whatever happened next. Hopefully, he wouldn't pack his bags and leave me.

I took a deep breath, dragged myself off my bed, and trudged down the stairs.

He greeted me with a wide grin and open arms. I strolled into them and allowed his cozy hug to comfort me. "The pizza will be here in a few." He released me, took my hand, and led me to the couch. "I'll be right back. Let me make you some tea. And then I'll give you your surprise."

I gave him a weak smile as I sat. I had a surprise for him too. Moments later he returned with a hot cup of chamomile tea with organic honey, lemon, and ginger. The only thing missing was a shot of tequila or something stronger to give me a boost of courage. When the pizza arrived, he placed slices on a couple of paper plates and met me in the den. He blessed the food, and we began to eat.

Chanelle say it, I thought. *Speak your peace and get it over with.* "Rick—"

He put his finger to my lips. "Me first."

I grinned, happy to push back what I didn't want to do, anyway.

"I was thinking of a way to take your attention off things, at least for a little while, and then a great idea came to me."

"What did you have in mind?" I inquired between bites of pepperoni, green olives, and pineapple.

"Well, years ago, when I was married, my ex and I bought a timeshare in Aruba. When we divorced, I kept it as part of the settlement. I usually rent it out because it's such a romantic place to visit, and I wasn't going to go alone. But if you're open to it, I'd love to take you. What do you think?" He held his breath while he waited for my response.

Aruba? Wow. I'd never been there before. Just the name alone sounded sexy. There was no way I could tell him about Sean now. But maybe getting away would be what I needed.

Maybe, just maybe, it would give Cynthia time to cool off and I could be gone when Sean returned to his old job. I was positive that Cynthia's hired gun wouldn't be able to follow me, although he'd laid off me lately. The more I thought about it, the more I liked the idea. "When would we leave?"

"Well..." He reached into his work bag on the floor. "I was thinking we could leave... tomorrow." And then he handed me two first-class plane tickets.

"Tomorrow? How in the world do you expect me to be ready by tomorrow?" My mind was racing. There was no way I could pull it together and be ready to board a plane in less than twenty-four hours.

"Calm down. All you need to do is pack your clothes and I'm taking care of everything else."

"What time would we leave?"

"Ten in the morning. We could be on the beach by five." His eyes begged me to say, "Yes."

I took a deep breath and then slowly exhaled and nodded. "Okay. It sounds like fun." My timid grin morphed into a toothy smile.

"Woohoo!" He jumped up, taking me with him and spinning me around. "We are going to have a great time and you'll finally be able to relax." He set me down.

His excitement was infectious, and I found myself becoming as enthusiastic as he was. "I have to call Michele. She's going to be so thrilled for me. For us."

"You call her, and I'll straighten up here."

"Wait. Don't you need to go home and pack?"

"Nope." He shook his head. "I knew you'd say yes, so my bags are packed and loaded in my truck."

I smiled at the man who was winning more of my heart with each day that passed. "Thank you," I said, sincerely.

He stopped what he was doing so he could wrap his arms around me again. "When we get back, we'll figure out how to stop this nonsense. I'm ready for us to get on with our lives, without all this drama looming over us." He looked deep into my eyes before his lips settled on mine in a passionate kiss.

"I'd do anything for you, Chanelle. I'd swim a swamp filled with crocodiles and alligators to get to you and make sure you're safe. You believe me, don't you?"

"Yes, I do." I pulled his face back to mine and returned the kiss.

CHAPTER 27

"Hey, Chele!" The joy in my voice tumbled out.

Michele chuckled. "Hey girl, what's got you so excited? You didn't sound anything like this when I was at your house."

I stood in my closet, snatching sundresses off hangers. "Rick. He's taking me on a two-week vacation to Aruba."

"You're kidding!"

"Nope, we leave in less than twelve hours." Arms loaded, I carried about a month's worth of outfits to my bed, dropping them in a pile and returning for more.

"That's fabulous. How did that happen?"

"He wants me to get me away from all this madness."

"Oooh, I love him for you. Wait, how are you getting all this time off work?"

"That's a perk of being a partner." I laughed, then said, "but seriously, Mr. Jeffries knows I'm always available. I have a ton of vacation time I've never used, and it carries over from year to year. My being off for an extended amount of time is needed right now."

"Well, enjoy yourself. I'll check on your house while you're gone."

"Thanks. And don't tell Andrea. She'll use her key and there's no tellin' what I'll come home to."

We laughed at my sister, both of us knowing her antics and what she was capable of. After chatting a few more moments, I hung up and started hunting for my suitcases in the basement.

"Hey, Sweetie," Rick called down. "You need any help?"

"I'm good. You've already done too much. I'll be ready before you know it."

After packing, we slept for a couple of hours, then drove to the airport for our six-hour flight, which was certain to be pure luxury. I was accustomed to flying coach, or maybe upgrading to business class, but first-class was a treat. Since we received priority boarding, the flight attendants served mimosas in actual glassware while the rest of the plane filled with passengers.

I peered out the window and watched the ground crew load our luggage, then turned to Rick. "Thank you, again."

"I should be the one thanking you. I get to spend fourteen days on a beautiful island with an even more beautiful woman, who I hope will be wearing little more than a bikini the entire time." The heat of his gaze seared me while he continued. "And who I hope will finally say the words I've been waiting to hear."

Knowing what he was talking about, I gave him a not-so-innocent glance. "What words would those be?"

He leaned in to me and his warm breath tickled my neck. "Tonight is the night."

"We'll see..." I bit my lip again, but this time for an entirely different reason.

He raised his glass and clinked it with mine. "Here's to us."

We stared at each other as we sipped our drinks. Then I laid my head back against the oversized comfy seat and took a long... slow... and deep cleansing breath.

As we taxied down the runway and the wheels folded into their hiding spots in the belly of the plane, my gaze journeyed back out the window. I visualized myself leaving my problems on the ground while we climbed through the clouds and into the blue sky far above everything that plagued me.

"Good morning, may I take your order," a short and portly man in a red and blue uniform asked us, mentally bringing me back into my seat. He handed us a laminated card with three hot breakfast choices. We both selected scrambled eggs and toast and within moments we were enjoying a surprisingly good meal. I sipped a couple more mimosas and began reading a novel on my Kindle until my eyes tired and I used Rick's broad shoulder as my pillow. I felt him kiss the top of my head before I drifted off in a peaceful sleep.

By the time we walked through customs at the tiny airport, my troubles were forgotten. Our cab driver zoomed us through the streets of Aruba while Rick gave me a little island history.

"Do you see the direction of the trees?" Rick tipped his head to mine and pointed to the postcard setting as we made our way to our five-star resort.

"Yes."

"You'll see that there's a constant breeze that causes the trees to grow in the direction of the wind. And because Aruba is basically a desert, they get very little rain. All the tropical foliage you see is imported."

I listened to him, and for the first time it was painfully obvious to me that he'd been here before. With another woman. His wife. Would he be thinking about her while he was here with me? "You know a lot about the island."

He covered my hand with his. "I know what's swimming through your head, Chanelle. You're the only woman on my mind and in my heart."

"You mean it?"

He squeezed my hand and pressed his lips to mine. "I mean it."

I grinned and settled in for the remainder of the ride to our new home for the next couple weeks.

I'd imagined what our room would look like. But this ocean front two-bedroom suite captured my breath.

"Rick," I whispered his name, breathless.

My mouth opened wide as I stood at the threshold of our Caribbean sanctuary. The open floor plan allowed my eyes to travel the expansive space. The kitchen with stainless steel appliances. The living room with cushioned wicker furniture and sheer white curtains that sailed in the breeze flowing through the open balcony doors. Walls adorned with colorful abstract art.

With unsure steps, I entered the suite and made my way to the bathroom. The marble his and her sinks were nice, but the star of the room was the stone and glass shower stall with multiple heads that would massage the stress from every part of my body.

The best part of the suite, though, were the views. A large wraparound balcony stretched from the master bedroom to the living room, overlooking the sparkling water and award-winning golf course.

Rick leaned against the doorway, a lopsided grin on his face as I bounced from room to room.

I stepped onto the balcony from the bedroom and leaned over the rail, gazing out into the turquoise Caribbean Sea, filling my lungs with the fresh salty air. Rick tipped the porter, then joined me.

"Isn't it beautiful," he said, coming up behind me.

I nodded. "I've never seen water so clear."

"And it's only going to get better. Come on, let's hit up the pool. I want you to see something." He clapped and rubbed his hands together and went back inside, opening up one of his suitcases and pulling out a pair of navy-blue swimming trunks.

"Yes!" I followed him inside and opened up my three

suitcases before finding my favorite orange and yellow bikini and matching sarong. I excused myself and went to the bathroom, where I changed and wet my hair so that curly ringlets fell right below my shoulders. I slipped my sunglasses on top of my head to hold back my hair, applied sunblock to my face and sun tanning oil to my body. I slid into a pair of thong wedges, filled my straw beach bag with all the essentials, and moments later we were strolling, my hand nestled in his, to the pool.

I'd wondered why our first stop on this picturesque island would be the pool and not the beach, but as we entered the wet area of the resort, I understood. The pool was majestic, with an infinity edge and a swim-up bar that included a popcorn machine and an ice cream dispenser. But it was the stone waterfall that captured my heart. It made the most tranquil sound as the falls descended from atop the mountain into the crystal waters below.

I claimed two lounging chairs underneath a straw-hut umbrella, while Rick grabbed a couple of towels from the towel stand. We spread them out on the chairs and then reclined. With closed eyes, I lifted my face toward the heavens and allowed the Caribbean sun to heal my wounded and broken spirit. I surrendered all my cares to God as I said a silent prayer of thanks to Him for allowing me to experience this dream of an island. I was sure I would have two weeks free of drama and fear.

"Would the lovely lady like a drink?" I opened my eyes to see the pool waiter standing over me, beaming. His bright white teeth, a lovely contrast to his deep blue-black skin.

I squinted and used my hand as a shield to block the sun rays that were blinding me. "Mmmm... what do you recommend?"

"Might I suggest the Aruba Island Dream? A tantalizing mix of flavored rums, mango, pineapple, and freshly squeezed orange juice," he said, his island accent welcoming us to his paradise.

"Oooh, that sounds yummy. I'll have that."

"And for you, sir?"

"I'll have the same."

"Thank you."

As the waiter walked away, I gazed at Rick with dreamy eyes. I believed him when he'd said I was the only woman he wanted. But this place felt magical. How could he not be thinking about his ex? I gathered my courage to ask the question that still plagued my mind. "Are you sure you're okay being here with me when it was a special place you shared with your ex?"

He stared at the tropical skyline, waiting several beats before he spoke. "It's been a long time since I've been to the island. When my ex and I first came here, we were so in love. By our last trip, our marriage was a shell of what it once was. I had hoped to recapture some of that passion." His smile and small laugh were somewhat whimsical.

"I wanted to remind her of what we once had in the hopes of having it again. Not only did it not work, but toward the end of our vacation she got a text from her boyfriend, while I had her phone." His eyes clouded over as he thought back. "Now that I'm here with you, I'm thinking of the possibilities of our future and I'm amped by it. I guess it'll take me a moment to shift my thinking and keep it in the present and future; not think about what happened here in my past. I know I'm rambling, but does that make sense?"

He'd opened up to me in a way I hadn't expected. And I was holding back on him. I shook off my mounting guilt and took his hand in mine. "That makes perfect sense. And I appreciate you doing this for me."

Rick looked down at our hands and then into my eyes. "Chanelle, I'm in love with you. I get that you don't want to hear it, but it's true. I would do absolutely anything in the world for you."

I felt warm inside. "I know you would. Let's enjoy the next two weeks and not think about your ex or my stalker. Once we get home, we'll work on a plan to bring this to an end."

"Agreed."

The waiter returned with our drinks.

I licked my lips and savored my first sip. "This is delicious."

The waiter bowed a little. "Thank you, Ma'am. It's our resort specialty."

Rick signed for the bill and started our room tab. Then we sat by the pool and talked for hours, ordering drink after drink. At one point, we got in the water and swam up to the bar. We ordered ice cream and ate our cones while swirling our feet in the water, enjoying the private time we shared. Several times we had to reapply sunblock so we wouldn't burn in the island sun. My fingers tingled when I rubbed the lotion into his muscular back. And my skin was on fire, and not from the sun, as he rubbed it on mine.

After we left the pool, we went back to the room and showered. Then we changed into our evening clothes and went into town. Our pool attendant had recommended a sunset dinner at the Flying Fishbone, so the hotel made the reservations for us, and the ambiance was almost indescribable. Most of the tables were on the beach or at the edge of the shore.

While we waited for our appetizers, we threw bread into the water and watched the small fish flock to the food and swim around our feet. As boats passed by, slight waves rolled in and gently lapped up our legs.

Sitting across from Rick, staring into his eyes through the glow of the table candles, while the sun traded places with the moon awoke feelings in me that I didn't know I had. I thought about my ex and how this was something we had never done in all the years we were together. And I felt cheated. I knew I had given Michael too many years of my life, but until now, I had no comprehension of exactly what I'd missed.

Instead of being bitter, I nixed the thoughts and returned my focus to the man in front of me. It was at that very moment that I felt myself tip over the edge of love. I was no longer fighting the feeling, but flowing with it instead. Rick was not a man who would hurt me, and I was going to enjoy being in love with him.

"A penny for your thoughts." His voice interrupted my internal dialogue.

I gave him a demure smile. "Just that this is the happiest and most peaceful moment of my life. And I'm so glad to be here with you."

He smiled back. "I feel the same way, Chanelle." He reached across the table and massaged my hands. "Sooo... do you think tonight will be the night when we can physically express how much we care about each other?"

I hated to dash the longing in his eyes, but I knew I still wasn't ready to take that step, especially as I held my secret. "How about we don't plan it, but let it happen naturally?"

"Is that your way of saying no?"

I laughed a little. "That's my way of saying when it's the right time, you won't have to ask."

He exhaled loudly. "Okay. I can live with that."

The waitress arrived with our order. A delectable feast of fresh lobster and salmon served with risotto and a medley of vegetables.

Our conversation took on a lighter tone as we chatted about the things we wanted to do while on our vacation. We agreed to do things he had never done before so we could build our own memories.

The next two weeks went by in a blur. Every day was filled with lots of fun in the sun. We spent time at the beach and in the pool. We parasailed, jet-skied, rode ATV's, toured the island, swam in the natural pool, snorkeled, and went scuba diving.

Every evening we had intimate dinners either on a sunset sail dinner cruise, at one of the several restaurants on the island, or on the beach. We did lots of shopping and shipped our purchases to Michele's home so we wouldn't have to take them back on the plane. The island had several casinos, and some afternoons we would enjoy the air conditioning and free drinks while playing the slots. I was saddened when I realized we only had one more night on the island.

"Hey, is everything okay?" Rick asked me as I sat curled up next to him on the couch, watching an old episode of NCIS Los Angeles.

"Yeah, I thought about how tonight's our last night and I got a little sad, that's all."

"I can't believe it's been two weeks already. The time flew by."

"Yes, it did." I was sure I would have found the right time to tell Rick about Sean. But the closest I came was when we were strolling along the beach, my hand in his, my head resting on his shoulder. We'd stopped to watch the sunset and held each other. I'd looked up at him and opened my mouth to confess, but he'd bent down and kissed me.

And that's what kept happening. Every time I got ready to open up and confess, he would do something or say something sweet to me and I couldn't risk telling him and then losing him. Now we were hours away from boarding a plane to head home, and he was no closer to knowing my secret than he was when we first arrived.

I knew I had to tell him before we left. Even if he was mad at me, he would have to sit next to me on the plane and I could try to convince him that I was still a good person with a good heart who made a mistake. I decided I finally had enough courage to be honest about my past and the reason for the stalking. I grabbed the remote and muted the television. Then I turned to face Rick.

I prayed he would understand, took a deep breath, and then said, "I have something I need to tell you."

~

The worry in Rick's eyes broke my heart. Would he have the same level of concern once he heard what I had to say? "Chanelle, what's wrong? Throughout this entire vacation, you've had these moments where you looked like you wanted to say something and then you don't."

He was so perceptive. "You're right. I've wanted to tell you something for several weeks, but I've been afraid of your response."

"Whatever it is, it won't change how I feel about you. I told you I love you. As a matter of fact, I have something for you. Wait right here." Rick jumped up before I had a chance to protest and went into the bedroom. He returned with a small box and plopped next to me.

He opened the box and revealed a flawless ruby ring in a platinum setting. "I have loved you since college. The day you walked into Lowe's and back into my life was the best day of my life. I hope you know by now that I'm not the same man you left all those years ago. I want to love you. Cherish you. Provide for you. Protect you. I know you aren't ready to say yes to marriage, but will you say yes to being my woman? With a promise of more to come. Let me love you, Chanelle."

I stared at him, in complete shock. I pushed all my former apprehension aside and was more than ready to be in a committed relationship with Rick. "Yes, I accept your promise to love me. To cherish me. Provide for me. And protect me." I smiled and held out my right hand. He slid the ring on my finger and sealed our commitment with a kiss.

"Oh, what was it that my beautiful lady wanted to tell me?" He gazed lovingly into my eyes.

"Uh, it wasn't important." I gave him a feeble smile. I knew that I would have to tell him about Sean, but clearly today was not the day. I hoped he would still keep his promises to me once he found out the truth.

"You sure?"

I pulled his face within inches of mine. "Yes, I'm sure. But there is something that is important."

"And what's that?"

I whispered as I nibbled on his ear. "Tonight is the night."

His eyes lit up. "You wouldn't play with a brotha's heart, would you?"

"I'd never play with your heart." I rose seductively, pulling him with me. "You asked me to let you love me. Now, I'm asking you to let me do the same." He followed me as I sauntered to the bedroom. I could feel his eyes watching my behind as though I didn't have on a sundress.

I led him to the edge of the bed and motioned for him to sit. "Don't move," I commanded.

I could practically see his chest thumping through his shirt as he anticipated what was to come. I set my phone to my "Slow and Sexy" playlist and did a striptease that would have made Holly Madison proud. We explored each other's bodies while we consummated our newly confessed love. But the best part of our night was snuggling in his arms as I closed my eyes to sleep.

CHAPTER 28

"TELL ME EVERYTHING. LEAVE NOTHING OUT," Michele said as she reached our table at our favorite bar and grill at the mall. Michele wanted to hear all about our vacation, so she and I agreed to meet for lunch and do some girl bonding the Saturday after I returned. I was still slightly skittish about being out in public, not knowing if I was being watched, but I had to push past living my life in perpetual fear.

"It was amazing." I motioned for our waiter. After placing our orders, we resumed our conversation. "You know all of my mistakes. My failed relationships. My bad choices. I don't deserve a man like Rick, but he's the best thing that's ever happened to me." I grinned like a schoolgirl with a crush.

"He is a great man for you, Chanelle."

I nodded. "I feel so unworthy of the devotion and intimacy and adoration he's pouring on me. And those two weeks together strengthened our connection."

"Sooo, did you finally give in?"

I blushed and giggled. "How could I not? And it was by far the most incredible time I've ever had with a man. Even in all my years with Michael, I never experienced anything as special as what happened with Rick. He's learned a lot since college. And he gave me this." I held out my hand so she could get a good look at my new ring.

She brought my hand up to her face. "This is gorgeous!"

"I know, right? It's what made me give in." I giggled again.

"Whew." She released my hand and leaned back in her seat. "That man loves you. Don't mess it up."

I frowned. I knew what she was getting at and she was killing my new-love high. "I'm not."

"Did you tell him about Sean and Cynthia?"

"Uh, I didn't get a chance to."

"Oh, then you *are* messing it up."

"No, I'm not." I objected to her assessment. "I looked for the right time to say something, but it never came. Maybe that was a sign from God to keep my mouth shut." I twirled my new ring around my finger, not even looking at Michele, while I tried to get her to understand.

"Seriously? You're putting the fact that you are being a coward on God?"

I scowled at my best friend. "That's unfair. Look, we were Cynthia and Sean free for fourteen whole days. I'm going to wait and see if, while we were gone, Sean talked some sense into his wife. I don't see a reason to spill my guts and risk my relationship if I no longer have a problem."

"I want to be sure I'm understanding your foolishness." She slowed her cadence down to a level that was almost insulting. "Your barometer for determining whether you still have a problem is when you hear from Sean, Cynthia, or a STALKER again? What if by then, it's too late?"

My lips formed a tight line, and I wished I was dining alone. "I hear you, but let's be done with this conversation. There's too much at stake for me to say something right now."

Her eyes pleaded with me, while she paused so the waitress could drop off our drinks and appetizers. "Chanelle, there's too much at stake for you to not say something."

But I vehemently shook my head. "Unh-uh. I've waited too long to find someone special and get my doggone picket fence and fairy tale ending. I hate to think that a decision I made months ago"—I threw my hands in the air in an exaggerated fashion to emphasize my point—"darn near a year ago, could come back to haunt me and ruin my future."

Michele, forever the optimist and unfazed by my theatrics, said, "I think you'll be pleasantly surprised by his response. Trust him."

I lifted my chin. "Nope. Now, do you want to see my pictures from our trip?"

Michele sighed deeply, and I saw disappointment etched in her face. She couldn't understand the position I was in because she already had the dream life. I was still trying to create mine. "Yeah, show me your pics."

"I'm going to pretend you're eager to see them." I whipped out my iPad.

"I do want to see them. I'm just worried about you. That's all."

My shoulders slumped. "I know. Let's just enjoy our day together and not think about the dark side of my life right now. Okay?"

She hesitated before saying, "Okay."

Our waiter arrived with our meals, and we began eating. Through bites of my jalapeno cheddar burger, I proceeded to tell Michele about our activities while in Aruba as I narrated the slideshow. Eventually, she lightened up and began enjoying her afternoon with me.

"Ben and I are definitely adding Aruba to our Bucket List." Michele declared after viewing the last picture.

"You're going to love it!"

We continued chatting, though in the back of my mind, I couldn't shake her words: *What if by then, it's too late...*

CHAPTER 29

"LET THE CHURCH SAY 'AMEN'," Pastor Sharpe said from the pulpit.

"Amen!"

"You may be seated."

Rick and I sat next to each other, and I was beaming. In all the years Michael and I had been together, he never once set foot inside of a church.

"Church, this morning's message is: How Honest Are You? How... Honest... Are... You?"

Michele, who was sitting to my left, looked over at me and I could feel her eyes boring into the side of my face, though I continued looking straight ahead.

Pastor Sharpe continued. "In today's society, people find all kinds of reasons to justify being dishonest. Some say, 'oh, it's only a little white lie'. But what did they tell?"

"A lie!" someone shouted.

"Or someone tells a lie by omission. What is that, church? They know the truth about something, but they allow you to think something different. They don't set the record straight. Well, I'm setting the record straight right now. A lie is a lie."

"Amen!" That darn Amen corner shouted their vocal agreement, as though they were perfect and never guilty of a little dishonesty.

"But what does God say? Proverbs 12:22 says: lying lips are an abomination to the Lord, but those who act faithfully are His delight. Are your lips lying, Church?"

"No," the lying Amen corner said.

"How can we change these lying lips? Simple. Tell the truth!"

"Preach!"

Pastor Sharpe continued to talk about the virtues of being truthful and how no good comes from lying.

Rick leaned in and touched my hand. "I like your pastor. She's on point. Without honesty, you have nothing."

My stomach churned.

"Do you have anything you want to tell me?" he asked.

I bit my bottom lip and shook my head, because I didn't trust my voice.

"Good," he continued. "I have nothing I'm holding back from you either." He squeezed my hand, kissed my nose, and grinned as he turned back to the sermon.

I took a deep slow breath and tried to shake off the guilt that could only be removed by telling a truth that I was too scared to say.

CHAPTER 30

"Boss Lady! You're back!" Patty exclaimed the following Monday. She came from around her desk and pulled me into her plump bosom. "You shoulda told me you was comin' back. I woulda had your office decorated."

I chuckled and returned the hug. "You're too kind, but I decided last night that enough was enough."

She lowered her voice. "Have you heard anything more from that stalker?"

I glanced around, even though I knew we were the only two in my suite. "Not a peep in well over three weeks. I'm thinking I'm in the clear."

Patty's sigh sounded like relief. "Oh, good, Boss Lady. I'm so happy this nightmare is over for you."

"You and me both."

"Did you ever find out who was behind it?"

"Uh, not really."

"Well, I'm glad it's done. You go get settled and I'll buzz Mr. Jeffries and let him know you're back."

"Thank you, Patty." I turned and strolled into my office. About five minutes later, I heard a familiar voice.

"Chanelle!" Mr. Jeffries entered my office and swiftly crossed the floor to hug me.

"Hello, Mr. Jeffries." I returned his embrace.

The older gentleman didn't waste any time. "I have a surprise for you." He turned to the door. "Come on in."

"Hey, Chanelle." Sean appeared at the entrance to my office and devoured me with his eyes.

I placed my hand on the edge of my desk to steady myself and pasted on a smile, pretending to be excited because Mr. Jeffries would be curious if I wasn't. "Uh, hey, Sean."

"Isn't it wonderful?" Mr. Jeffries offered. "I was thrilled when Sean called and told me he was returning to Michigan."

"Yes," I managed to choke out. "It's wonderful. Welcome back."

"Well, I'll leave you two to get caught up." Mr. Jeffries gave me a second hug and exited my office.

"Chanelle, it's so good to see you after all these months." Sean took a couple of steps into my office and glanced at the table in the corner. If he was looking for an invitation to have a seat, he wasn't getting one.

I studied him and did a gut check. Nothing. Nothing about me was still interested in him. I'd found the man I loved... and who was free to love me back.

And that man was now strutting through my door carrying a bouquet of roses. Yellow and white roses. The same kind of roses Sean had sent me, giving me the worst case of déjà vu I'd ever experienced.

If it was possible, I would have crawled under my desk and hidden until both of them left.

"Hey, Sweetie," he said, brushing past Sean as though he weren't in the room, handing me my flowers, and planting a big kiss on my lips.

"Uh, hey, Babe. What brings you by?" I stammered.

"It's your first day back and I'm proud of you."

Sean lost his smile and coughed, announcing his presence. "Oh, uh, Babe, I'd like you to meet one of my co-workers." *And my ex-lover who I'm praying doesn't say anything.* "Sean, this is my... boyfriend, Rick."

Rick extended his hand. "How you doin'?"

Sean looked like he was in physical pain when he accepted Rick's greeting. I held my breath. "I'm good. You have a very special woman." He stared at me a harder than he should have and longer than was comfortable.

Rick placed a possessive arm around my waist and forcefully pulled me to him. "Tell me something I don't know." He bent down and kissed me again. If he'd lifted his leg like a dog, he'd have been less obvious in marking his territory.

"Sweetheart, I have to get to work," he said. "But let's go out to dinner tonight and celebrate your first day back."

My grin was warm. Genuine. "I'd like that. You pick the place."

"Okay, Babe." He kissed me a third time. "It was nice meeting you, Shane."

"Likewise. And it's Sean."

"My bad. Sean." Rick winked at me and with the swag that made me hot for him, he sauntered out of my office.

"So, how long has that been going on?" Sean demanded when the main doors to my office suite closed behind Rick.

"It's none of your business," I hissed. "I told you that I wasn't waiting for you to figure out what you wanted to do. Not to mention, your *wife* hired someone to *threaten* me in order to get me to back away from you. Why would you think I'd stick around for that?"

He walked up on me. "I tell you that I'm leaving my wife for you. Walking away from my marriage for us to have a chance together. And this is what you do to me?" His low tone shook me a tad.

I'd never seen this side of Sean. I swallowed my rising fear.

"That was your choice. I never asked you to leave her. And you need to back away from me. Now."

"I came back to Michigan for you. This isn't over. We aren't over." Slowly, he leaned in and placed his wet lips on my forehead. Then, with his hands in his pockets, he began whistling as he strolled out of my office. Leaving me dazed and wishing I'd stayed home.

CHAPTER 31

"TELL ME ABOUT YOUR COWORKER?" Rick said over our candlelight celebratory dinner at Black Rock.

Although, with the way my first day back had gone, I didn't see anything worth celebrating. "There's nothing to say. He's just someone I work with."

Rick took a bite of his T-bone steak and chewed methodically before speaking. "Chanelle, do you remember the night I came to your house after we saw each other in Lowe's?" When I nodded, he continued. "And I told you about how my marriage fell apart?" I nodded again. "My wife was a cheater. A liar."

"I remember." I chomped on a forkful of my salad and tried not to squirm.

He sliced another piece of his steak. "And remember when we were sitting on your couch and I told you I know when you're being dishonest?"

I almost choked on a piece of lettuce. "Yes."

"And your pastor, she preached on honesty, right?"

"She did. But what point are you making?"

He placed his arms on either side of his plate. "Our

relationship will never work if we're not truthful with each other." His usually warm hazel eyes darkened. "If you have anything you need to tell me, now's the time."

I absently twirled my promise ring. I could hear Michele's calm, rational voice telling me not to create a problem where one didn't exist. He'd understand. "I... uh..."

My eyes darted behind him and landed on a couple who looked like they were in a heated argument. The woman had tears in her eyes. She reached for him, but he jerked away, threw his napkin on the table, and stormed out. She placed her head in her hands and her shoulders began to quake.

Would that be me? Would he walk out on me? I didn't think so... but... Could I risk it?

Michele's voice began to fade as Andrea's took over. She was telling me that I'd be stupid to open my mouth and ruin the best thing that had happened to me.

"Chanelle?" Rick called me, drawing my attention away from the sobbing woman, and interrupting the battle that was warring in my head.

I raised and lowered my shoulders. "I... uh... there's nothing to tell."

He stared or was it a glare? I wasn't sure. But he said, "Nothing?"

My gaze journeyed to the woman dabbing her eyes, down to my ring, and finally, to Rick's waiting face. As I slowly shook my head, I committed myself to my deception. "Nope. Nothing to tell."

"And the guy in your office? The one who was looking at you like you belonged to him and looking at me like I was in the way? You've got nothing to say about that either?"

I wished I could hide behind my water goblet. I took a long sip to keep from biting my lip. I ignored the warning bells in my head. "Like I said, he's just a colleague."

"For the sake of our future, I hope you're being straight with me, Chanelle."

"I am." I placed my glass back on the table and reached for his hands. "Now can we go back to enjoying a beautiful dinner?"

"Yeah," he said, still giving me a look that let me know he wasn't buying what I was unconvincingly selling.

CHAPTER 32

"GOOD MORNING, CHANELLE," Sean said, parked in my doorway.

It was Thursday, and I'd successfully avoided him for a couple days, but Mr. Jeffries had given me another major prospect and the only way for me to win the account was to work with Sean. After all, that was the reason he'd been rehired.

"Good morning. Please, come in and have a seat at the table." I stood and came from behind my desk.

I didn't want him in my office. I didn't want him anywhere near me. But working with him wasn't optional. I needed him to stay focused on the task and leave behind all thoughts of rekindling an intimate relationship.

"Please leave it open," I instructed, when he had his hand on the handle to push the door shut.

"I thought you'd want it closed so we wouldn't be interrupted."

I bet you did. "Patty will make sure we're not disturbed." I met him at the table. "Have you given any thought to how we can start outlining this account? This is a very important client for Mr. Jeffries."

"You sound so formal. I was hoping we could spend some

time catching up." He pulled out one of the rolling chairs and sat, leaning back and resting his left leg on his right thigh.

I gave a very loud sigh. "Sean, I don't have time to chat. We have to get the ball rolling on this."

"You're going to pretend we didn't have anything? That there was no chemistry between us?"

I threw my hands in the air and tossed my pen on the table. "I'm not pretending anything. Yes, we had amazing chemistry. But it's over now. Why can't you respect that? Not to mention, again, that your *wife* threatened me. Where is she anyway? Were you finally able to talk to her? Because I haven't heard from her in a few weeks." I hoped by mentioning Cynthia, I could take his focus off us. Besides, I needed to know if I should still be worried.

"Cynthia moved back into our house in Virginia when I relocated here. I don't know what's going on with her these days, but she's being served with divorce papers today."

My eyes widened. "Wow, so you're going through with it?"

"I told you, I want a chance with you." He reached across the table to touch my hands and I snatched them back like I'd been stung.

"Sean," I began, exasperated, "that's no longer possible. Back to Cynthia. How do you think she's going to take the news?"

He seemed unaffected by my rebuke and shrugged. "No clue." His cell rang, and he checked the number. "But, I guess I'm about to find out." He swiped the screen to the right and before he could say one word, I heard Cynthia yelling.

"Are you freakin' kiddin' me? You're divorcing me? For that tramp?"

"Calm down," Sean said, though I doubted she would listen. "She's a good woman, and our divorce has nothing to do with her. We've talked about this."

"If it wasn't for her, you'd be here with me, right now. I was willing to forgive you and start over." The ache in her voice triggered my guilt... until I heard her vengeance. "But I see how it is. So both of you better watch your back. You tell that slut I am *not* through with her."

"Cyn—"

Sean placed his phone on the table. Unable to face me, he kept his head down. "I'm sorry. Chanelle."

I sat with my elbow on the table, my finger resting on my upper lip and my thumb on my chin. I sighed, heavily. If it were possible to kill with a glare, Sean would be dead. Because, though the sun was streaming brightly through my windows, inside my office the atmosphere was as gray as the skies before a tornado. The nightmare that I'd begged God to end was accelerating, and I wondered how in the hell all of us would make it out alive.

"Michele, I never thought I'd say this, but Sean is as loco as his wife," I said, sitting in her family room and doing what we did best. Gossip and eat.

"Cynthia is after you because you slept with her husband and he's divorcing her? And Sean is after you because you've moved on with your life and don't want him? This is ridiculous."

"You think?" I tipped my pop can and chugged. "This kind of stuff only happens to me. But I'm thinking maybe I should call Steve."

"For once, you are saying something that makes sense. Are you finally going to tell Rick?"

I paused with my can in mid-air. "You're kidding, right? I told you how Rick was acting when he came to my office. And then when we had dinner and he asked me point-blank if there was anything to tell about Sean and I couldn't bring myself to do it. Now I can't tell him."

"You've dug a hole for yourself." She took a bite of a tortilla chip with guacamole.

I was ready with a sarcastic comeback, but instead I released a loud exhale. "I know. And there is no way out of it without somebody getting hurt. Physically or emotionally. Or both. That's why I need to talk to Steve."

Michele pulled out her phone. "How long do you plan on hanging out with me?"

I'd come by her house when I'd gotten off work and had already been here for a few hours. "Not much longer. I told Rick I'd be home by nine."

She cocked her head. "Home? Sounds like you two are living together."

I giggled because I liked the thought of living with Rick. "I guess we kinda are."

"Do you still have him sleeping on the couch?"

"He's been upgraded to the guest bedroom," I said, smiling.

She raised a brow. "But not your bed?

I shook my head. "Not yet."

"So no more since Aruba?" When I shook my head again, she continued. "How are you holding out? And why are you holding out?"

My answer was a smirk. "My conscience. Too much going on for me to keep adding layers of emotions." I pointed to her phone. "Call Steve. I'd like to see if he can come by while I'm here. Otherwise, maybe we can meet up tomorrow."

Michele dialed her brother, and after finding out that he was working the second half of a double shift, he agreed to meet at my office the next day. With the one condition that he was dressed in plain clothes.

"Are you going to tell Steve everything?" Michele asked.

"I'm not sure yet. Probably. Maybe. I don't know..."

"He's heard and seen it all. Tell him. Besides, he knows you. He won't judge."

I wasn't sure about that. I'd judge me if I were him. "We'll see. Look, I'm going to get out of here. I'll let you know how things go tomorrow." I stood, gave my bestie a hug, then made the short drive home.

Fortunately, Rick didn't bring up any prickly topics, and we had a peaceful night. But the next morning, sitting across from Steve in my office, I was feeling anything but calm.

"What's been going on, Chanelle? And don't beat around the bush." He sat with his arm on the back of the chair. And for reasons I couldn't explain, this man who'd known me since I was in diapers had my nerves on edge. Growing up, he was the cute brother I'd always wanted. I was sick thinking about how my truth could tarnish his view of me.

"Promise not to judge?"

"Have I ever?"

I gave a partial smile. "You got me there." I inhaled a quick breath, held it, then slowly let it go. "Okay. Here's my life for the last nine or so months." I told Steve everything. The affair. The bad dates. Reconnecting with Rick. The Stalker who seemed to have vanished. Cynthia calling and being outside my home. The shooting lessons. My lies to Rick. Sean returning to Michigan and his possessive behavior. And I concluded with Cynthia's indirect threat to me. I couldn't look at him, so I didn't. I knew it was bad but saying everything out loud made me feel like a horrible person.

It was Steve's silence that caused my frown to deepen in my mind. Finally, he rested his elbow on the table, rubbing his chin. "Is this an on or off-the-record conversation we're having?"

I didn't know I had options. "I'd love for it to be an off-the-record brother-sister discussion."

"You want Steve, your brother, to fix this and not Steven, the cop?"

My nod was tinged with a bit of trepidation. "Yes."

"What are you most concerned about?"

"Honestly?"

"Honestly."

My eyes fell on my framed degree hanging on the wall while I debated what to say. Because what I truly wanted could have life-changing consequences. "Sean. He has me most concerned. I have to work with him almost every day and he's not hearing me when I tell him we're completely over."

"Hmmm. I thought you would have said Cynthia."

I shook my head. "She's in Virginia. Sean is here. In my face."

He bobbed his head, slow up and down nods. "I'll handle him."

"What are you gonna do?"

"Don't worry about it. You need plausible deniability. Leave it to me. He's done being a problem for you."

I shot forward in my seat and whispered. "You're not going to hurt him, are you?"

It was his smirk that made my leg shake. "Would you care?" He squinted at me.

I eased back into my chair, creating distance between myself and my almost brother. "I, uh, I... I wouldn't care, *care*, but, I mean, I wouldn't want him to get hurt."

"Look, lil sis," he began, exchanging that smirk for a crooked grin, "don't sweat it. Go about your business and let me do what I do." He patted my leg and stood.

I nodded and rose with him. After giving him a hug and escorting him to the door, I rushed to my couch, flopped down, and called Michele. "Has Steven gone crazy?"

Her chuckle was a blend of humor and confusion. "What are you talking about?"

I cupped my cell phone and said in a hushed voice, "I think he might do something to Sean."

"What? That's not Steve."

"I didn't think so. But I told him everything, and he told me he would 'handle Sean.'"

"He would never put his career on the line like that. I'm sure that's not it." Michele spoke with a confidence I didn't share.

"Maybe."

"Act natural and let whatever's going to happen, play out."

Natural? Impossible. I was more anxious now than before I decided to call Steve. Still, I said, "O... K..., I'll talk to you later."

After hanging up, I chewed on my fingernail, thinking about what I may have done. Did I set Sean up to get hurt without realizing it? I thought about how Steve was when we were growing up. He was the same age as Andrea and had been on the gangsta side of the law until he got in trouble in high school and made a hundred-eighty-degree turn. He'd always been an honorable officer, with awards to back it up. I hoped that my mess wasn't going to have him flip back to the shady side of life.

But six hours later, my fears became a reality. "Chanelle." Mr. Jeffries entered my office and quietly pushed the door.

"Mr. Jeffries, is everything okay?"

He remained by the door and crossed his arms tightly across his chest. "No. Sean's been arrested. I heard from his boss at Image."

My eyes widened and my mouth opened. "He's been what?"

"Arrested." Mr. Jeffries was usually jovial, but this somber news seemed to have sapped his joy.

This moment was why Michele had cautioned me to act natural. "Oh my gosh, for what?"

"Embezzlement from his employer in Virginia."

"Excuse me?" I'd thought his arrest was because of Steve. But how could Steve have anything to do with Virginia? Maybe this was a freaky coincidence. "I can't imagine Sean being arrested for anything, let alone embezzlement."

"Well, he was. He was picked up about an hour ago."

I was in a daze. "I, I don't understand."

"Apparently, there was a complaint filed against him and a bench warrant for his arrest. He was pulled over for a traffic violation on his way back from lunch and when they ran his license, the warrant popped up."

Okay, so this *was* Steve. But how did he create a false charge and get a warrant for Sean's arrest so quickly?

Mr. Jeffries stared at me. I knew I needed to give an appropriate response. But I wasn't sure what that would be because I was kinda happy. I chewed on my bottom lip before saying, "That's awful news. Is Image going to stand by him?"

He shrugged. "No idea. But that's not something we can tolerate. I'll be pulling him from all future projects until he's able to clear his name. And if he can't, then he will no longer be a consultant for our firm."

I felt a mixture of relief and disloyalty. I'd betrayed a former friend, but at least now I wouldn't have to see him every day.

Mr. Jeffries misread the look on my face. "Don't worry, Chanelle. I know how close the two of you were. But we'll get someone else to partner with you. Sean was excellent, but no one is irreplaceable. Not even you or me."

He laughed, but I didn't. Enfolded in what he'd said was a warning to me. If he ever found out about my indiscretions, he'd terminate my partnership and not ask any questions.

I gave him a smile that probably looked more like a grimace. "Well, keep me posted."

Mr. Jeffries nodded and walked out of my office. I picked up my cellphone to call Steve and saw a text from him. It read: *Everyone has skeletons.*

I was no longer comfortable talking about this at work. I grabbed my purse and stepped out into the open area of my suite. Patty wasn't at her desk, so I left her a note that I was taking off a little early and to call me on my mobile if she needed to reach me. Then raced to my car and called Steve.

"What did you do?" I asked the second he answered.

"I told you I'd handle it. Wanna meet?"

I was amazed by how chilled he was because I was trying not to flip out. "Yes, the park around the corner from my house?"

"See you there in fifteen."

I didn't even bother to say goodbye. I bowed my head while sitting behind my steering wheel and said a quick prayer. Then sped to the park to wait.

CHAPTER 33

"STEVE, WHAT DID YOU DO?" I asked for a second time, panicked.

He was now wearing his uniform and chuckled. "Settle down." He slipped onto the bench next to me and placed his palm on my trembling leg. "I didn't do anything. His background did it for me."

My frown creased my forehead. "What are you talking about?"

"Here." He handed me a white envelope. "Take a look at this."

"What is it?"

"Read it and see."

I opened it and gasped. "Sean has a rap sheet?" I read through the list of charges and darn near had to pick up my mouth, which was close to touching the ground. Wide eyed, I looked to Steve. "Sean did all of this?"

"Allegedly. The warrant for his arrest was real."

I closed my eyes and put my head in my hands. "This is insane. There's no way he embezzled money from Handle Marketing."

Steve shrugged one shoulder. "He'll have his day in court. He's being extradited back to Virginia. Authorities there have already been notified, and the paperwork is in process for his transfer."

I whipped my head back and forth several times. "I won't believe it. That is not the Sean I know."

"Look, I can't answer that. You said you had a problem, and I told you I'd take care of it. Let me know if you hear from Cynthia and we'll deal with her. But at this point, if Sean was the only one you were worried about, then you should be good."

Tears filled with relief clouded my eyes. Or maybe they were from sadness because I didn't know Sean as well as I thought. But I could sort out my feelings later. "Steve, I don't know how to thank you. Tell me you didn't do anything that would put your job in jeopardy."

"Never that. I'm not the guy I was years back. I'm all about law and order. But if you dig deep enough into people's past, you'll always be able to uncover something you can use. And your boy proved that to be true." He stood and tousled my hair, the way he did Michele. "I gotta get back to work. You know how to find me if you need me." He kissed the top of my head and sauntered out of the park, leaving me sitting on the bench and wondering what to do next.

CHAPTER 34

"THAT WAS DELICIOUS," Rick said, licking the last of the barbecue sauce from his fingers.

"I'm glad you enjoyed it." I smiled, taking our plates into the kitchen and loading them into the dishwasher.

Rick followed me. "Let me help you clean up."

I swatted him. "Absolutely not. You've done so much for me lately. Let me enjoy doing this for you. Why don't you go into the den and watch a little TV? I'll join you as soon as I'm finished in here."

"You sure you don't want some help?"

"I'm positive. Now go." I shooed him away.

I hurried and straightened up the kitchen, then snuggled up next to him on the couch. "What are you watching?"

"Nothing, just flipping through the channels. Do you have anything you'd like to watch?"

"Well, you know how I love me some ratchet reality TV." I laughed.

"Absolutely not. I value my brain cells and I will not waste them on that garbage."

He was so adamant that I didn't tell him I watched all the shows. The Housewives, Basketball Wives, Love and Hip Hop. All of them. "How about a movie?" I offered.

"Now, you're talking my language."

I slid off the couch. "Okay, you pick it and I'll pop some popcorn."

"K. Comedy or Drama?"

"Hmmm... Let's do a comedy. I could use a good laugh." I hummed on my way to the kitchen. For the first time in months, I felt normalcy in my life. Just as Steve had told me, Sean was taken back to Virginia. In my heart, I didn't believe he was guilty of what he was being accused of doing. But being Sean and Cynthia free for the past week eased my guilt substantially. I'd managed to keep my secret from Rick, and his trust in me seemed to be growing. We'd had a great couple's weekend with Ben and Michele, and we were enjoying a Sunday evening before we started our workweek. Yes, my life had made the U-turn I'd wanted and was headed in the right direction.

I whistled as I grabbed the jar of popcorn kernels from the cabinet, poured some into the air popper and turned it on. I glanced at my cellphone laying on the counter and saw I'd missed a call. I dialed my voicemail before grabbing a bowl to catch the popcorn. I froze in my tracks when I heard the voice.

"Hey, Chanelle. It's me. Sean. I only have a minute to talk. Literally, that's all they give you in jail. But I wanted you to know I didn't do what I'm being accused of, and my name will be cleared soon. Though, I'm pretty sure Mr. Jeffries won't be taking me back. But, um, I also think you should know Cynthia is blaming you for my arrest. I tried talking sense into her, but she's not listening. Being locked up, there's nothing I can do to help you, so I thought I'd warn you. I tried telling the officer in my block, but to him, I'm a just con, so he's not listening. Cynthia is hell-bent on making you pay. I—I—I'm sorry, Chanelle. I never meant for this to happen to you. I love you.

And I wanted us to be together. I still want us to be together. But you should watch your back. I'll try to call you later. Bye, Love."

Moments later, Rick strolled into the kitchen. "Babe, what's taking you so long? The movie…" His voice trailed off when he saw me standing in the middle of the kitchen surrounded by popcorn. "What happened?"

He noticed the cellphone still in my hand and took it from me. "Did that guy call you?"

I was trying desperately to snap out of my catatonic state. "Um, no. No, he didn't. I, um, I…" Think, Chanelle. I willed myself to come up with a believable story.

He held both of my arms; concern etched across his face as his eyes searched mine for answers. "If it wasn't him, then what has you so frightened?"

I gently slid my phone from his hands and set it on the counter. "Uh… I… uh… um, I got a voicemail from work. Uh, Patty, um, Patty said she won't be in tomorrow. Her husband got hurt at work today and he's in the hospital."

"Oh, no! That's terrible. Is he going to be okay?"

I settled into my lie, careful not to bite my bottom lip. "Oh, yes," I said, quickly. "He's—he's going to be fine. He should be able to come home in a day or so."

"That's good news." Rick pulled me close. "You had me scared. You looked like you'd seen a ghost or something."

I was scared my voice would betray me the second I opened my mouth, so I took several deep breaths to calm myself. "All is well." I removed his arms from around my waist and headed to the closet to grab the broom and dustpan. "Why don't you go back into the den and restart the movie. I'll clean up this mess and be there in a sec."

"Okay. Don't take too long." He kissed me and sauntered out of the room. But not before stealing a glance at my cellphone.

Rick swallowed my lie this time, but it didn't go down easy

and he was a very smart man. I knew next time I wouldn't be so lucky.

CHAPTER 35

I TURNED on the water in the sink in the downstairs bathroom. "Hey, girl," I said in a hushed tone.

"Hey. Why are you whispering?" Michele asked.

"I don't want Rick to hear me. I got a voicemail from Sean and I lied about it."

She huffed. "This makes no sense. A relationship built on lies isn't a relationship."

"Look, I didn't call you for a lecture," I said with far more attitude than I should have had. "I called because I need your help."

"You've got a lot of nerve. You don't want to hear my opinion, but you want my help."

"Exactly. So can you meet me tomorrow for lunch?" I ignored the irritation in her voice. She had every right to be agitated with me.

"Fine," she relented. "When and where?"

"Champs. Tomorrow at noon."

"I'll be there."

"Thanks. Talk to you later."

〜

"Over here." I stood slightly and waved to Michele to join me in a booth in the back of the restaurant.

She snaked her way through the tables. "What in the world do you have on?" She scooted onto the seat and placed her purse beside her.

"What do you mean?"

"I mean, you look like you're dressed to drive a 1960s convertible with those oversized dark glasses and that scarf." Michele's shoulders heaved with laughter.

I cut my eyes at her. "Shh... lower your voice. I don't want anyone to recognize me."

"It's official. You have lost the little bit of mind you had left."

"Whatever." I pulled my cellphone and a piece of paper out of my bag. "Here, listen to this." I pressed play on Sean's voicemail and handed the phone to Michele.

Her mouth dropped when she heard the message. She handed the phone back to me. "Oh, my God." We paused while the waiter took our orders. "Did you call Steve?"

I removed my sunglasses, setting them on the table. "Unh-uh. He's helped me enough." I let a moment pass before I added the real reason I'd invited her to lunch. "I thought about this a lot last night, and I have an idea."

"I'm listening..." Though her lowered eye and tipped head told a different story.

I fiddled with my napkin because I knew what her response would be to what I said next. "I think we should go after Cynthia."

Michele threw up her hands. "Are you crazy?"

I winced. "Don't football players say the best defense is a great offense?"

"I have no idea. But it doesn't matter. You're not a football player. And this isn't a game." Michele stopped talking while the waiter brought our salads. "Let me make sure I have this straight. You don't want to do the logical thing and call the police. Or even call Steve again. Instead, you'd rather confront Cynthia?"

"Well, when you say it like that, you make me sound ridiculous."

"That's because you *are* ridiculous. Chanelle, this is not a good idea."

"But think about it," I pleaded with her. "No one would see it coming." I sat back as though I'd said something profound. "I think my idea is absolutely brilliant."

Michele stared at me, drawing out an already uncomfortable moment. "I'm at a total loss for words."

I ignored her. "Plus, I've been holding on to some information that may be useful." I touched the piece of paper I'd removed from my bag and slid it across the table.

She looked down at it. "What's this?"

With a triumphant grin, I said, "That is the license plate number from Cynthia's car. I wrote it down the day she was in front of my house before I went on vacation."

"O... K... And what do you propose we do with this?" The way she hunched her shoulders told me she didn't understand why this was great news.

"We use it to track her down. Duh..."

"Uh, why can't you ask Sean where she is?" she said. Then she added, "Duh," for emphasis.

"Because he's locked up. It's not like he's at a country club and can make calls whenever he feels like it. If he calls me again and I can get the information, then fine. Otherwise, let's use this,"—I pointed to the paper—"and track her down."

She stared at me. "You're serious about this."

"I'm absolutely serious. I'm guessing it's a rental. And even though she's been leaving me alone, she must be coming back to town, or she's going to put that stalker on me again. Otherwise, why would Sean warn me to watch my back?"

I knew it would take some coaxing to get Michele onboard with my plan, so I played the one card I had that I knew she wouldn't resist. I slowed my voice way down and placed a tear on standby. "Michele, I need you." I sniffed. "I need this to end and I can't do it alone. Please help me. Please." I sniffed again.

She let my pleas hang for a few and I crossed my fingers under the table. It was when she sighed loudly that I knew she'd have my back. "And there's no way I can convince you to call Steve?"

"Like I said, he already helped me out. And we have enough to do this ourselves. But if we can't find the information on our own or it gets too dangerous, then we can call Steve."

This time her sigh was followed by crossing her arms. "I'll help you on one condition."

I exhaled the breath I'd been holding. "Anything. You name it."

"I'll help you if you come clean with Rick. About everything." Now it was her turn to lean back in the booth.

Ugh! I knew she would pull a stunt like this. Fortunately, the waiter arrived with our entrees, which bought me time to plan how I was going to respond.

I placed a fresh napkin in my lap and blessed my meal. "Okay. But I get to decide when."

"That works. As long as it's within the next week."

"How about the next two weeks?"

"Agreed." She held out her hand.

"Agreed." I accepted and gave her a firm shake. "Now, let me tell you my plan."

We huddled, and I told her how we were going to bring Cynthia down and get my life back.

CHAPTER 36

"Do you have to leave?" I asked. It was Sunday evening, and Rick and I were doing what we loved to do; cuddle on the couch in the den and watch television. But he'd soured my blissful evening with his announcement that he was staying at his house tonight and leaving early in the morning to drive to Chicago for a contractor's convention.

He squeezed me closer. "I'm so sorry, Babe. But I have to go."

"And you're leaving tomorrow?" I pouted. "Why didn't you tell me about it sooner?"

"I only made the decision today. Max and I go every year and it always leads to a lot of business. I was going to cancel my reservation because of what was going on with you, but since we haven't heard from him in weeks, I figured you'd be safe. Besides, I'll only be gone for four days. Please try to understand."

"I'm trying, but what if they pop back up while you're gone?" I whined.

Rick frowned and pushed away a little so he could look into my eyes. "They? I thought it was one guy?"

Uh-oh. "Well, it—it is the one. But what if he's working with someone?"

Rick's body tensed. "Have you heard from him and not told me?"

"No," I answered quickly. Maybe too quickly. But, technically, I was telling the truth. I'd only heard from Cynthia and Sean.

"And you would tell me if something was still happening, wouldn't you?" His stare never left my face. Not even to blink.

I gulped. "Of course. Of course, I would tell you."

"I'm serious, Chanelle. Is there anything you're *not* telling me?"

His look was so intense that I had to look away. Michele and I had worked out a plan. I just needed a little more time. Once this was over, I'd tell him everything. "Rick, there is nothing to tell you. That guy, whoever he is, hasn't reached out to me in weeks." I gave a light laugh. "Maybe he realized he had the wrong person."

He looked at me sideways. "Mmmhhhmmm." He stood and brought me up with him, holding my hand as we made our way to the door. "I'm just a phone call away. Call me if you need me." He folded me into his arms and weakened my knees with his kiss. "I have something to give you." He lifted his shirt, pulled his nine-millimeter out of its holster and held it out to me.

I stared, but didn't dare touch it. "Why are you giving me your gun?"

"You may need it. You said it yourself, you're a natural shot. I'm sure everything will be fine, but just in case..."

I didn't budge. And I definitely didn't lay my hands on that weapon. "Thank you. But I'll be fine. I don't need a gun." I smiled, reassuring him that all was well.

"I'm sure you're right. But, if you do need it, I want to make sure you have it." He unclipped the holster from his belt, placed the gun back inside and laid it on the table by the front door.

He kissed me again and walked out, closing the door behind him.

~

After Rick left, I dressed for bed and called Michele.

"I don't know if this is a good thing or a bad thing, but Rick will be out of town for the next four days. He's going to a work convention."

"Are you scared?"

I'd changed into my pajamas and was sitting cross-legged on my bed with the gun in front of me. "A little. But it's not like I've heard from anyone other than Sean for a while. And if I look on the bright side, at least now I don't have to worry about Rick finding out what we're up to. I'm sure we can bring this to a head and have it resolved before he returns. Are you all set for tomorrow?"

"Yes. I took BJ to my mother's for the week. And we're in the height of our busy season at work, so Ben will be working late nights for the next month. He won't be home to ask me any questions."

"Perfect. Okay, I'm going in to work tomorrow and then I'll be by your house."

"Chanelle, it's not too late to change your mind." I heard the warning. I ignored it.

"I can't live the rest of my life looking over my shoulder. One way or another, this ends. Soon."

"Somehow, I knew you would say that."

"Thank you so much for doing this with me." My appreciation was sincere.

"I need to have my head examined."

I chuckled. "Your head is fine. I'll talk to you later." I figured it was best to hang up before she told me she'd changed her mind.

I placed the gun in my nightstand drawer, then gave it some thought, and removed it from inside the drawer and set it on top of the table, close to my bed before nodding off into a fitful sleep.

~

Michele and I were ready to begin Operation BAM, also known as "Operation By Any Means." Because I was getting my life back, by any means necessary. If I hadn't already taken so much time off work, I wouldn't have gone in at all today. But I went in and did my best to focus. Around noon, Mr. Jeffries walked in.

"Hello, Chanelle. I'm glad I caught you. I'd like you to meet Sean's replacement, Lynette." I peered behind Mr. Jeffries to see a tall, curvy woman with long blond hair and olive skin, dressed in a linen suit.

I pointed to the chair in front of my desk, offering her a seat. "Hello, Lynette, it's nice meeting you."

"Likewise. Sean spoke very highly of you." She unbuttoned her suit jacket before planting herself on the soft leather.

Mr. Jeffries glimpsed the Rolex on his arm. "Chanelle, would you mind bringing Lynette up to speed on what you and Sean were working on?"

Yes, I mind, is what I thought. But I did the dutiful thing and smiled. "Of course, Mr. Jeffries."

"Thank you." He turned to Lynette. "I'll be back in about an hour and we can continue with our tour."

"Certainly, Mr. Jeffries," she said.

I waited for him to close the door, then intertwined my fingers, placing my forearms on the desk. "Tell me about yourself, Lynette. How long have you been with Image?"

She began listing her pedigree. But all I could think about was the fact that it was my fault Sean had lost his job. Well, it was his fault for whatever went down in Virginia. But I blamed myself for having Steve look into it.

I forced myself to listen to her ramble and was thrilled when Mr. Jeffries reappeared and escorted her from my office. I checked the clock every ten minutes and as soon as it changed from four fifty-nine-to-five o'clock, I packed up my belongings, bid a quick goodbye to Patty, and scooted out the door.

As I stepped into the elevator, I called Michele. "I'm leaving now. I'm on my way."

"Cool. I'll be ready."

"Were you able to make the calls we discussed?"

"Yup. I'll fill you in when you get here."

I said, "Okay," and pressed the 'off' button.

Twenty minutes later, she had her garage door up; I pulled in and parked next to her. She was already sitting in the driver's seat of her mom-wagon, also known as the dreaded minivan. Before I could sit down, I brushed animal crackers out of the front seat.

Michele started the engine. "Here." She handed me a large manila envelope as she backed out of the garage and hit the button in the van that lowered the door.

I opened the envelope and began reading. "Wow. Your cousin, Elisa, got all this?"

"Yes, and she said you can expect a bill. She put her job on the line to get you this info. Everything you have in your hands is hot off the press. It was faxed to me right before you arrived." Michele merged onto the highway and directed the car toward downtown.

I flipped through the pages. "This is a gold mine. How did she get all of this?"

"Well, you know she works for Speedy car rental and her boyfriend, Martin, works for a collection agency and he'll do anything for her. I gave her Cynthia's license plate number, and we caught a break. The car belongs to Speedy. Elisa pulled up Cynthia's account and got the credit card number used to pay for it. Then she gave the credit card number to Martin, and he was able to get a report of all of her transactions for the past ninety days. Judging by the report, she returned the car a day after you and Rick left for Aruba and she went home to Virginia. And it looks like she's been back and forth a handful of times, but most recently, she came back into town a few days ago. That's probably why Sean gave you a heads-up call. Anyway, she rented from Speedy again. This time she has a white Malibu. The license plate number is in the fax. And she's staying at a Motel 8 near downtown, which is where we're going now."

I searched through the papers and found the license plate number. "Here it is. QWX495."

"This is our exit." Michele came off the freeway and made a few turns.

About two miles later, we had the Motel 8 in view. She backed into a space at the far end of the parking lot and we scanned the area for the white Malibu.

"What's the number again?" Michele asked.

"QWX495."

"That might be it." She retrieved a pair of binoculars from her bag and pointed to a white car on the other side of the lot.

"Let me see." I snatched the binoculars from her hands and looked through the viewfinder. As the license plate number came into focus, a wide smile spread across my face. "That's it. We found her."

"Don't get too thrilled. Remember, she's dangerous."

Michele's comments sobered my spirit and erased my smile. "Right."

"What now?" she asked.

"Since we don't know which room is hers, we wait. We are

officially on our first stake out. Did you bring any snacks? I haven't eaten since breakfast."

"I can do better than snacks." She reached into a cooler behind my seat and pulled out two turkey sandwiches, two bottles of water, and a bag of chips.

I unwrapped my sandwich, and took a big bite of my first meal for the day. "You're awesome. You keep your eyes on Cynthia's car while I see what else is in these documents."

"K. You must really be stressed and hungry. You didn't even bless your food before you attacked your sandwich."

"Oh, right. Thanks." I paused in mid-chew and prayed. I reviewed the packet and noticed several charges paid to "GID Investigators".

"Hey, look at this." I showed Michele the papers. "This has to be the company she hired. Although, I'm surprised he wouldn't be in a cash only business."

"A hit man who takes credit payments? Doesn't he know paper trails are bad for his kind of business?"

"Apparently not. I wonder how we can find out—" I cut myself off in mid-sentence. "Look!" Cynthia stepped out of her motel room, the door slamming behind her. She put her cell to her ear and walked briskly to her car, not wasting any time backing out of the spot.

"Duck," Michele shrieked. We slipped down in our seats so Cynthia wouldn't see us as she sped by.

"Follow her," I shouted.

Michele dropped her sandwich, threw the car in drive, and trailed her out of the parking lot.

I was anxious. I didn't want to lose her, but I also didn't want her to see us. "Slow down... Speed up... Switch lanes... She's gonna see you," I yelled.

"Would you stop barking orders at me? You're making me nervous," Michele shot back. "Eat a chip and keep your mouth busy. I got this."

I shoveled potato chips in my mouth by the handful. Anything to keep myself from talking.

When Cynthia turned down a street with burned-out buildings, I pressed a few times on the door lock. "Where in the heck are we going?"

Michele shrugged. "Chanelle, I'm not sure about this."

I didn't want to say anything, but I was second-guessing myself. "Let's see what happens."

After three minutes of doing our best to stay out of Cynthia's rearview mirror, she pulled up in front of what looked like an abandoned warehouse in the middle of the block. She rolled to a stop behind an old, dark colored Buick.

Michele parked at the end of the block, and we waited for Cynthia's next move.

"That looks like the same car the guy was driving the day I saw him at the gun range," I whispered.

"Maybe this is his office." She spoke so softly I could barely hear her.

Once again, we slipped down in our seats. A scruffy man wearing a dingy white T-shirt, with a huge beer belly, and a cigar dangling from his lips, appeared from inside the building and surveyed the street. His eyes paused briefly on our van while he took a long drag on his cigar and scratched his gut. I grabbed Michele's hand while I held my breath, releasing both when he turned his attention to Cynthia. He gave her a big hug and a swat on the butt, then the two of them walked inside.

"Now what?" Michele asked.

"How should I know?"

"Well, you need to think of something. Clearly, they are still communicating with each other. This means that at this very moment they are plotting their next steps against you." She jabbed her finger at me.

"Don't you think I know that?" I snapped.

She placed her hand on my shoulder. "Don't yell at me. I'm

in this with you. All I'm saying is we need to figure out what we're going to do next."

I backed down. Michele's calm tone, combined with her soothing touch, was like a tranquilizer for my anxiety. "You're right. I'm sorry. I guess I didn't think this through."

Her glare and raised brow told me she agreed.

"Gimme a minute. I'll come up with something." I chewed on my thumbnail. "We need a way inside that building without being seen."

"Any ideas on how we can do that? Because I'm all ears."

"I got it." My voice grew strong as a plan formed in my mind. "Let's wait until they leave and then break in and see what we can find. I bet he has a file on me. Maybe we can figure out what their next step is going to be."

Michele threw her hands on top of her head. "I swear I lost my best friend. Would you tell her I'm looking for her?"

I rolled my eyes. "I'm serious, Michele."

"I am too. This is ludicrous. Let's just call Steve."

"No." I shook my head in disagreement. "It's like Andrea said, I'm a punk if I don't get this under control on my own. Steve took care of Sean for me. I can handle it from here. Besides," I pointed to the roof of the building, "it's one story and it's flat. I remember years ago, I did a community center restoration project, kinda like Habitat for Humanity. Anyway, I learned that a lot of commercial buildings have ladders in the back that pull down. It's how contractors get onto the roof. And I'm sure we'll be able to find a way inside if we enter from the top."

"This is not some scene out of a spy movie. You are a corporate executive. The stuff you're talking about doing is crazy. For goodness' sake, you were never even a girl scout."

I gave her my best comeback. "And neither were you."

"True. But I'm also not the one suggesting breaking into the building of a known stalker, and possible *killer*, by climbing on the roof."

"Come on, Michele. We've already come this far. Let's see it through to the end." I begged. I couldn't do this by myself.

After a silent standoff, she gave in with a sigh. "I'm sure I'll regret saying this, but fine."

"Thank you!" I gave her a jubilant hug. "We'll need to go by your house so we can change clothes. I'm glad we wear the same size. Like you said, I'm corporate. There is no way I can climb onto that roof in my Dolce and Gabbana suit." My hand swept down my body.

"That's my point. You wore a cream suit and Louboutin's to a stakeout. Why would you wear that, anyway?"

I shrugged. "I dunno. I guess I wasn't thinking when I got dressed this morning."

"Mm hmm. And now you want to climb on a roof."

"Yes. And finish my sandwich." I took another bite, and chewed slowly, giving myself time before I responded. "Michele, you act like I don't realize that what is happening is very serious. I'm well aware of the risks I'm taking. And the risk I'm asking you to take with me. Okay?"

Michele inhaled through her nose and exhaled slowly through her mouth. "Okay."

Michele and I watched the door for another two hours before Cynthia emerged with the dirty-looking man. He pulled her into a long, creepy hug.

I scrunched my face and hunched my shoulders. "Eww."

They got into their respective vehicles and drove to the corner. Michele started the ignition but didn't move. When he went right and Cynthia went left, Michele asked, "Which one should we follow?"

"Cynthia. Let's see where she goes."

Michele made a left, and we tailed her to a liquor store and back to her motel.

"Maybe she's in for the night," I said. "Let's head to your house so we can change."

She opened her mouth before quickly clamping it shut. I could imagine the things she wanted to say as she drove.

"I'm glad Ben isn't home," she mumbled, raising the garage door and easing inside. "The last thing I need to do is answer questions about my outrageous evening that isn't even over yet."

She wasn't looking for a response, so I didn't offer one. We changed into black leggings, black long sleeve turtleneck tops, black socks, and black boots. She had two hair scrunchies, and we used them to pull our hair back.

As we got back into the minivan, I asked Michele if she had any mace and a flashlight.

"I believe so. Let me check." She ran inside the house and reappeared with two cans of mace, two mini flashlights, a camera, and a small device I couldn't identify.

"Here." She got in and handed me the items.

"What's this?" I examined the gadget.

"A portable scanner. I use it for our business receipts, but I thought we might need it."

"Good idea."

We chatted about trivial things as we retraced our route to his office. Anything to keep our minds off of what we were about to do. All too soon, the building with several busted windows came into view. "Let's circle the block before we get out," I suggested.

"K."

We cruised around the block, our necks twisting from side to side as we surveyed the area. When we didn't see any cars and we were confident we were the only ones on the block, we parked across the street from the building. "You ready?" I asked.

"No. But I'm going to do it, anyway."

As I placed my hand on the door handle, I heard my ringtone. I dug my cell out of my purse and the caller ID said "unknown". Michele and I glanced at each other, her eyes as wide as mine.

"Should I answer?"

"Would you usually answer?"

I nodded. "Unfortunately, yes."

"Then, answer."

I took a deep breath and placed the phone on speaker. "Hello?"

CHAPTER 37

"You know who dis is. You prollay thought you was done wit' me, didn't cha?" Cynthia slurred.

Michele and I looked at each other. "Cynthia, what are you talking about?"

"Don't play stupid wit' me. Or maybe you ain't playin'. I know you went on yo' lil vacation to some island. I know yo' every move, you piece ah trash. And I know you the one behind Sean gettin' locked up."

I tried hard to hold back my sigh. "Cynthia, what's happening between you and Sean is not my fault, including him being in jail."

"If you ain't have nothin' to do wit' it, then how you know he in jail?"

"*You* just said it. Look, I was wrong for what I did. I own that. But it was months ago. Whatever's going on between you two has nothing to do with me, now."

"You know," she began, taking a long pause before she continued. "I always did hate you, but at least I used to think you was smart. But you dumb as a box of rocks because you believe what you sayin'. Don't you get it? Me and Sean, we had problems. But we coulda worked on it. After you came along, he changed his mind. He ain't wanna work on us no mo'. It's tricks like you, who think you can sleep wit' a woman's husband and then just walk away." She paused again, and sounded like she was taking a swig of something. "You crossed the line on me, and now I'm 'bout to cross the line on you." And with that, she hung up.

I fell back in the seat and closed my eyes, my breath coming in quick, unsteady inhales.

Michele slipped the phone from my sweaty hand and placed it on the console. "I know you wanted to 'flip the table' on her, as you put it. But I'm not so sure we should approach her right now."

"You're right. We shouldn't." I swiped a terrified tear, then squared my shoulders, and sniffed. "And before you tell me to call Steve, I'm going to remind you that I'm not. Because here's the thing, Michele," I said, my voice trembling, tears now streaming down my face. "I want this to be over. For good. I don't want to have to press charges against her for stalking and then deal with all the legal rigmarole. And that's exactly what I would have to do if I called Steve. He already told me that he operates above board."

I sniffed again and reached for a tissue from the box on her dashboard and dried my eyes. "So I'm calling on my inner Andrea and I'm handling this bit—" I caught myself and said, "chick, myself. I don't know how this is going to play out, but the one thing I will *not* do is live in fear. If you want to back out, I'll understand."

Michele's eyes were filled with kindness and support. "We agreed when we were kids that a real best friend is ride or die to the end." Michele pointed between us. "*We* are doing this together."

I looked at Michele. There were no words strong enough to

explain how much I loved her. I squeezed her hand and simply said, "Thank you."

"Come on. Let's do this."

I took a cleansing breath. We grabbed our items and dashed across the street to the backside of the building. As I anticipated, there was a ladder. We had to jump up to reach it. After a few tries, I was able to hold onto the bottom rung and pull it to the ground. Once on top of the roof, we looked for a way inside. In the far corner, we found a door and crossed our fingers that the door was unlocked. Unfortunately, it wasn't.

"Darn. Now, what are we going to do?" I asked.

"Let's try this." Michele reached inside her pocket and pulled out two nail files.

"What are we supposed to do with those?"

"Pick the lock. We've seen it done on TV lots of times." Michele started wiggling the files around in the lock.

"Michele, this isn't TV. Do you know what you're doing?"

"How hard can it be? On TV they have the lock cracked in less than thirty seconds." Ten minutes later, she was still trying to get the lock open. "Boy, this is a lot harder than it looks on TV."

"Give it here. Let me see if I can do it."

"Gladly." She handed me the nail files and then I spent ten minutes trying to open the lock. I brushed a few strands of hair out of my face. "We need a new strategy." I looked around but saw no other option.

"Maybe this is a sign that we shouldn't be doing this," Michele said.

But I shook my head. "Nope. This is a sign that we need to try harder." After another twenty minutes, I heard a click. "Yes." I turned the knob and the door opened. "Whew. Finally."

"You always were persistent."

I smiled. "Is there any other way to be? Let's see what we can find and get out of here."

I turned on my flashlight and we held hands, tiptoeing down the steps, which led to what appeared to be a maintenance room. On the other side of the room was another door. I tried the door and it opened. I peeked my head out first and looked both ways down the narrow hall. There were no lights on, so I pointed my flashlight in the direction of the longer end of the hall and together we ventured out into the unknown. It was a small building and there were only four office suites. "How are we supposed to know which is the right one?" I said.

Michele looked to her right. "Didn't the papers say 'GID'? This has to be it." She pointed to a door with a peeling nameplate that read, "Get It Done Investigators."

She tried turning the doorknob but, as expected, it was locked. "You got the other door open. I'm going to get this one." And after fifteen minutes, we heard the 'click'.

"Good job." As we stepped inside the cluttered office, I said, "Phew. It stinks in here." I gagged and covered my nose.

"What did you expect? You saw what he looked like." Michele searched for the light switch, but when she reached to turn it on, I grabbed her hand.

"Unh-uh. Let's leave it off and use our flashlights."

"Good point." She turned on her little light, and scurried over to the junky desk, rifling through the papers. I followed the direction of my light and headed toward the old file cabinet behind the bureau.

A couple moments later, we both said, "I found something."

"You first," I told Michele and looked over her shoulder.

"He's been taking pictures of you. Look."

I gawked at numerous pictures of myself. There had to be at least seventy-five photos. I picked them up and flipped through them. Me with Rick. Me with Michele. Me driving. Me in the parking garage at work. Rick and me at the gun range. Me at the grocery store.

I shivered. "What the hell? Do you have your camera?" When

Michele nodded, I continued. "Let's spread them out and take pictures of the pictures." I fanned the photos on his desk and Michele began snapping. "Make sure you get pictures of his desk in the background."

"Got it."

As Michele took the pictures, I opened the file with my name that I'd found in the drawer. He had several notes of conversations he'd had with Cynthia. The file was so thick that it was best to scan the pages and review them when we got back to Michele's. As I was scanning the last page, we heard footsteps in the hall and the sound of a man on the phone. We froze.

My voice was barely audible. "What are we gonna do?" We frantically looked around the room, but there was no decent place to hide.

"Under here," she said.

We turned off our flashlights. I snatched the file and scanner while Michele stuffed the photos back in their folder and grabbed her camera. We crammed ourselves into the small space beneath his desk, and I prayed.

The footsteps drew closer, stopping in front of the door. Slowly, the knob turned, and the door creaked open. "Humph. I could've sworn I locked this," we heard him say.

I pushed up on my chin to stop my teeth from chattering.

He flipped on the light. "Cynthia, I told you I got this." He paused. "I'll have this wrapped up by the end of the week." Another pause. "No, nothing will blow back on you." In a few short steps, he was standing in front of his desk. I looked at the floor and his scuffed loafers were inches from my face. My heart stopped.

We heard him sift through the papers on his desk and grab what sounded like a set of keys. Then he turned and headed back to the door. "If you want me to kill her, I'll kill her. Don't make me no difference. The fee is the same." The light switched off and he closed and locked the door behind him. It wasn't until we heard the sound of his retreating footsteps that we exhaled.

"Let's get out of here," I said.

Michele waited while I re-scanned the final page and returned the file to the drawer. Then we cautiously exited the office, remembering to lock it behind ourselves. I turned to go back the way we came in, but Michele tugged on my arm. "Wait. Why not leave through the front door?"

I hesitated. "What if there's some alarm on it? I say we go back the way we came."

"Okay."

We raced each other back to the maintenance room, up the steps, through the door, onto the roof, and down the ladder. We didn't slow down until we were safely inside the van. Michele gunned the motor and sped back to the safety of our side of town.

CHAPTER 38

WHEN BEN ARRIVED home around midnight, he took one look at the Chinese dinner cartons, our outfits, and all the papers on the floor, said he didn't want to know what we were up to, and went to bed.

"This is like the night that won't end," Michele moaned. It was well after two in the morning and we'd been in her basement for hours going through the documents that we'd copied.

"Yeah and I'm exhausted." I gulped my Pepsi and stretched my arms. Much of the information we had confirmed what we already knew. Cynthia blamed me for the breakdown of her marriage. She'd responded to an ad on Craigslist, and that's how she found this guy. She'd paid him fifteen hundred to taunt me and right around the time Sean was arrested, she paid him an additional five hundred for what he referred to as "investigator discretion." As far as we could tell, that meant he could do whatever he wanted, up to and including death.

I rubbed my eyes. "You know, I'm going to call Steve. This is bigger than I can handle. Andrea is just going to have to call me a punk. At least I'll be a punk who's alive."

"That's the first smart thing you've said in months!"

I rolled, then narrowed my eyes and pursed my lips at my best friend. "I hate it when we have these 'I told you so' moments."

She chuckled, probably relieved that my insanity was over. "We've both had a very long and exhausting day. How about we put this away for now and look at it with fresh eyes before you talk to Steve?"

I yawned. She had a point. I was so tired, I was seeing double. "Okay. But I'm still going into the office. I have my weekly meeting with Mr. Jeffries and if my attendance doesn't improve, he's liable to rescind my partnership." I half joked.

"He wouldn't do that. You're too valuable to him. Are you going home in the morning before you head in?"

"Yes. I certainly can't go in wearing this getup." I pointed to the all-black outfit I had borrowed. I headed toward her spare bedroom in the basement. "Good night." I was sound asleep almost before my body hit the mattress.

"Wake up. Chanelle, wake up." In my haze, I felt someone shaking me. "Wake up. It's nine. You're late."

"Huh?" I willed my eyes to open. I was so exhausted.

"Get up. You still have to get home and get dressed."

"Home?"

"Yes. You're at my house. Remember, you spent the night?"

Slowly, Michele came into focus, and the events of yesterday replayed in my mind. "Oh, no. I'm late." I sprang out of bed and hunted around for my shoes.

"That's what I've been trying to tell you for the last five minutes."

I was frantic. "No. No. No. I don't wanna be late. Do you have anything I can wear?"

"Of course I do. Hop in the shower and I'll find you something." Michele sprinted out of my room, and I snatched a washcloth and towel from the bathroom closet and took the quickest shower in history. Fortunately, I was a regular overnight guest at her house and kept an overnight kit in her spare bedroom, so my morning routine wasn't too disrupted. When I stepped back into the bedroom, Michele had placed a black pantsuit and new underwear on the chair. I dressed, did my makeup, slipped on a pair of her heels, and was out the door and pulling into the parking structure at work in less than forty-five minutes.

"Good morning, Patty," I said, breezing by her and heading toward my office.

She looked up from her computer. "Hey, Boss Lady. You just missed Rick's call."

I stopped cold in my office doorway and turned to face her. "Rick called?"

"Yeah. I told him you weren't in yet. Then, he asked me the strangest thing."

"Wha—what did he say?"

"He wanted to know how my old man was doin'."

"Oh. Um, wha—what did you tell him?" I was as nonchalant as I could be with the fear that was walking up my spine.

"I was a little puzzled because I thought it was odd that he was asking 'bout my man, but I told him he's doin' good."

"And... was that the entire conversation?" *Please say "yes."*

"No. Then, he asked how I was doin' and said he was sorry to hear that my old man had to go to the hospital after gettin' hurt at work."

"Oh. And then wha—what did you say?"

"Well, then I figured out you must've used me as some sort of cover story. And I don't wanna know what you was tryin' to cover because it ain't my business. So, I said we is all doin' fine and thanks for askin'. Boss Lady, I don't care if you need to use me. Just in the future, please tell me. Okay? I can do a much better job if I have a heads up."

I smiled and relaxed. I could always count on Patty. "Thank you. I'm so sorry. I promise I won't put you in that position again."

She returned the smile. "Anytime, Boss Lady. You got about five minutes before your meeting with Mr. Jeffries."

"Thanks," I said.

Patty returned her attention to whatever was on her computer screen, and I went inside my office, dropped off my bags, then walked to the break room to fix a cup of coffee before going to my meeting.

The meeting was brief, and within an hour I was on my way back to my office. My plan was to call Steve and set up a time to meet after work, and then call Rick. But when I got to my suite, Patty said, "Hey, Boss Lady, you have a visitor. I figured it'd be okay if he waited in your office."

I frowned. She knew it was a no-no to leave people in my office without my permission, but when I opened my door, I understood why she did it. "Rick. What are you doing here?" I closed the door behind me and rushed over, embracing him.

"We didn't talk yesterday, and I missed you." His grin was wide, showing off his one dimple in his right cheek.

"Awww. I missed you, too."

He hugged me back, then handed me a bouquet of red roses.

I gave him a deep kiss. "You spoil me. These are beautiful, but what are you doing here? You're supposed to be in Chicago."

He sat down on the couch and motioned for me to sit next to him, which I did, still holding my flowers. "I couldn't concentrate. I called your house for hours last night and you never answered. I got worried, so I drove back this morning. Where were you? And why didn't you answer your phone?"

"Oh. I spent the night at Michele's. Ben is working late this week, so we had girl-bonding time. Nothing special. We do it often when they're in the middle of their peak season. Why didn't you call my cell?"

"I did. It went straight to voicemail."

"I never heard it ring." I got up, placed my flowers on my desk, and reached inside my purse for my phone. It was dead. "See." I showed him the blank screen. "I didn't realize it was off." I placed it on the charger and returned to my seat next to him; still grinning and happy about my surprise visit.

"Um-hmm." Rick paused. "Chanelle, I'm going to ask you something and I want you to give me a straight answer."

I frowned, my eyes searching his face for the direction of this conversation. "I'm always straight with you."

His smile was replaced with his own frown. "No. You're not. You're keeping something from me."

"What makes you say that?"

"A feeling I have. I can't do lies. If we're going to work, we have to be transparent with each other. Don't you agree?"

I nodded. "Of course."

"Then tell me what you're hiding."

I stuttered, feeling like the air in my office was evaporating. "I—I'm not hiding anything."

His body tensed and his jaw tightened. "You're lying. So I'm going to ask you one last time. What. Are. You. Hiding?"

I bit the inside of my lip, rubbed the back of my neck, and picked at imaginary lint on my suit. So many things ran through my mind. He was right. It was time to let the chips fall wherever they were going to land. After about sixty seconds of deafening silence, I mumbled, "I know who's stalking me and I know why."

"What?" he bellowed and jumped up.

"Shhh. Lower your voice, please." I patted the seat, but he continued to stand.

"Who is doing this to you and why didn't you tell me? And when did you find out?" His voice remained at the same extra loud volume.

"Please, lower your voice. I'll tell you everything. Promise." I patted the seat again and this time he sat back down, but perched himself on the edge. I reached for his hand, but he pulled away from me.

"Talk."

I could feel the clouds hovering over me and there was nothing I could do to stop the torrential downpour that was coming my way.

So, I began talking. "Several months ago, long before you came back into my life, I had a brief, very brief, insignificant affair with a married man."

He cocked his head and glared. "Did you know he was married?"

I hated that I had to nod. "And I knew it was wrong, but I did it. Anyway, he and his wife moved away, and that was it. I went on with my life and he did, too. Or, so I thought. But then he called me. He told me he was coming to Michigan and wanted to see me. I told him no and that I had moved on. That's when I found out who was behind the dead rat and the phone calls. Apparently, he told his wife about us, and said he wanted a divorce. They were already going through problems. I'm pretty sure she was doing her own thing on the side, but that's irrelevant to her. She blames me for her situation getting worse and she hired someone to threaten me." The truth poured out of me in a long ramble. I could feel the steam coming off his body.

He never moved. "How long have you known?"

"Umm..." I kept my head down because I didn't have the courage to look at him. I twirled my promise ring. "Umm... For a while."

"What's 'a while'?"

"Umm..." My heart raced, and if I hadn't already been sitting, my knees would have buckled. "Umm..." I swallowed and exhaled. "Since before our vacation."

"What?" he yelled and jumped up again. "And you found out how, again?" He began pacing the length of my office.

I repeated what I'd said seconds earlier. "Her husband called me."

He stopped pacing long enough to stand over me and glower. "And that day when we were sitting on the couch, and you said the office was on the phone?"

"That was Sean; he's the husband. He was telling me that he was moving back to Michigan."

"Wait. Sean? Is that the guy who was in your office on your first day back? The guy who I said looked like he was more than a coworker."

I gulped, then nodded.

"Mm hmm. And that day in the kitchen. When you said Patty's husband had been in an accident?"

I continued to play with my ring. "That wasn't true. I had just received a call from him again. He was calling me from jail and telling me that his wife blamed me for him being arrested."

He frowned. "Arrested? Why was he arrested?"

"Umm," I began. I didn't want to tell the truth, but I'd come this far. No need to hold back now. The chips were already falling. "He'd made it clear he didn't care that I was happily involved with you. He said he wasn't giving up on us. That's when I talked to Steve, Michele's brother, and asked if there was anything, he could do to help me. Turns out, Sean had a warrant for his arrest, and Steve executed the warrant. He was extradited back to Virginia to stand trial or whatever. But he called me from jail and told me to watch my back."

"Let me make sure I understand. You've known for weeks who was responsible for the threats against you. And you didn't trust me enough to tell me?"

"It's not like that," I pleaded. "I did trust you. I *do* trust you. I was scared that you would judge me. And I didn't want you to leave. You were adamant about faithfulness, and I didn't know how to tell you that I'd made a mistake. I didn't want to lose you. I needed you. I need you. I am sorry that I kept this from you."

The volume of his voice had returned to normal, but he was still seething with anger as he looked at me. "So am I, Chanelle. So am I. You looked me in my face and lied to me. Not once. Not twice. But multiple times. You know, people make mistakes all the time. I understand that you could get caught up and make some bad choices. I would've never passed judgment on you. But, what I can't forgive is you lying to me. If I can't trust you, then I can't be with you." He turned away from me and marched toward the door.

I bounced up and ran after him. "Rick, I'm sorry. Please don't leave. Please stay." I grabbed his arm, but he shook me off.

He gave me a final look, disappointment brimming in his eyes. "I'm sorry too, Chanelle. You are not the woman I thought you were. Goodbye." He turned and walked out of the door. And out of my life.

CHAPTER 39

"It won't end well." Pastor Sharpe's words of caution played on a loop in my mind. I sat at my desk, staring through the office window, and for the millionth time, told myself this was not my life. I closed my eyes, pinched the bridge of my nose, and sighed. Staying at work was useless. I collected my items, told Patty I wasn't feeling well, and left.

I stopped at Chipotle, and ordered a vegetarian burrito bowl and lemonade to go. Twenty minutes later, I was home, sitting on the couch in my den, mindlessly flipping through the channels. I settled on a court TV program, and made a futile attempt to enjoy my lunch.

After about an hour, I picked up my home phone on the table next to the couch and dialed Rick. It rang a couple times before I heard the instructions to leave a message. Wow, he pushed me to voicemail. I left a rambling apology and hung up.

This was even worse than I thought. With the phone still in my hand, I clicked the "on" button to call him again, and heard a busy signal. Thinking that was odd, I turned the phone off and tried again. Same busy tone. Returning the phone to its cradle, I reached for my cell in my purse. Before I could process why my phone had suddenly stopped working, I heard the sound of my front door opening. I panicked momentarily until I remembered Rick had a key.

"Rick? Is that you?" I sprang from the couch and raced to the foyer and skidded to a stop. This man wasn't Rick. I was face-to-dirty face with the grungy man Cynthia had hired. I was looking at The Stalker.

"Nah, I ain't Rick. I'm Brutus. And it's time we had a little chat."

He was as wide as a wall and was blocking my escape through the front door. I immediately looked at the hall table and my heart hit my wood floors when I remembered the gun Rick had given me was upstairs in my bedroom.

As he moved toward me, I backed up and then spun on my heels, sprinting up the steps toward my bedroom. As I reached the top of the stairs, he caught my leg, causing me to fall, and the carpet burned the side of my face as my head bounced down the steps. I struggled to catch the banister for leverage and kicked him off me. He fell backwards to the bottom, giving me time to regain my balance and dash to my room.

I slammed and locked the door behind me and ran to my nightstand. With shaking hands, I reached for my gun. But before I had a chance to snatch it, my door flew open and Brutus clutched me from behind and threw me onto the other side of my king-sized bed. I screamed.

"Things will go much smoother if you stop fightin'," he growled, coming toward me.

Pouncing on top of me, he pinned my arms over my head and bent down to kiss me. Twisting my head from side to side, I did my best to avoid his chapped lips from touching my face, but when it looked like it was inevitable, I spat in his eyes.

"You're gonna pay for that!" he bellowed, punching me in my face. It felt like bone fragments from my busted nose had traveled up my nasal cavity and pierced my brain. Blood immediately pooled in my mouth and I had to turn my head to the side so I wouldn't drown in my own fluid.

He grabbed the bottom of my shirt and wiped his face, then punched me harder than a boxer in the ring, this time darkening my eye.

"Get off me." I mustered as much strength as I had to push him away, but he was a man possessed and immovable.

"Stop fightin'. Can't nobody hear ya and you just makin' things harder for ya self." He sat up enough to adjust his straddle over me. While he fixed himself, I saw the opportunity to knee him in his most private part. "Arrgh!" he yelped and grabbed his wounded jewels.

I took advantage of the moment and kicked him one more time. As he doubled over, I flew off the bed and ran around to the other side, back to my nightstand. I once again reached for my gun and this time I was successful. With perspiration stinging my eyes, I cocked the trigger and pointed it at him.

"Now, who's gonna pay? Put your hands behind your back and get up." I took a couple deep and jagged breaths to steady myself.

He began rising slowly, then lunged toward me, reaching for the gun to snatch it from my trembling hands. As I jerked back and out of his reach, the gun slipped from my fingers, firing into the wall behind him and sliding underneath the bed.

We fell to the floor, both of us scrambling to be the one to retrieve the weapon. I grabbed the gun as he yanked my legs, flipped me on my back and dragged me toward him. He got back on top of me, with the gun between us.

Each time he slammed my head into the floor, I lost a little more consciousness. I knew I had mere seconds before I blacked out. I squeezed my eyes shut, exactly the way I had been taught not to do it, and pulled the trigger.

The pounding of my head into the floor stopped and for the second time that day, he fell to his side and off of me.

I heard a blood-curdling scream. "Chanelle!"

"Michele?" I answered weakly, then passed out.

CHAPTER 40

"WHERE AM I?" I moaned, only able to look around the room with my eyes because my head felt like it was anchored to my pillow.

"Welcome back, Ms. Slate. You're at First General Hospital." An elderly woman in a nurse's uniform smiled down at me. "You had us scared for a moment."

"Wha—what happened? Why am I here?"

"You were in a very bad fight. Lucky for you, your friend saved your life." She nodded in the direction of Michele, who was sleeping in the visitor's chair.

"How long have I been here?"

"Four days. You were in a coma for the first few days, but you started coming around yesterday."

"A coma?"

"Mm hmm."

"Ooh," I groaned. "I feel like my face is about to pop off."

"That's natural. I just changed your morphine drip, so you should feel some relief soon."

"Was the rest of my family here?"

"They've all been in and out. But that lady right there," she said, pointing at Michele, "she never left."

I tried to sit up but felt a sharp pain shoot through my head and screamed out in pain.

"Chanelle?" Michele said, jumping up and hurrying to my bedside. "You're awake. Oh, my God. You had me so worried." She leaned over the side rail of the bed and gently kissed my forehead.

"Relax, Ms. Slate," the nurse said in an overly soothing tone, gently pressing me back into the sheets and adjusting my pillow. "You'll feel best if you try not to move. The doctor will be in shortly and she'll be able to give you more info." She placed a remote next to my hand. "Here's the call button. Use it if you need to reach me." She gave Michele a reassuring pat on her shoulder and left the room.

"Can you tell me what happened?" I asked, weakly.

Michele's eyes clouded over. "You don't remember anything?"

"Not much."

"Well, you were attacked in your home. Do you remember that?"

I closed my eyes and tried to think back. "Kinda... I think Rick and I had an argument." I paused. "Yes, we argued because he said I wasn't honest with him."

My eyes popped open and I glanced at Michele. "Does he know what happened to me?" I asked, my voice shaky.

Michele's tone was heavy with sorrow. "I called his office and left a message with his answering service. But I never heard back."

A tear trickled onto my pillow. "Well, did you try him again?" I couldn't imagine Rick knowing I was in the hospital and not coming to see me. Even if he was still angry.

She reached for my bruised hand and tenderly held it between hers. "Honestly, Chanelle, I didn't think about it. All I

234

could focus on was watching my best friend fight for her life. And praying that she won. Can you remember anything else?"

More images of that day began to play in my mind. My voice was hardly a whisper. "I left work early, grabbed some lunch, and went home... I called Rick, but he didn't answer. I heard my front door open and thought it was Rick, but it wasn't him. It was..." I gasped as the rest of my memories came flooding back. "The stalker. He was in my home! We fought and... the gun. It went off," I wailed.

With tears in her own eyes, she began, "I don't know how to tell you this, but..." Before she could finish her sentence, my hospital room door opened and two men, with badges hanging from a chain around their necks, walked in.

The senior of the two greeted me. "Hello, Ms. Slate. I'm Detective Watson and this is my partner, Detective Brunson. If you're up to it, your doctor said it would be okay if we asked you a few questions." Both men approached my bed.

I would have rolled my eyes if they didn't hurt. "You do know I was in a coma, right?"

"Yes, Ma'am." He spoke in a lowered tone of voice. "I promise, we'll be less than five minutes. All we need you to do is tell us what you remember about your incident."

I felt woozy, compliments of the morphine drip finally doing its job. "My memory is hazy, but I'll tell you what I can." I slurred as I recounted the information I'd shared with Michele.

"And that's it? You don't remember anything else?" the younger detective, who was much less sympathetic, asked me.

"I'm sorry. I don't."

He asked, "Did you realize that you shot Mr. Cowan?"

"Who is that?" I squinted.

"Brutus Cowan. He's the gentleman who was in your home," Detective Watson said.

I felt some of my sass return because they had exceeded their five minutes and I wanted to go to sleep. "If you're referring to the pervert who stalked me and later assaulted me in my home, then you're not speaking of a gentleman. And to answer your question, no, I do not recall shooting him. At least not specifically. He was on top of me, pounding my head into the floor, and the gun was between us. I heard the gun go off, but I couldn't tell you if he got shot or if I did."

"That was when I got there and saw her on the carpet next to her bed," Michele interjected.

The officers looked at Michele, who was standing by the head of my bed, like she was my bodyguard. "And you are?" Detective Watson inquired.

"Mrs. Michele Burke, Chanelle's best friend. I'm the one who found her nearly unconscious, and half dead, on the floor."

"Please, go on." Detective Watson had out his little notepad and was feverishly writing down Michele's statement.

"To back up a little, I called Chanelle's office and her assistant told me she'd left early. She thought Chanelle and her boyfriend had gotten into an argument, and Chanelle seemed distraught. I figured she would've gone home, so I went by to check on her. I have a key to her house and let myself in. That's when I heard some sort of commotion coming from upstairs. I ran up the steps to her bedroom and I saw Cowan on top of her, banging her head into the floor. Next thing I knew, I heard a gunshot, he fell over, and she passed out. I called nine-one-one and the EMS brought her here. I have no idea what ended up happening to him. For the record, I gave my statement to the police officer who was here a couple days ago while Chanelle was still in a coma."

"Since Mr. Cowan has now died, this case has been turned over to homicide," Detective Brunson said.

"He died?" I asked.

"Yes, Ms. Slate," Detective Watson said. "He passed away this morning. It's our job to determine if this is a case of homicide or self-defense. Do you have any idea why he was in your home? Did you know him? Earlier you referenced that he was stalking you?"

"Because he was," I said.

"Do you know why? And did you report it to the police?"

I was silent. I knew I should tell the truth, but really, how much of the truth did they need to know? To tell them everything would include breaking and entering into Cowan's office, illegally obtaining credit documents, having an affair with someone else's husband, and utilizing Steve to help get Sean arrested. I could get innocent people in trouble. And I could also come off looking as guilty as Cowan and Cynthia. I had to choose my words very carefully. I cleared my throat, praying that the medication wouldn't make me say something I was trying to keep to myself. "Well, I didn't notify the police because he told me that he would hurt my family."

"And do you know why he was stalking you, as you put it? Were you in a relationship with him?"

"Absolutely not," I rushed to answer. I took as deep a breath as my cracked ribs would allow. "I dated a married man months ago. His wife blamed me for the breakdown of their marriage. She's the one who hired Cowan."

Detective Brunson touched his wedding band, and I felt like I should've had a scarlet letter branded on my hospital gown. "Can you prove any of what you're saying?"

Of course I can prove it, I thought. But how do I clear my name without getting myself into trouble? "She blamed me because she called me and told me. Her husband also warned me that she was out to get me." I suddenly remembered that Sean had left me a message to be careful. "And I saved the voicemail from her husband if you'd like to hear it."

"That would be helpful," Detective Watson said.

I looked to Michele. "Do I have my cellphone?"

She shook her head. "It's at your house. And your house has been taped off as a crime scene."

I looked back to the detectives. "If you can get to my cellphone, you'll hear my proof."

"Do you have anything else?" Detective Brunson asked.

I thought hard. "My assistant. My assistant was there when Cowan first called me." I gave him Patty's contact information.

"And is there anything else?"

"Well..." I hedged. "Um, he has an office on Third and Cass. I believe it's called 'Get It Done Investigators'. I'm sure he has a file with my name on it."

Detective Watson squinted his eyes and furrowed his brows. "You're sure there's a file, huh?"

I looked as sweet and innocent as I could with a puffy face, broken nose, and a black eye. "Uh-huh. And that file will probably have notes on who put the hit out on me. If you can find that, then that would clear my name, right? And maybe you could even arrest Cynthia." I tried batting my eyelashes at him, but they seemed to be almost swollen shut.

"One step at a time. We're going to follow up with the leads you've provided. If what you're saying is true, then you would've had every right to defend yourself in your home. But don't leave town when you're released from the hospital. We'll be in touch soon. Get well." The detectives turned and left the room.

"Michele, what if they come back and say that I committed cold-blooded murder? You don't think that would happen, do you?"

"Of course not. I saw what was happening to you. He was literally beating you to death. I'm sure that everything will all work out. I'll be back. It was too soon for the detectives to come and question you. I'm going to make sure that no one else comes in for the rest of the day."

She left to find the doctor, and I did my best to find sleep. My head was pounding, my heart was racing. I was scared and I wanted Rick. No, I needed Rick.

Michele returned with the doctor, who gave me an update

on my condition. Though I had been badly injured, none of my injuries were life-threatening. There was slight swelling on my brain, but no permanent damage. Even though my nose would have to be fixed, the doctor was hopeful I would be released within a week, two at the most. That news was the first comforting thing I'd heard all day. She turned up my morphine dose so I could sleep, and before long, I was sleeping like a newborn baby.

CHAPTER 41

"HOME SWEET HOME," Michele sang.

"Kinda," I responded with a slight smile and slowly stepped inside my front door into the foyer. I'd ended up staying in the hospital for two weeks. Thankfully, once the swelling on my brain went down, my recovery was swift. I'd finally been released with minimal home care instructions.

Yesterday, the crime scene tape had been removed, and I was free to return to my home, though it would be another couple of days before the carpet company could come out and replace my bedroom flooring. The police had checked my story and cleared me. They recommended to the DA that no charges be filed against me, and instead they went after Cynthia.

I'd received a call from Detective Watson right before I was discharged from the hospital. Cynthia had been arrested. They fully expected her to be charged with conspiracy to commit murder. Apparently, in addition to the files and pictures Michele and I discovered, Cowan also recorded phone calls with Cynthia that Michele and I had overlooked. Lucky for me, the detectives never asked me again how I knew about Cowan's office and his files, and I never volunteered that information.

Michele walked ahead of me to the den and placed my bags from the hospital on the floor in the corner. She said, "My mom has been keeping BJ for me. I need to swing by her house and pick him up. I'll be back after I get him settled at home with Ben."

I eased myself into my recliner. "No, Michele. You have been away from your family for much too long. Go home. I'll be fine."

Michele looked skeptical. "Are you sure? I feel funny about leaving you here alone. Why don't you come home with me? At least until they finish cleaning your room."

I shook my head. "Unh-uh. I have almost a clean bill of health. No charges were filed against me. Cowan is gone. Sean is gone. Cynthia's been arrested. This is the best I've felt in a long time. I may be moving a little slow, but I feel like I'm on top of the world." I paused and thought about the hole I felt in my heart. "The only thing that would make this day better is Rick. But I guess he meant it when he said he couldn't forgive me."

On one hand, there were no words to describe how elated I was that my nightmare was over. On the other hand, I was filled with a sadness unlike anything I'd ever felt before because I hadn't heard from the man who made me the happiest I had ever been. I missed his smile and his comforting arms. I missed his companionship. And most of all, I just missed him.

Instead of feeding into my pity party, Michele admonished me. "He would have been there for you if you'd have let me call him." She headed to the kitchen while I stretched out in my recliner.

I'd been so hurt that Rick didn't respond to Michele's message that I tried shutting my heart to him. But for the last few days I missed him so much that I was ready to admit I was wrong and willing to humble and humiliate myself to win him back.

Michele returned with a cup of chamomile tea. "Here you go. Everything will be fine. You get some rest and I'll call you later." She paused to look at me and her eyes began to tear. "I'm so happy you're okay. I don't know what I would have done without my best friend."

"Don't go gettin' all sentimental. You know I'm on too much medication right now. You'll have me cryin' and I won't be able to stop." I tried to chuckle as I looked at my bestie. But I was overcome with emotion. "You are the best friend I have in the world. Every woman needs a ride or die, and I'm so blessed that you're mine."

Michele bent down and gave me the biggest, warmest hug I'd had in a long time. And I needed it. The floodgate of tears that I'd been holding in since the day I was taken to the hospital was finally unleashed. "I love you, girl," Michele said.

I sniffed and wiped my tears with the back of my hands. "I love you too, my sister from another mister." I said the phrase we'd been saying to each other since middle school.

"Let me get going." She dabbed her eyes with a tissue from the coffee table. "I'll check in a little later."

"Thanks for everything."

"Anytime." She turned the corner and walked out the door.

I breathed a little easier when I heard the sound of the door lock. I looked around the room and that's when it hit me that the last time I was in my home, I'd been attacked.

I fought back the panic that threatened to sweep over me and raised from my seat. I ambled to the foot of the stairs and stood there for a moment, looking to the top. My eyes landed on the step where I'd been caught and dragged backwards. I brought my hand to my face and touched the remains of the carpet burns. My heart rate increased.

One step at a time, I climbed the stairs, feeling accomplished when I reached the top. Then I stared at my bedroom door at the end of the hall. It felt like everything in my body paused. My heart. My breathing. My everything.

"You can do this, Chanelle. Count to three and open the

door." Silently, I counted and took the few steps until I was standing in front of the door. I drew in a sharp breath and slowly turned the knob.

As soon as my room came into view, images of my terror flashed through my mind like a trailer to a horror movie. I saw myself being thrown on the bed, fighting for my life. Being punched in the face. Struggling with him over the gun.

I crept over to the side of my bed where Cowan had met his fate. It was the huge bloodstain that had saturated my carpet that made me place my hand over my mouth and take in large gulps of air to keep my breakfast down. I had never seen a crime scene before, but this was not what I pictured. I had second thoughts about going home with Michele until my bedroom was repaired.

I turned and shuffled out of the room, slamming the door shut behind me. Then made it back down the steps as quickly as my injured body would take me.

As I reached the bottom step, my doorbell chimed. Fear, once again, blanketed my body. The only person who knew I was back home was Michele, and she had a key. With uneven breaths, I tiptoed to the door and peered through the peephole. My heart skipped.

It was Rick.

~

"Hi." I spoke softly.

His forehead creased with concern as he took in my nose splint and still bruised eyes. He gently cupped the side of my face. "Baby, what happened?"

"I met the stalker. He lost."

He pulled me into his arms. "Oh my God, Chanelle. Are you okay?"

I closed my eyes and clasped my arms around his waist. This

was the comfort I'd needed for over two weeks. "I'm fine," I managed to choke out.

After several moments of holding me tightly, he pulled back. "May I come in?"

"Oh, yes." I stepped aside so he could enter. After closing the door, with our initial greeting behind us, we stood awkwardly. Neither of us seemed to know what to say or do next.

He reached for my hand. "Please, tell me what happened."

I looked down at our hands and nodded. "Follow me." I led him to the den and sat next to him on the sofa.

He noticed my drink on the table in front of us. "What are you drinking?"

"Chamomile tea. Would you like me to fix you a cup?" I made a move to stand, but he placed his hand on my leg.

"You rest. I'll do it," he said.

He went into the kitchen, and I relaxed against the couch. I was glad Rick had come by. No. I was ecstatic. But cautious. Because I didn't know why he was here. Had he only stopped by to pick up some of his things?

"I made you a fresh cup, too," he said when he returned and placed two mugs of hot tea on the table in front of us before sitting.

I folded my hands in my lap, suddenly shy. "Thank you."

More awkward silence.

I watched the up and down rhythm of his chest as he breathed. "Chanelle. What happened?"

My inhale was deep. There was so much I didn't want to relive. The days in the hospital, worried that I'd never be normal again. The awful realization that I'd taken a human life; that I'd had to fight for mine. But as I looked at Rick, the way he leaned toward me, concern written in his eyes, for the first time in weeks, I felt safe. I exhaled slowly and recounted everything that had happened since he'd walked out of my office.

He took my hand. "Baby, I'm sorry I wasn't there for you. That I let a stupid argument stop me from protecting you."

"Rick, it's okay. You couldn't have known." I paused before I frowned, the question I'd been wondering written on my face. "What made you stop by? I thought I'd never see you again."

"I missed you," he said, simply. "My parents have a cabin up north and I went there to clear my head. I unplugged from the world. I thought if I took a few weeks to myself, it would be easy to walk away from you. It wasn't. As I was driving home today, all I could think about was you. So, I came straight here. I'm very disappointed in you, Chanelle, but I'm not ready to throw away what we were building. I love you too much."

My heart leapt. "I love you and I missed you, too. And I'm so very, very sorry for not being honest. I was scared to lose you and by keeping things from you I almost did. I truly, truly, truly apologize. Will you please forgive me?"

He caressed my face and held my eyes with his. "Of course I forgive you. But you have to promise me something."

"I'll promise anything." I beamed at him.

"No more lies. We keep it one hundred with each other from here on out. Okay?"

"Yes. I will always tell you the truth. And I'll start now." I confessed everything. I began with how Sean and I met, and I stopped right before I retold him about Cowan breaking into my house. Rick held back a laugh when I told him about our adventure on top of the roof. Now, that I was safe and no longer in danger, I had to agree that it was a little humorous.

"I'm sorry I wasn't there for you," he said again.

"I know you would have been if you had known. But what's important is that you're here now."

"And I'm not ever leaving. I mean that." He stood, gently pulled me up and held me close. Only this hug came with a tender kiss. And for the first time in my life, everything was right with my world...

EPILOGUE

IT HAD BEEN six months since my ordeal had come to an end. I'd had to testify at Cynthia's trial, which I did gladly. She received a fifteen-year sentence for conspiracy to commit murder. I saw Sean at her trial. Mr. Jeffries told me Sean had been cleared of all charges, but he'd decided to stay in Virginia. He'd only been at her trial to see how much time she'd receive. Apparently, she'd been behind the embezzlement case and was going to have to stand trial in Virginia.

I was finally back on track at work, and Mr. Jeffries was happy to have one hundred percent of me. Patty was still complaining about all of her aches and pains and her crazy family. Michele was back to spending time at home with her family now that my shenanigans had come to an end.

Andrea was still Andrea. About a week after I returned home, I invited her over for dinner and updated her on my life. She feigned sympathy and then asked for a loan. Like I said, Andrea was still Andrea.

My bedroom and master bath were completely redone, compliments of Rick. It had taken about a month for us to truly put the past behind us, but we did it. And now we were in a very peaceful place. I was sure that my engagement was on the horizon.

"Hey, Sweetie, something smells delicious," Rick said, joining me out on the deck where I was grilling pork chops.

"Hey, Babe." I greeted him with a peck. "Dinner is almost ready, so go wash your hands."

"Yes, ma'am," he joked and saluted me, then set his sunglasses and phone on the table before heading through the sliding patio doors.

As he strode out of the sunroom, his phone rang. "Babe, would you catch that?"

Still smiling, I said, "I got it." I glimpsed the caller ID, and it read, "Unknown."

"Hello?"

"Who is this?" a female voice asked.

"Who is this?" I responded with my own question, and a bit of attitude.

She smacked her lips. "Rick's wife. Twyla."

My neck twisted as my hand went to my hip. "Excuse me, but don't you mean his ex-wife?"

"Once a wife, always a wife. Now is Rick there?" The demand in her tone angered me as she continued. "Because I need to speak with my husband."

I know this chick is not serious, I thought. "My man is unavailable at the moment, but I might mention that you called. Would you like to leave a message?"

In a tone drenched in so much sex I squirmed—and not in a good way—, she said, "Yeah, as a matter of fact, I do. You tell him we're not over. I'm comin' back to claim what's mine. He knows the number; have him call me."

I yanked the cell away from my ear and stared at it as the home screen reappeared.

"Babe, who was on the phone?" Rick asked, walking up behind me and nuzzling my neck.

I spun to face him. "Your ex-wife. She said call her." I shoved his cell into his chest. "She wants you back."

His jaw dropped, and in an instant, the peace of my life shattered. I stormed into the house and up to my bedroom to call Michele because I had a problem; and she was the only one I trusted to help me handle it.

HANDS OFF

Enjoy an excerpt at
monicalynnefoster.com
While you're there, join my mailing list for future releases and
exclusives.

Monica Lynne Foster is a woman's fiction and inspirational author. She enjoys writing novels that give readers time to suspend reality and immerse themselves in pure fiction, simply for the joy of escaping day-to-day life. She also writes inspirational devotionals that give hope to its audience.

facebook.com/authormonicalynnefoster

twitter.com/authormlfoster

instagram.com/authormonicalynnefoster

amazon.com/author/monicalynnefoster

goodreads.com/authormonicalynnefoster

bookbub.com/authors/monica-lynne-foster

AN INTERVIEW WITH MONICA

Who are your favorite authors? I have several. Many who have inspired me for years. I'd have to say that at the top of my list, I really enjoy reading Victoria Christopher Murray, Reshonda Tate Billingsley, and Kimberla Lawson Roby. I love how they have series that I'm able to follow. I begin to feel like I know their characters.

What inspires you to get out of bed each day? I enjoy life! I believe that we all have just one life to live and we should spend our time doing the things that bring us joy and happiness.

When you're not writing, how do you spend your time? I'm a self professed workaholic. My husband and I own a gas contracting business and I have a natural body and hair care company. So when I'm not writing or reading, I'm typically working or spending time with friends and family.

Do you remember the first story you ever wrote? Actually, I do. I was about seven years old and wrote a four-page story called Charlie and the Dunce. That was over forty years ago, so while the particulars of my story are a little fuzzy, what I remember most is the fact that my family supported me. I remember reading my story to them and receiving praise for my work. In hindsight, I have no idea if my writing was any good, but that was a defining moment for me. I fell in love with writing and embracing my very active imagination!

What is your writing process? I like to call myself a visual writer. I see my writing as scenes in my mind's eye, so I literally close my eyes and visualize what my characters are doing in that moment. And then I write what I see.

What do you read for pleasure? I enjoy reading the same genre that I enjoy writing, Adult Fiction, Chick Lit, Women's Contemporary Novels. I love novels that are adult and yet clean.

Tell me about your Chanelle Series. I absolutely love my Chanelle Series, for several reasons. Chanelle is a powerhouse of a woman. On the outside. Beautiful, lovely home, great family, true friends, a boss at work. But on the inside, she's a hot mess. She has relationship drama that many women can understand. And she pulls her best friend, Michele, into her shenanigans. What's great about this series, is the bond between the friends. And how no matter what outrageous situation Chanelle gets herself into, her best friend is right there by her side.

What book are you working on next? I am working on the third book in the Chanelle Series, For Better And For Worse. This book focuses on the marriage of her best friend, Michele. Michele's husband finds himself in deep trouble and on trial for murder, and the strain of his trial creates problems for their otherwise happy marriage. I love this book because it explores the ups and downs of the marital relationship. On the one hand, you'll root for them. On the other, you'll tell her to drop kick him to the curb. But in the end, it's her decision. Just like a real old-fashioned marriage! LOL

What do your fans mean to you? Fans are everything! I write because I enjoy it and I want to share with others. I hope that the break from reality that I feel when I'm writing, is the same break from reality that my fans get to enjoy when they're reading.

BAD CHOICES BOOK CLUB GUIDE

Michele was Chanelle's bestie. She was Chanelle's voice of reason and yet Michele was also in her corner from beginning to end. Do you have a ride or die bestie that always has your back? Discuss.

Chanelle was very successful at work, but her personal life started out a mess. How is it that a woman can be put together professionally and in control of her career and yet her personal life is so out of control?

If Chanelle's boss, Mr. Jeffries, found out about her relationship with Sean, do you think she should have been fired? Discuss your reason(s) for your answer.

So many women want a man like Rick. A man who steps up and takes care of her when she's in need. Discuss the characteristics that showed that Rick was a good, strong man.

Cynthia was obviously a woman scorned. Hiring a hit man was over the top. But would she have been justified in confronting Chanelle about what happened between Chanelle and Sean, even though it was months after the fact? Why?

Rick thought it was important for Chanelle to learn how to protect herself with a gun. What are your thoughts on using a gun for protection? Do you believe women should know how to shoot a gun?

Chanelle may have been able to avoid a lot of pain that she caused herself if she was just honest with Rick about her past and the reasons why she was being stalked. If you were in Chanelle's shoes, would you have told Rick, or would you have tried to handle the problem yourself? Why?

Rick took Chanelle to Aruba, a romantic island that he used to visit with his wife. If you were Chanelle, how would you have felt about going to the same place that he took another woman that he once loved?

Rick and Chanelle's relationship moved very quickly. Do you think it's possible in real life to have an instant connection with someone and have your relationship move at warp speed? Discuss your answer.

www.ingramcontent.com/pod-product-compliance
Lightning Source LLC
Chambersburg PA
CBHW071131170626
46809CB00002B/577